MW00479425

THE WAITRESS

NINA MANNING

Boldwood

First published in Great Britain in 2022 by Boldwood Books Ltd.

Copyright © Nina Manning, 2022

Cover Design by Head Design Ltd

Cover Photography: Shutterstock

The moral right of Nina Manning to be identified as the author of this work has been asserted in accordance with the Copyright, Designs and Patents Act 1988.

All rights reserved. No part of this book may be reproduced in any form or by any electronic or mechanical means, including information storage and retrieval systems, without written permission from the author, except for the use of brief quotations in a book review.

This book is a work of fiction and, except in the case of historical fact, any resemblance to actual persons, living or dead, is purely coincidental.

Every effort has been made to obtain the necessary permissions with reference to copyright material, both illustrative and quoted. We apologise for any omissions in this respect and will be pleased to make the appropriate acknowledgements in any future edition.

A CIP catalogue record for this book is available from the British Library.

Paperback ISBN 978-1-80162-222-6

Large Print ISBN 978-1-80162-223-3

Hardback ISBN 978-1-80162-221-9

Ebook ISBN 978-1-80162-225-7

Kindle ISBN 978-1-80162-224-0

Audio CD ISBN 978-1-80162-216-5

MP3 CD ISBN 978-1-80162-217-2

Digital audio download ISBN 978-1-80162-218-9

Boldwood Books Ltd
23 Bowerdean Street
London SW6 3TN
www.boldwoodbooks.com

For my beloved Phyllis, from your Pearl.

PROLOGUE

I stood at the edge of the broken window as shards of glass crunched under my sandals. I felt a piece slice through my shoe and into my toe – a sharp pain then the slow warm trickle of blood. I welcomed the pain. I had yearned for it. It was a distraction from everything else that I was trying to contend with. But now, finally, there was nothing more to distract me; I knew what it was I needed to do. I was acutely aware of the crowd that was forming beneath me. Were they chanting? Egging me to do it? It was hard to tell; they were so far away, so very far below me. It was funny how my fear of heights had suddenly disappeared. Where I usually felt fear, I now only felt numb.

I took a small step forward and I looked down. My thoughts turned to the line from *Peter Pan* – 'To die would be an awfully big adventure' – the one part of the film that had always struck a chord with me. For here I was, ready to take the step into the unknown. What was waiting for me? What would it feel like? Whatever it – death – was, it had to be better than the alternative. Staying here amongst the madness and chaos.

I could hear the tiny voices of the crowd and I wondered what they were saying. It was all such a blur now. I didn't need to know. I edged further forward; both of my feet were now teetering over the edge. I surprised myself at how calm I felt; the beginning of the day seemed so far away, and I could no longer recall the steps I had taken to get here. But it didn't matter any more. Too much had gone on recently. Was this finally the end? Surely I could not survive this next part. Because maybe I wasn't supposed to. Because maybe this was finally it.

For a brief amount of time, I had been the luckiest girl, now I was standing here, wishing I didn't exist.

I listened to the voices calling me, telling me to do it. I took a deep breath – heard the crackle of glass under my shoes as a thousand faces from my past and present shot before my eyes. I took one final step, so it was only air between me and the ground. I instantly felt my stomach being pushed into my chest, then I simply floated down.

Down.

Down.

1

NOW

People look at me and think, she's just a waitress, but really, I am so much more than that. I hear snippets of conversations, feel the energy from each person around the table, and I can tell if they are happy, sad or anxious. It is me who changes them from hungry to full, from skittish to comfortable. I am there to tend to their every need. Some people would just ignore these facts, and pretend being a waitress is just another job, but waiting tables takes skill, precision, and patience. You must know the exact moment the customer has made their decision and approach the table with a smile, as though you hadn't just been surreptitiously watching and waiting for the final person to lay their menu down, satisfied with their choices. You need to be aware of when a wine glass has become too low and top it up with finesse and grace, as though you had barely been there, whilst also watching out for a hand over a glass to indicate that person has had enough. Then you wait patiently as they eat their food, looking for a single clue that someone was not entirely satisfied. You can be at their side in a moment, quietly assuring them it is fine for them to send the dish back and you will replace it immediately, and no, they will not be charged for their inconvenience.

I had been an exceptional waitress once.

Now I was just good enough.

Because sometimes we get things wrong. And sometimes we make mistakes.

2

NOW

Her face was pure and angelic. She was smiling. She was always smiling. That was the most appealing thing about her. I mean, who wouldn't be mesmerised by that winning smile? A real bobby dazzler, my dad would have called her. If he had ever met her. Such a small, tiny thing. Gone far too soon.

Someone cleared their throat and the image of her face that had been dancing in front of me disappeared. She was gone. Again. I wondered when she would return to me.

I looked to my left, to the stranger who was waiting for me to say something, do something. I wasn't sure what I needed to do. Suddenly I felt self-conscious.

Click-click. A man behind a camera was standing a few feet away, taking my photo. Had he been watching me intently? Had I said anything that might have sounded strange or out of context to him? It was happening more and more, the visits from her, and I let myself get swept away in the illusion, trying to make it feel as real as possible.

I looked at the man next to me again. What was his name?

Hendrick. That was it. It was a rare name, not one I had heard before. It made me think about Jimi Hendrix and that Hendrix would have been a better name, more rock and roll. But then this guy didn't look particularly rock and roll in his navy suit and white shirt. So maybe he was more suited to Hendrick. I could feel myself getting warmer; it was probably just the weather and the fact I had been standing outside in the heat for almost twenty minutes now and I desperately needed a drink. Something to calm my nerves, maybe. Surely there should be some champagne or something; wasn't that what was supposed to happen at these events, someone pops a comically sized bottle of champagne?

Why was I suddenly feeling as though I couldn't speak up? Tell this Hendrick dude to hurry up, or better still, fetch the oversized bottle of champagne he must have forgotten he had in the boot of his car. I had always managed to converse articulately enough in front of a small audience; it was part of my job as a waitress, confidence came with the role. It did once, anyway. And as I stood in front of the camera and this stranger, Hendrick, I suddenly felt as though I wanted the ground to open up and swallow me. I had fantasised about being popular; not necessarily famous, just well-known and respected, yet the reality of the attention was overwhelming, and I could feel a swelling in my head. This was all out of sync; it wasn't meant to be, surely? There she was again, a tiny glimpse, just dancing in my peripheral vision. I shot around, to catch her full-on, but she disappeared.

'Are you okay?' Hendrick asked. I looked at him properly, tried to plump my face into a smile, to look as though I were ready to engage in a normal interaction, so he could see I was just a normal woman, here to receive my prize.

Surely this was it, someone had taken my photo a few times, he was talking, saying something that sounded official, and he was holding a key – another photo opportunity. Click-click. I went to take the key from him. The one that must belong to the grand house that was behind us. The house that I had won and was now the owner of. I nodded my thanks and went to walk away from the glare of the sun and the camera lens that kept catching my eye and making me feel all squirmy inside, back to where I had parked my little blue Fiesta on the driveway. I would bring my overnight bag out, and go inside, perhaps make a cup of tea if there was no sign of alcohol. Why didn't I think to bring something with me? But Hendrick from the competition company who was hosting this ceremony and who was also my chaperone, grabbed my arm firmly and dragged me backward, almost lost his charming host demeanour for a second, but quickly pulled it back in time as the camera started up again.

'Hey, Kit, we're not done yet,' he said through a painfully inane smile. 'Now smile.'

I turned to the short stout man behind the camera for what felt like the fiftieth time and put on the happiest face I could muster. 'It's not going in the paper or anything, is it?' I said, trying to keep the panic out of my voice. The last thing I needed was to start drawing attention to myself. If anything, this win was a blessing in disguise. At least here I could hide away a little; no one could find me if I didn't want them to.

'No,' Hendrick said. 'Just for the website. To prove to others that people do win these prizes. That it's not a hoax.'

I had always thought these things were a hoax. That they just advertised these grand prizes but that no one ever won them, that someone just pocketed all the money at the end. But here I was, living proof. Such a shame, I thought. If only this could have happened a year or so ago, I could have been the right person to fully appreciate it. At the very least, the year-ago version of me would have deserved it.

A two-million-pound house would come in handy for someone

who was settled with a partner or kids, maybe. But this massive place just for me? I wasn't sure why the universe had picked me or this time in my life to bestow upon me such an expensive gift. But for whatever reason, I had to accept that it was meant to be. Sometimes things happened that just didn't make sense. Good things. Bad things. Very bad things.

I wasn't hard up, that was the important thing to remember. I was doing just fine and had been living on just my waitressing wage. Sure, I relied heavily on the tips, always opting for the evening shifts because people were more generous after a few bottles of wine, but that was the nature of the industry, and anyone who didn't leave at least 10 per cent of the bill in a restaurant was the devil incarnate as far as I was concerned. Luckily all the restaurants I had ever worked at had been renowned for good tippers. Even Citrus, the one I currently found myself working at. I didn't relish working there, but it hadn't been my choice.

I suppose most people would just stop working if they suddenly found out they were the winner of a two-million-pound house – which also came with a cash prize of twenty thousand pounds. Hendrick nudged me, a little too hard, I thought, but as I looked at him, ready to express my frustration at the length of time this was taking, he gestured to the camera.

'Just one more, please,' he said and so I pulled my face into something that I thought resembled ecstatic joy.

Click-click.

I thought of all the people who might look at the website and see that image, or one of the many other photos that had been taken, and what they would think. There's a woman who has nothing to worry about any more. But they would be wrong. Then there were the people who I didn't want to see the photo. Was this a bad idea? Perhaps I should ask Hendrick if he could stop the photo from getting published anywhere.

Hendrick handed me the key to the house in what he clearly believed to be a dramatic manner and the photographer snapped one final photo before he slung his camera over his shoulder. He mumbled something to Hendrick which I didn't quite catch, and Hendrick's face formed into a frown. He nodded quickly and waved the photographer away.

'Here we are then, Kit Lowman. The place is officially yours.' Hendrick turned back to me, the wide smile back on his face.

'Is there something I should sign? Something to say it belongs to me now?' I asked, still wondering how it was possible for me to not only own a house but for it to be this size.

'You did all you needed to do when you responded to the initial email and then signed the paperwork we sent you.'

He began rooting around in his man bag. 'Here is the final paperwork with our signatures.' He pulled out a large wad of A4 papers; they were clipped neatly together into a large booklet.

'You've probably read it all, I imagine?'

I gave him a blank look. It was too much for me to think about. I had ignored most of it and skipped to the important parts about me being the prize winner and coming here today to accept the prize.

'No? Oh, okay. You don't need to read it all tonight.' He noted my face drop at the sight of so much paperwork. 'In fact, at all. You have the prize now, it's all yours.'

Hendrick turned the pages and presented the final one to me.

'Anything else you need to know is in the emails I sent.'

'Emails?' I questioned, thinking of my inbox full of some two thousand unread messages plus spam. I shuddered at the thought. Modern technology, for all its convenience, unnerved me to my core and so I ignored it whenever I could.

'Yes, check your spam, but most should have gone to your inbox.'

I took a deep breath and scratched my neck; the heat of the day had finally got to me.

'Look, you can always call me if you need to know anything, don't look so worried!'

It was mid-June and had been over 25°C for most of the day. I felt a tired warmth wash over me. It was barely 6 p.m. but I was ready for bed. I glanced back at the huge house that I knew hardly anything about, but which was now, apparently, mine. Hendrick had talked with real animation over the phone when he called to tell me I had won.

What I did know was that it was a fourteenth-century mill house, Grade II listed with extensive grounds, a tennis court, and a swimming pool. All the furniture was included, but it was the gardens that had intrigued me the most when I saw them in the photo Hendrick had shown me when I bought the tickets from him. They were enchanting, like something straight out of a fairy-tale book I'd had when I was a child. The front cover depicted a garden scene that was just so similar to the one surrounding this house. When I was younger I had stared at the front cover, imagining myself walking through the garden. Right at the edge of the house stood a willow tree that hung over a small lake with a tiny bridge that took you from one side of the lawn to the other and gave the building its name – Willow Cottage. It stood behind, gazing over the lake like a proud parent. I looked at the lake now, and I wondered just how deep it was.

Hendrick cleared his throat behind me.

'So, it's all yours, then.' He was holding out another set of keys. The actual keys to the property, not the one key he had held up for the sake of a photo. 'Would you like me to talk you through all the locks?'

I looked at him and wondered if he had someone at home waiting for him. He seemed in a rush.

I shook my head. 'I'll figure it out. There's one for every door I presume?'

Hendrick nodded. 'Right then, I'll be off—'

'Could you just take a photo of me, please?' I interrupted just before he turned back towards his car in the driveway. I suddenly felt I needed to mark this occasion, with a photograph just for me, that I could keep on my phone and look back on, because that was what you did, wasn't it? I remembered when I was a child, the sound of a camera clicking and being wound on was a permanent fixture in my memory. My parents captured every school race, every present opened on Christmas morning. They were so proud of me. Amongst the chaos of what my life had become, there was a sliver of an emotion that was driving me to mark the occasion, making me realise I would regret not creating a memory with a photograph. Who knew if one day I would want to look back and remember? Would I see the fear in my eyes, would the image spark something visceral?

'With the house in the background,' I added as Hendrick placed all the paperwork and his briefcase on the grass in an awkward manner. I thought about who I would send the photo to and then I felt a sudden wave of sadness as I realised I wouldn't be sending it to anyone.

'Sure.' He took my phone from me, and I pulled myself into another pose that felt just as wrong and uncomfortable. Even after twenty or so photos I still didn't know how I was supposed to look when I had just won a house.

He handed me my phone back. 'I took a few. Hopefully, there is one you will like.'

'Thanks.' I scrolled through them quickly, searching for the one that showed I was thrilled, that this was where my new life was about to begin. But in each shot, I wore the same tired and worn-out expression, a slight variation of my life's failures in each image.

Then I remembered it didn't matter how I looked because I wasn't going to share this win with anyone. But I would keep hold of the photo and maybe one day, not too long from now, I could share this picture and this memory with someone. I still had hope, if nothing else.

Hendrick stooped to pick up his briefcase and then the paperwork, which he handed to me.

'Thank you.' I clutched the mound to my chest.

'Enjoy your new home,' he said as he turned towards his car. I noticed it was modest: a blue Ford saloon. Why did I presume he would drive something flashier just because he'd handed over a property worth two million to me? I wasn't entirely sure.

Suddenly he looked back at me. He put his hand inside the breast pocket of his suit jacket and took out his mobile.

'Actually, let's swap numbers, in case you need anything, or have any questions.'

'Okay,' I said because it seemed a reasonable thing to do. I put my mobile number into his contacts, and he called me straight away. I saved his number under 'Hendrick – the admin guy'.

We stood for a second and I smiled, wondering if I was supposed to offer him a cup of tea or something. But a lot of my things were still at my flat in Bournemouth. All I had with me here was my overnight bag, with the notion that of course, I would want to stay here straight away. That was what I was supposed to do; I was merely following some sort of hypothetical protocol. There was no one to tell me what to do. This was adulting at its absolute finest. Should I stay in the mansion I had just won or go home to a tiny yet very comfortable flat? Yet there was a part of me that yearned for the security of it. Here was unfamiliar. But that could do me some good; unfamiliarity was a distraction and I desperately needed to distract myself. And of course, I was here now. I could always go back to my seaside flat if I felt at all unsure.

Now I knew Hendrick was going to leave this time, I felt a pang of worry. I would be all alone. But I righted myself quickly. I was not the sort of person to worry about being alone. If anything, this was a test and one I would gladly accept. I needed to find myself amongst all the guilt, remind myself that I was someone who deserved to live. There she was again; every time I began to imagine a life where I could move on, she caught up with me. Why was that, I wondered? Was it because I was never going to be able to forget? I had ruined so many lives. Yet here she was, still flitting around in my peripheral vision, like a guardian angel. But I was not worthy of one of those.

'I will definitely call you if I need something,' I told Hendrick firmly, so he knew that this wasn't just a pleasant exchange of numbers. This was an unusual situation and I had once been a strong independent woman who knew her mind, who knew what she wanted. I never wanted to rely on anyone. I felt a sliver of worry crawl from the pit of my stomach; suddenly, and with remarkable force, it began to paralyse my limbs. I shook my legs out and watched how Hendrick was back at his car in a few strides, throwing his briefcase onto the passenger seat. I wondered what woes he carried, did he have many life regrets, was he bearing a heavy heart? He waved as he drove away and I stood there watching the dust from the gravel swirl in the air and felt jealous of that dust, at how it could be disrupted and then so easily fall and settle some-where new. This was a good thing, I needed to remind myself. I was thirty-one years old, and I didn't need anyone to prop me up. I could manage this next episode of my life.

And it was okay if, from time to time, I thought of *him*, if the images of who he and I were when we had been together occasion-ally crept into my mind. I didn't allow myself to hold them there for too long; they were fleeting, sweeping through my mind, resting for a moment where I could almost reach out and touch them before they floated away. And for a few moments afterward, I felt the dull ache of loss, for someone and something that had once saturated my life, that was no more.

3

THEN

He looked at me from the table where he sat with his work colleagues. He seemed to be the alpha male; I could tell from his body language. He had only sparkling water with his meal, the others had all had at least one beer and a glass of wine. I felt his eyes on me as I circulated the area I had been assigned to at Mirabelle, the restaurant where I worked. It was one of the best restaurants on the south coast and had won multiple awards, including earning one Michelin star. I had worked there for almost a year and had settled in well. I had been building up a rapport with a family who had eaten at the restaurant a handful of times and were becoming weekly regulars. The little girl was particularly sweet and loved the spaghetti Bolognese. On their third visit, I had requested to serve them, and they became my regulars. They had very specific needs that I had become accustomed to, and they began to trust me as the one to attend to them. Waitressing had been my life for so long and it was what I was good at. We often had business types in at lunchtime and I knew how to handle them.

'Kit, you take section C, look after the tycoons,' Bret, the maître d', had said at the beginning of my shift. It was a particularly quiet lunchtime, unusually so, as though the universe had aligned, and the gods had all worked their magic to bring us together in that room that day. And so, because of the quietness, I was more available to the table for the entirety of their meal. Each time I took a drink order, dropped off a water glass, and brought them another napkin, he seemed to extract a little more information out of me: what was my name? How long had I worked here? What time did I get off?

I could sense another set of eyes on me that lunchtime. Another waitress. Courtney. Petite with bleached blonde hair, but a hard face, sunken cheekbones, and majestic green eyes. Some would say it was a strong look. She didn't even seem as if she tried very hard with her appearance. I was surprised Bret and Denim hadn't pulled her up on some of her jewellery, which I considered to be slightly excessive for a waitressing job. Should she be wearing that many bangles and an eyebrow piercing? It was a health and hygiene risk if nothing else. But management didn't seem to pick up on it, and besides, she had a way with the customers, and that seemed to matter more.

I considered Courtney to be a colleague, but in the few months she had been here, she had barely stretched to saying more than a few words to me. We'd had one interaction when she'd first begun that had stuck with me because it was the longest conversation we'd had to date. She'd asked me how I'd got into waitressing. I told her I had fallen into it but loved it and had been doing it for about ten years. She asked what my parents thought about me doing that as a career and I said they fully supported it. My parents were happy that I had found something that I enjoyed. After that, there had been little to no conversation. And I could sense her dislike for me as if she thought she were better than me. It didn't matter what I did or said, Courtney remained po-faced with me at all times. I could only take this to mean she had some issue with me and me only. I had seen her laughing and joking with the kitchen staff, especially Matt. But I would say her dislike for me escalated when I started dating Tom. I would feel her eyes bore into me whenever he and I were together.

At the end of my shift, on that first afternoon of my first encounter with Tom, he was waiting outside in his silver Lamborghini Urus. No words were spoken as he opened the door and I slid into the passenger seat. He drove us to a private members' hotel with an indoor and outdoor spa. It was only when I woke up in the emperor-sized bed the next morning that he revealed he owned the hotel. I wouldn't say he was flash with his money; he *was* money. It was ingrained into every piece of his life, from what he wore to how he acted to what he ate; there was no escaping it. He didn't try to play it down, but he didn't try to inflate it either. It was what it was. He was rich. And I wasn't. Except I would be, if I stuck with him, he told me. *Stay with me*, he would ask over and over until I found I no longer went home after work, I would go straight to his house or the hotel or we would get on a plane and spend my two days off from the restaurant in Brussels. He would work and I would eat giant grilled mussels and drink Belgian beer that was so strong I was floored after two bottles. He laughed at me, called me a lightweight, and said that I needed protection. He would protect me, he said. Would he have done, though, I wonder, if I had given him the chance? But I didn't. His name was Tom Bridely, and we were inseparable for just a few short months.

Until, one day, we weren't.

4

NOW

The floorboards in my new house creaked. It still felt strange referring to it as my house when I had only been here a few hours. I stood on the landing on the first floor and rocked back and forth, distributing my weight onto my back foot and then my front foot. The floorboards grumbled their response back at me. I began to familiarise myself with the noise in case I ever found myself lying in bed at night and heard it. I shuddered at the thought, at the size of the property, and how it would be possible for someone to be in the house without me being aware. These were the things I needed to prepare myself for, should it ever come to it. Not enough time had passed between what had happened then and what was happening now. It was as though I had been lifted from one part of my life, but I was still carrying all the emotion from the other. All the fear.

I listened to the noise beneath my feet and was thankful when the practical, logical side of my brain kicked in. It was a loud enough creak for me to consider how much bringing in someone to fix it might cost. I had briefly thought about the running costs of the house. I had a small amount of savings, and the extra cash that came as part of the prize would need to last me. I would have to be careful with it. My wage as a waitress, as happy as I was with it, was certainly not enough for the upkeep of a house this size. But I did okay on tips at Citrus, the new restaurant I had been working at. It was a far cry from the exclusivity at Mirabelle.

At Citrus, there was talk of a promotion to maître d' three days out of five. I declined without any hesitation. I needed to remain as inconspicuous as possible. I needed to be able to fade into the background of the restaurant. I had dyed my hair a dark brown. It was almost goth-like in comparison to the sunny golden highlights I had streaked through my hair a few months ago. But this way, people didn't tend to look at me for too long. My dream of working my way into management and then maybe owning a restaurant would have to wait. I just needed to get through each day right now. At Mirabelle, I had been made to prove myself before gaining the maître d' title. And the job had nearly been mine until it had stopped, just like everything else had at that time. A big full stop to signify the end of that part of my life. That was why I was here, alone.

At least the house was now a bonus. I had always wanted to live out in the countryside. I loved the sea, it was calming and healing, but there was something mysterious about being amongst greenery and woods. Here I felt not only as if I could heal but that I was safe too, wrapped up in the arms of the forests that surrounded me. Perhaps this was all meant to be.

I wondered if this was a gift from the universe. A place for me to grieve and repent all at the same time.

I moved my feet again on the floorboards.

Creak. Creak.

I peered through the window on the landing out onto the garden below. There was no breeze. The trees stood statue-still. Not one leaf moved. It was as though someone had pressed pause on a film. Which, in a way, was how I was feeling about my life. I had pressed pause on everything. And everyone. And now here I was, living a life in limbo. Waiting for the storm to pass.

I listened to the silence until it numbed my ears. Then I shifted on the landing. The floorboard let out one last creak as I stepped away and began to walk down the staircase. At the bottom, the hallway opened up into two; the whole effect from the staircase to the hall was like the letter T. From the bottom of the stairway, the kitchen and utility were to the left, and then a separate corridor to the side led to the sunroom and pool. To the right were a study, a formal sitting room, a dining room, and small snug.

I couldn't quite take in the enormity of it, the size and the space that was suddenly all around me, and that it all belonged to me. Suddenly I could hear Tom's voice in my head. 'Suits you, babe.' It was the sort of thing he would say, and I imagined him here, looking at the house and me in it. He would be pleased that I had finally allowed some opulence into my life. That was the sort of thing that would have impressed Tom. I closed my eyes briefly to allow my mind to rid itself of the image of him. When I could no longer feel or hear him, I continued walking down the stairs until I found myself outside and standing and basking in the last bit of the sun of the day. It had cooled down significantly since I had been out here with Hendrick earlier. I turned and looked at the house. Again, trying to feel something, some connection to the place. Maybe it would come with time. In the same way some mothers couldn't bond with their babies straight away.

My sister, Jude, hadn't been able to bond with Emily, her first-born. It was a long, stressful labour that gave her the blues for weeks afterward. I hadn't been through labour, but this house was the closest thing I had to a baby. I had to learn to love it. For all its creaking and groaning. There were worse things to worry about with a house of this age and size.

I would, of course, at some point decide what to do with the house. Would I sell it, rent out the rooms maybe? But for now, living in it seemed the most obvious option. It belonged to me, and as much as I had come to appreciate my cosy studio flat in town, this was the house I had always dreamt of living in. Besides, I had become accustomed to staying in large houses when I was with Tom. His idea of the sort of house we should live in differed from mine. He loved new modern architecture, roofs at sharp ninety-degree angles, and floor-to-ceiling glass windows. The relationship would never have worked for that reason alone, but of course, there were many other reasons as well, ones I couldn't dwell on for too long.

I was probably just imagining the way Hendrick had lingered for a few seconds before he left, as though he'd wanted to say more to me. I knew I appeared somewhat withdrawn, and that people might find that disconcerting. But something had changed for me. The people who knew the old version of me were no longer around, so this new peculiar version of myself was all anyone got to see. Was he genuinely concerned for me? Did I radiate an oddness that worried him? I was sure I hadn't imagined the strained look on his face as if he hadn't quite finished what he had to say to me. I was still perceptive enough to sense what someone was about, even after everything that had happened. I was stripped of my confidence, and I had a genuine fear that some terrible fate awaited me, but I was still able to see through a person's skin and feel their psyche. My instincts hadn't failed me yet. Thank goodness. Who knew if I would need them out here all alone?

I was tired, though. Sleep was almost non-existent these days. The moment I fell into a deep sleep, I was awake again within minutes, then I would snooze for several hours, waking very early in the morning. Then I wouldn't be able to get back to sleep, so I would get up, and that was that. My day would start at 6 a.m. Then I was shattered by 8 p.m., and the whole cycle started over again. So maybe my tiredness was the cause of my overthinking everything. It had all happened so quickly. I felt as if I had only just entered the competition.

Yet here I was, in this house of dreams, but my nightmares had followed me.

I had brought some basics with me – a duvet, a couple of blankets, toiletries, my laptop and Kindle, and a bag of paperbacks, although I was sure I wouldn't relax enough to read them. But they were my comfort items, and just knowing they were there gave me some hope that someday soon I might reach for my Kindle purely for relaxation, and not because I was trying to distract myself.

The first night sleeping anywhere new was always a challenge for me. I would doze on and off, waking to look at the time only to become stressed about how little sleep I was getting. Couple this with not sleeping anyway, and I was sure I was in for a long night. I had spotted the champagne in the fridge and the plastic glasses in the hamper on the kitchen counter, a welcome package meant for more than one. I could feel a bubble of tension rising from the pit of my stomach. This was a family home. It at least deserved to have two people living in it. But I was going to be living here alone, so very alone. I couldn't help it, I allowed an image of Tom to creep into my head, of the two of us here together in this house. But I soon shook that away. Trying to keep that idea alive was not healthy. Besides, I deserved to be alone. The sooner I became comfortable with that notion, the better.

So far, I had popped my head around the doors to all the rooms and thrown my overnight bag and duvet into the master suite, where a large double bed was. The headboard was against a wall which was papered with golden bird patterns. It was not something I would ever have considered for myself, but it looked good and I was glad it was there; it made the room feel a bit grand... special.

Maybe being somewhere new would help me deal with the

insomnia that had developed over the last month. Not surprisingly, of course. Only people who can come to terms with the horrors that they created can sleep well at night. I wasn't sure when I was dreaming and when I was awake half the time. It was alarming how one day everything could be normal and the next day your whole world had shifted. Everything that was once so easy, like closing my eyes and getting seven or eight hours' sleep, was now a hardship, a test I had to endure each night. And while what had happened was still on my mind every day for most of the day, this was going to be the state of my life from now on. I wasn't sure I would ever sleep soundly again.

I tried to focus on the house. On the win, and what living here could mean in the long term, although it was hard to see beyond the end of each day now. But the house was the distraction I needed and at times my mind gave me some respite and allowed me brief fleeting moments to just be. If I tried hard enough, I could make those moments last for minutes. So, I wandered from room to room and tried to take in everything about the house, the way it smelt: old wood mixed with new fabrics. The furnishings were a bit mismatched, which I felt suited my personality. I was only ever one for symmetry and uniform at the restaurant, so I had always enjoyed feeling rebellious outside of work. I looked at the geometrically patterned rugs scattered around and wondered if they were to my taste.

Most of the people I knew my age had settled with their significant others, had bought paintings from local artists and hung them on their walls, landscaped their gardens at the weekends and bought bright cushions to put on their gaudy-coloured sofas. These people seemed to know themselves, they knew their tastes and they knew what they wanted their world to look like. But what about me? My life had been full enough for me just a few weeks ago, but now it felt small and empty, and this was emphasised more inside the cavernous walls of this mansion.

I found my way outside the front door to admire the garden, the part of the house that had charmed me so much when I had seen it in the photograph that Hendrick had shown me when he'd sold me the ticket. I stood in the garden and thought back to that day at Mirabelle. It had been quiet, but that wasn't unusual for a May bank holiday when everyone was enjoying themselves at the beach. Hendrick had come in by himself and ordered sparkling water at the bar. I had cleared up around him and stopped suddenly when I saw a book poking out of the top of his briefcase. *Women Who Run with the Wolves* was one of my favourite books. I carried a copy around in my own bag often and would sometimes read it on my lunch break. So, when I saw it just sitting there in his briefcase, I was immediately drawn to him. I struck up a conversation easily, asking him about the book, and he told me how he was enjoying it. He had only just started it and was reading it because he and his girlfriend were experiencing a period of difficulty in their relationship, and she had requested he read it to help them get through this sticky patch.

'She thinks I will understand her better,' he had told me, and I assured him that he would, 100 per cent. After that, we fell easily into a conversation about other things, and it wasn't long until Hendrick told me that he worked for ABC Wins, where the prizes were all huge houses scattered across the home counties. He'd had a rubbish day of sales and should have hit his target and hadn't yet. He'd shown me the website, and there was a selection of houses to win: one in the Cotswolds, one in London. But I already had my eye on the one in Dorset, where I already lived. The thought of a country retreat had been very tempting to me.

'So, people actually win these houses, do they?' I quizzed Hendrick. Even though I had read up on this kind of competition before, I wanted to check I wasn't going to be throwing my money into a pot that never actually saw anyone win.

'Oh, yes, all the time. The business makes a massive profit even with a prize worth this much.'

'Two million.' I stared at his laptop screen. 'For a house.' I had thought of Tom at that moment; how he wouldn't have flinched at that price. But we had still only been together a short while by that point, and I was still astounded every time I walked into one of his properties or we checked into a hotel of his choosing. I couldn't imagine owning something of such value, whereas for Tom that was his normal life.

I bought five tickets from him in the end. Not because I expected to win, but because I felt sorry for him, and because I was suddenly invested in him and his girlfriend getting their relationship back on track. I believed in love, I truly did. Maybe I was feeling altruistic and imagined that by considering someone else's narrative, my relationship with Tom would magically evolve into what I needed it to be. I spent twenty-five pounds that afternoon – all of my tips from the few tables we'd had over lunch – and I came out with a two-million-pound property. A very nice little investment, some might say. I had never considered myself a winner; I was one of life's losers in many ways: I hadn't succeeded at school, I had flunked my A-levels, and had lived in a poky flat for most of my twenties...

I tried not to linger too long on the other thing, the major factor that made me not just a loser, but a liar and a criminal. I was living my life under a blanket of deceit. I didn't deserve to be in the lap of luxury. I didn't have a lot to offer the world, but I was fine with that. What I did as a job was enough and always had been. There seemed to be this incessant need in life to get on and 'become' something, to excel and reach some higher level where you could look down on the rest of your peers, family or friends and say, 'Hey, look at me, I made it!'

But what was wrong with us all just being content with the simple things? A few friends, a steady income to buy the things I needed and maybe a few extras from time to time. But mostly, to have a purpose, to feel as if I was doing something worthwhile. Serving people, making them feel comfortable and watching them leave full and satisfied – often happier than when they arrived – was all the buzz I needed in life. I wasn't sure what it was that Tom saw in me when we first got together. Why would he pick someone who had lower career expectations and who had done so little with their life? But it wasn't long before I worked it out. Before I worked him out.

I walked along the small driveway and in front of the lake where the tiny idyllic bridge linked the drive to the patches of grass on the other side. That then opened onto a larger patch of grass situated at the side of the house that was as big as a full-size football pitch. It was then that I saw her. Racing across the lawn, still the same age. Six years of fanatical fun. Running as though she could never stop. I wasn't surprised that she had followed me here; she had been in my mind's eye for the last month, always standing within a few feet of me, but here she was able to run. I had never seen her run that way before, with so much space around her. She faded to nothing, as quickly as she had appeared, and I was left feeling slightly bereft – as I always was – that it didn't ever come to more, that she would always only visit for a few seconds, and then she would be gone again. I always felt as if I had so much to say to her, but the words would never properly form. Besides, would she even hear me? Would I be able to communicate with her?

I walked across the bridge and found myself standing where I had just seen her. I looked where the grass led around to the back of the house, where I saw a series of outbuildings and a large open barn. I immediately thought about a party I had been to in my early twenties and wondered how I could replicate something similar here. But then who would come? The reality was that there was no one. There had been of course, not so long ago, but they had all faded into the background. They were there still, simmering away. Occasionally I would get a text or even a call – which I wouldn't answer – and I would ignore them.

I was stuck, wishing they would disappear so I wouldn't have to ever admit to them what had gone on, how not only my life was in tatters but the lives of others, and all in such a flash, a moment that came and went in a second. Yet I also silently craved for them to congregate around me, to hold me, as I slowly told them what had happened. For them to bear the brunt of some of the pain as well, and then give me advice, tell me it would all be okay eventually. But the terror always overtook the rational side of my thoughts. In the end, all I imagined were looks of pure disdain on their faces. And the words, 'Kit, how could you? What have you done?' echoing around me as they too tried to take in the enormity of it all.

I peeked in through one of the outbuildings. The window was thick with dirt on either side so I could only just make out the silhouette of what looked like an assortment of garden tools. I shuddered at the thought of having to maintain the huge lawns and borders, then I felt the weight of the property overwhelm me again. What had I taken on? What was I thinking? I didn't need the worry of such a place when so much else was going on. Was this going to bring even more stress? On the outside, it looked like the perfect house, a fairy-tale. But what if it became a house of horrors with leaks and holes and draughts? I wasn't sure I was ready for this. I had never been ready for this. This was why I had always been so happy with my little flat by the sea. I wandered back onto the main lawn and tried to take in its splendour. Wasn't this one of those moments when I should be drenched in happiness, delirious with excitement? Shouldn't I be saying over and over that I couldn't believe this had happened to me and I was so grateful? But my mind was too busy with thoughts of dread. Because although I had won, and something special and amazing had happened to me, all I could think was that something terrible needed to happen again, to balance out the good.

5

NOW

My eyes tried to adjust to the space around me, but the thick darkness blotted out everything. Panic rose in my chest as I realised I was unfamiliar with the room and unsure where the light switch was. I cursed myself for falling asleep without prepping for when I woke. But I hadn't been thinking ahead; I had thought that the most appropriate thing to do was to toast myself in my new house with some of the champagne that had been left in the welcome hamper. I had also hoped that this would help me sleep better. I knew better than that now I had woken. But last night, the only way to get past the worry had been to drink. Then suddenly, after several drinks, I began to think that this could all work out. Something about a new home and a new start made me believe I would be rewarded with the most basic of needs, to fully switch off and recuperate. But it wasn't to be. I was awake in the middle of the night again, with only my painful thoughts for company, as well as the beginnings of a hangover.

I grappled around for my phone. The bed was low to the floor, so my hands grazed the carpet but didn't meet anything. Next, I felt across the bedsheets. All the while, I forced myself to remember what the room looked like, where the door was so I could get up and walk towards it, but my mind was blank. I began to panic; my mouth felt watery – a side effect of the alcohol I had consumed. How long ago, I had no idea, but long enough that the effects were wearing off.

Finally, my fingers skimmed the cool smooth case of my phone and relief flooded through me. I lit up the screen. It was 1.33 a.m. I had managed just over four hours' sleep. That had to be a record. I shone the torch in my bag which was next to the bed and found my charger. I stuffed it into the nearest plug socket, then turned on the bedside lamp. I perched on the end of the bed and sucked in a few big lungful of air into my chest until it no longer felt restricted. Then it suddenly came to me why I had woken. A noise. I knew there would be plenty of things to get used to in a house this size, but it still unnerved me all the same.

From where the house was situated, I couldn't see my neighbours and they couldn't see me. Would anyone hear me if I screamed? The night was still, with no wind, no rain. Perhaps it had been an animal knocking over a bin, that was the sort of thing that happened in the countryside, wasn't it? I was loath to move from the room and tried to summon the courage to start skulking around an unfamiliar house. I knew I needed to get up because trying to sleep now was a no-go. I would be thinking about whether it was indeed a noise I had heard and then I would be catastrophising until I had exhausted every possible scenario.

Was it possible that someone other than Hendrick knew I was here? Had the photo gone out already on the ABC Wins website? There would be some people who would be more than upset if they saw me living it up in the lap of luxury after what I had done. But would they come here for me? I hadn't gone out of my way to hide at Citrus, which wasn't too far away from Mirabelle. It was in the same area.

But still, the echo of the noise was in my head. What was it, a bang, a smash? I couldn't quite say. I had been told on more than one occasion that I had a pretty vivid imagination. I spent a lot of time alone as an adult. So, I had plenty of time to imagine all sorts of things. Listening to the goings-on outside my flat on Friday and Saturday nights as people made their way home from the pubs was always a good opportunity to lie and imagine what they looked like, what the story was. Especially if it was a couple arguing. My imagination served me well as a child, when I had needed to talk myself out of a few tricky situations, much to the disgust of my older sister, who – because my excuses were so well delivered – would be the one who ended up getting the blame.

Thinking about Jude made me think about my parents and the many words still unspoken between us. I wondered if I would ever be able to tell them the truth. The pain of the lie sat like an indigestible piece of food, redundant in the pit of my stomach.

As I stood to make my way to the bedroom door, I thought about Jude again. How, if she were here now, she would be hiding behind me, and the old me would be laughing whilst I waltzed out into the unknown, with Jude's desperate fearful whispers in my ear. It had felt good, back then, to not have real worries. The only fears were the ones my mind had created. But that fearless tigress had almost disintegrated.

I moved out of the bedroom and paused whilst I remembered where the light switch was. Once the landing was illuminated, I felt a little more in control. Whoever or whatever had made the noise would be exposed. But the thought of a 'whoever' was too much to deliberate at such an hour, in new surroundings. Again, I reassured myself. No one knew I was here. If I wanted to just hide out and be forgotten for a while, surely this was the place to do it. I hadn't wanted to tell anyone about the win and I didn't want anything to change. Not again...

I arrived downstairs and found myself in the hallway, which felt stark and cold. Again, too big for just one person. How would I fill that hallway? With a hundred umbrellas? Tables upon tables of white lilies? Their presence would go unnoticed by anyone, pollen dripping onto the hard wooden floor. The space only reminded me that this was a family home and the hallway deserved to be filled with guests coming and going, people mingling at parties. I tried to imagine a party with me as the hostess milling about, but I just couldn't conjure it up. It wasn't going to happen any time soon. There was no one I would call on, not now. I went to the front door and looked through the panes of glass into the night. What was I thinking, sleeping here alone tonight? Thoughts of the past began to creep in, the what-ifs plaguing me. What if I hadn't broken it off? I would have someone here with me to share the darkness with, to wander the rooms with and absorb the newness. There would be two bodies for the unfamiliar sounds to bounce off.

I thought I knew what I was doing when I decided to go it alone, but standing here in the cold and dark, I was no longer sure. I walked back the other way through the hall and into the lounge, checked the patio door was locked, and then wandered into the sunroom, checking that door was also locked. I had checked all of this once as soon as the sun began to set. It was just first-night nerves. I would be fine once the sun rose. Things always felt more intense at night. When I felt as though I was all alone and no one else in the world was awake except me, mulling over the same thoughts: how did I let it happen, how did I become this monster?

I climbed the stairs, but kept the landing light on, and left the bedroom door ajar. The room was bathed in a little light and I felt a sense of security. But I knew sleep would not come. I would simply have to go back to bed, close my eyes and wait for morning.

6

NOW

The tables were bare save for the bright starched tablecloths. Maisie, the manager of Citrus, had probably been in since seven o'clock this morning, waiting to receive the linen delivery. She was efficient and pristine in her own appearance and was steaming wine glasses at the bar as I walked through the double doors and headed to the office to drop off my bag. No personal items allowed in this restaurant.

'Good morning, Kit,' Maisie said loudly, a strained happiness in her voice, as though she liked her job just enough. I suddenly longed to hear the bustle of Mirabelle's, to hear Denim's French accent, the way he would rush to get as much into a sentence as possible, always keen to know how I really was and what I had been up to.

'Nice and early, that is what I like to see,' she added cheerily, and I wished I could match her chirpiness. I wished I could break through this veil of despair to the person I was before. I wished I didn't have to match her forced joviality; I hated that we were the same in that sense. Happiness in my job had come so naturally not long ago and now here I was, somewhere entirely new, trying to fit in, trying to find that edge where I balanced harmoniously between being an impeccable worker and enjoying the shift as well as trying to blend into the background a little. Not showing I was too capable because I didn't need the sort of responsibilities I had been aiming for at Mirabelle. I didn't need to be the centre of attention any more. I would only greet guests as and when I had to; the rest of the time I was happy to blend into the background.

Besides, I didn't find the job as easy as I once did. Something had stopped clicking. It was inevitable, really, the memories were still so acute. If I had half a mind, I would have chosen a new occupation because, right now, I felt as if I was walking through very sticky mud. Each small job I did, I was acutely aware of the very act of it. But this was better than not doing anything at all. This was better than sitting at home and being alone with my thoughts. I had to keep busy, and this was the only way I knew how. This was all part of the redemption, the path I needed to follow to come out the other side a better person.

I smiled at Maisie and made my way to the office, past the large ottoman that was home to the perfectly folded napkins, toothpicks, spare teaspoons, colouring pencils – all the things customers asked for. I could hear the commotion of lunch being prepared through the hatch. I was not yet fully acquainted with all the kitchen staff. Gray, the sous chef – short for Graham, I presumed – and his brigade of three chefs were moving at speed around one another but with such dexterity and grace I could watch them all day. I envied their seamless dance routine and the formula they had instilled in their own little space. Being able to create a sense of order and continuity without anyone looking over your shoulder must be a satisfying experience for them. I longed for that in my world again.

Maisie was a good manager, but I could often sense her watching me, as though she was expecting me to do something out of the ordinary. Did she know who I really was? People talked in this small town. I knew I should have taken a new job further away from Mirabelle. But this was my home, and I couldn't bear to leave it. Too much had changed already, and this was the only constant thing I had in my life right now. But with Maisie's eyes on me, I wondered why it was she watched me. Perhaps it was that she was waiting for me to make a mistake. But I was far too vigilant now. Every aspect of my life was carefully thought out and planned. There would never be another mistake.

'Got nothing on, Kit? Tonnes of dishes need doing in here.' Someone's voice filtered through from the kitchen, a lightness to their tone. Did they know my name, had we been properly introduced? I couldn't remember. I had been here a matter of weeks and I was not counting the days to mark an anniversary of working here. I didn't feel as if I had anything to celebrate. Mirabelle was the place I had once felt so at home.

The voice belonged to Cheryl, another chef. She was friendly like everyone else here but there wasn't that connection that I had felt with Den and Matt and all the other staff at Mirabelle. Courtney not included. But I had accepted her obnoxious ways and would have continued to. But it was Courtney who had won in the end. She still got to go into Mirabelle every day and feel the energy of the place. Despite its zesty name, Citrus lacked fizz.

I smiled at Cheryl. It was her attempt at banter, and of course there were plenty of other jobs that needed my attention in the restaurant, and it seemed that was the interaction over with. In a way, it was for the best, I shouldn't be allowed to have fun. Working here shouldn't be about the banter. I needed to focus on my work and concentrate. Especially because of the way things had ended at Mirabelle.

I tied my pinny around my waist then picked up a large grey plastic tray, filled with freshly polished cutlery.

I began the meticulous job of laying the cutlery in perfect symmetry on the fresh white linen, letting my hands brush against the starched fabric. That was one thing that was similar about the two restaurants, the way the tables were set out, with an extra raised section at the back. It brought back memories that were overpowering. Almost crippling sometimes.

Tiredness overcame me, and I pressed my hands on the tablecloth and imagined I was back there in Mirabelle, as though I would feel the presence of the people who had once sat there. I lingered, hoping my strange actions went unnoticed. But I was suddenly aware of being watched and so I raised my head instinctively towards the window and there, only for a fleeting second, was Courtney. She had paused, looked right in at the restaurant. I was certain she had seen me sitting at the table and then, as I lifted my eyes to meet her gaze, she walked quickly away. It had all happened in a flash, but my stomach twisted. Anything or anyone associated with Mirabelle was a stark reminder as to why I was working here. I was trying to make a new life. It didn't mean I had forgotten, I would never forget, but it was almost as though Courtney was trying to rub it in my face. She had meant to be there. It wasn't an ideal situation for me, but I couldn't turn back time; I had to take this penance. There were worse places I could be, like prison.

Denim had given me a very basic reference – enough to get me this job – which was good of him, and I realised I could have been a lot worse off. He knew what had happened had been a tragedy and one he had tried in many ways to avoid, but I had let him down. I had let everyone down.

And now Courtney knew where I worked. How long had she known, and would she care enough to try to make my life difficult? She had what she wanted: me out of Mirabelle and out of her life. Surely that was enough for her, wasn't it?

I knew I was good enough for that role and so did she, but it had all been snatched away in an instant. Everything about that one moment had changed things forever. It had been my dream to make maître d'. I used to think that if I got promoted above her, then I would have been Courtney's superior and she would have learnt to respect me, like me, even. But now all I wished for was for things to be how they were. I would take Courtney's sly looks and snide comments over this – my new empty life – any day. I would even be happy for her to be maître d'. Oh, how painful and tormenting it was to wish for time to rewind itself. My alternative reality felt within reach, as though I could just about touch it with my finger-tips. I would never have been able to assert myself over Courtney and even if I had gained the promotion, she would have continued to have given off an air of superiority, as though she was winning at life, no matter what I did.

Maisie's voice cut through my thoughts and brought me back into the moment. 'Are you okay?' she asked, a curious look on her face as she stood before me.

'Yes.' I laughed off her comment. 'I slept a little lightly last night, and I was just taking a moment.' I was suddenly aware of myself and how I must look to others. It was never something I had considered before, I'd always had enough confidence to do my job and go about life with a certain amount of personality, but that had all evaporated. I was a shell of the woman I'd once been. Maybe Courtney knew that. Maybe that pleased her. But here, here I had to be able to hide how I was really feeling. I had to learn how to smile through the pain.

'Well, after your moment, can you check the ladies' toilets for me, please?' she asked curtly before walking away. I winced at her words.

I looked down at the table and nudged the cutlery so it was exactly in line with where the chair met the edge of the table. The act felt good, and I was catapulted back to a time with Tom – this

had been one of his habits whenever we had eaten out. Now would
have been the time to have someone around to depend upon, to
share the burden of the worries, to discuss the vivid images that
came at night and then kept me awake until dawn. But it could and
never would be Tom, so I had to stop dwelling on what could have
been. I knew you couldn't change people.

I moved slowly away from behind the table, placing the chair
back carefully. Maisie must have had a sixth sense because the
ladies' facilities did not look up to scratch. I fetched fresh toilet roll
and refilled the soap dispensers. I straightened up the hand towels
and nudged the little vase of flowers into the corner. I clocked my
face in the large mirrors. I had stopped looking at myself since it
had happened – unable to see the woman who was responsible for
doing something so unimaginable. *How can you live with yourself?* I
thought, and hurriedly left the room.

Back out in the restaurant, one of the other waiting staff had
arrived. He was holding another large container of cutlery and
looked unsure what to do with it. I ushered him to the ottoman. He
had only been here a week. I filled up a metal jug with boiling
water from the coffee machine and showed him how to dunk the
cutlery in the water and polish it up with a waiting cloth. He
nodded and mumbled his thanks. He seemed like a very intro-
verted young man, and I wondered what his life had been like up
to this point. I wondered if he'd had a happy upbringing. Right
now, I would have swapped anyone's life for my own, regardless of
how pathetic or unappealing it seemed from the outside. Surely
what I was experiencing inside had to be far worse than what
anyone else was going through. I heard Maisie clapping her hands,
her way of telling us that we needed to get a wriggle on. Then I
looked at the time: there were fifteen minutes until service. I let out
a small sigh of relief, I would be distracted for the next few hours at
least.

Without speaking, I took a handful of fresh cutlery and finished setting up the restaurant.

* * *

The shift was as hard as each one had been since I'd started. But I made it through. I hadn't just walked away and sunk into the background of society. I saw enough of those people on the streets in the town centre, people who had maybe come down south to make a living but had been forced to opt out of life for one reason or another. I wondered how close I was to that sort of life. Maybe it was the win that had saved me. But could I truly allow myself to fall so far? I wasn't sure I could. These feelings I was having, they were totally alien to me, but things happened to people all the time that changed their lives for the worse. I knew I was someone who had to keep busy and so I felt lucky that I had the restaurant; it was all I was living for. It wasn't perfect, but I had to accept that nothing would be from now on.

I half wanted to offer to stay on this evening, pull another shift. I'd be dead on my feet, but at least it might help me sleep better tonight. Suddenly the thought of returning to the new house filled me with a sense of dread that I hadn't felt in a long time. Images of me sitting alone for hours flashed before my eyes and made me want to weep. I looked around the restaurant at the staff that were remaining, wondering if I could possibly bring myself to ask someone over. But that would be too much, because then people would see my huge house and wonder how a simple waitress could afford such a place and why it was that I was still working in such a humble job when I had all this wealth. I sure as hell wasn't ready to trust anyone with my secrets.

So instead, I gathered my things slowly and Maisie handed me and the other waiting staff our tips. I looked at the money in my hand and thought of the mansion I now lived in and owned and the £20,000 sitting in my bank account. It felt silly and wrong to take the tips. I didn't need it. Some people had worked hard to earn the money to tip me and here I was taking it from them whilst I sat on a small fortune. But to turn down the money would open the flood gates to questions. So I smiled and thanked Maisie.

I stuffed the notes into my purse and headed to the door. I glanced over my shoulder at two of the other waiting staff, deep in conversation. Were they talking about me? I felt the familiar pang of paranoia hit me as I stepped outside.

The afternoon air still lingered with the warmth of the day, and I thought about everything that had been happening around me whilst I had been working: couples walking hand in hand in the park, families picnicking on the sand. All very normal stuff that was missing from my life now. I longed for that old life – would I ever experience it again?

But for now, I was on my way home. I had to get used to calling it that and become used to living there. It was *mine*; I had won it. And maybe I deserved a little lightness amongst the dark. Perhaps this was a little salvation to help me through the bleaker days. Or perhaps this was the beginning of the end of what had been a month of berating myself. This could only be a good thing, and good things came to good people, didn't they? I knew I was a good person deep down. I had just done that one bad thing, and so far, I had got away with it.

7

THEN

The first few months with Tom were heaven. If I could have bottled and sold that feeling that came with a brand-new relationship, I would have been richer than he was. The notion that every insignificant move I made or slight nuance was being registered by another person, and making their insides dance, gripped my stomach, sending flights of butterflies bursting out of me on a regular basis. Normal behaviours suddenly became a conscious act; knowing I was being watched and my quirks and rituals were one by one being added to the list of reasons why Tom was slowly but surely falling for me. But he had yet to say those words. And I was not the sort of person to declare my feelings unless I was sure.

I would finish up at Mirabelle, and he would be there at the front door in yet another new and expensive car, much to the envy of my colleagues and, of course, Courtney. We would get dinner late at a restaurant he knew stayed open until the early hours of the morning and we talked until late into the night. I was delirious with it all.

I asked him about his family, but he would always change the subject or just stare blankly into the distance and so I never pushed him for more.

He talked of marriage and children. I laughed it off because that was so far into the future.

'How about a dog first?' I half joked when we were in bed one night.

'Our parents didn't let us have any pets growing up,' he said. 'We found one stray in our grounds and brought it into the house. I don't know what happened to that dog, but I never saw it again.'

'Your parents killed it?' I said, shocked.

'I don't know. Maybe.'

'So what do you think happened to it?' He had mentioned a 'we' – did he have siblings? But Tom had turned over and begun breathing softly. I wasn't sure if he was asleep, but I got the impression he did not want to talk about it any more. From then on, it was obvious to me that Tom had things he would rather not tell me. And I wanted to respect that. But I also needed to know more about the person I was falling for.

The best times, though, were when we would get a takeout and go back to his place in Sandbanks and eat out on the terrace overlooking the sea. On my days off, he made time for me by clearing his diary for hours so we could be together, and his attention would be solely on me. Wasn't I lucky? my mum told me when they had spent a weekend in his company. And I was. I couldn't believe he had chosen me. It was almost perfect. His thick shiny hair, his wide smile and eyes. The way he was just a few inches taller than me and could kiss the top of my head. It felt reassuring, I felt a sense of protection that I had never experienced before. I had just a few doubts about him. But they would iron themselves out once Tom realised he could trust me.

Tom took us to a lodge in the forest. He shot pheasant with my father and barbequed with Stanley, my brother-in-law. Jude had eyed him carefully as she'd relaxed in the hot tub on the Saturday afternoon. 'Don't you think he's maybe a bit too good to be true?' she had slurred into my ear after several glasses of champagne.

I had laughed away her comments. Everything *did* seem too good to be true, but I wasn't about to admit that to my sister. She thrived on always being right – which she rarely was – but she spent an inordinate amount of her life trying to prove me wrong. I was riding on waves of pure euphoria – every glance, every graze and touch with Tom felt as if I were being electrocuted; my senses were so heightened to everything and anything he said or did. Just the scent of his skin sent a torrent of shocks through my body. Nothing that anyone could have said at that point could have made me see beyond that. Except me. I had a lot of questions and I wished Tom would answer them.

Later that evening, Tom had ordered a platter of mussels, crabs, scallops and prawns to be delivered from a local seafood restaurant. It had unnerved my father to the point he had inspected each crustation with a meticulous eye; his fear of contracting food poisoning was palpable, to me at least. He said nothing, just nodded enthusiastically at Tom and thanked him afterwards, having only scraped a sliver of crabmeat onto some brown bread and butter.

Tom told me, Mum and Jude to sit back and relax as he and the boys would be clearing up. I watched Dad's eyes double in size, having lived in the lap of luxury with my mum for the last twenty-five years where he had barely needed to lift a finger. I feared he would not know what to do. But he found his way around the kitchen, putting away the knives and forks that Tom washed. Stanley didn't bat an eyelid; he was heavily engrossed in a cricket match on the TV when Tom went over to him, said something quietly in his ear and then I watched as Stanley stood sheepishly and shuffled awkwardly over to the sink with empty champagne glasses. Tom certainly had a way of getting people to do what he wanted them to do, I had thought in that moment.

'Stan rarely helps me clear up. What kind of hocus pocus was that?' Jude slurred; she had drunk far too much champagne with dinner. When I had told Jude about this trip that Tom was planning to get to know my family better, she had immediately got her children, Josh and Emily, booked in with her mother-in-law for the weekend so she could enjoy everything that Tom had on offer. It had been a weekend of indulgence and Jude had taken full advantage.

'He's a little bit... *Sleeping with the Enemy*, isn't he?' Jude observed as Tom folded a towel neatly and adjusted it to a perfect angle on the oven door. I thought about the film starring Julia Roberts and then I had to agree that yes, he had brought a certain amount of order into my world. But amongst all the lust, tenderness, hilarity and conversations that went on into the early hours of the morning, I had perhaps pushed that element of Tom's personality to one side to assess later. I felt a rush of heat across my chest as Jude made comment after comment about how Tom rearranged the cushions after he had been sitting against them, and how the bathroom had been immaculate after she had gone in there after him that morning. I cringed at her words. I did not need her bringing these traits to my attention. Was Jude trying too hard to focus on things about Tom she knew I might find uncomfortable? Or were these traits she found endearing? There had been times when I was with Tom when I wondered what exactly it was that was drawing me to him, that made me want to stay with him. Because even though I was trying my best with him, I knew it would never be enough, unless he gave some of his true self back to me. The frayed edges would soon start to show and all it would take would be one firm tug and everything we had become would unravel.

The evening continued with an enthusiastic game of charades

and many more drinks were had. Dad looked visibly shocked as Tom kept his beer glass topped up and Mum thanked Tom too loudly every time he arrived at her side with the wine bottle. He appeared to be the perfect host: able to keep everyone happy with food and drink and yet still seem calm and relaxed enough. Rich, charming, handsome, the three classic qualities in a man that a woman looked for, surely? To everyone around me, he was the ideal partner. But they couldn't see the things that I saw, that I felt. I had to keep them a secret because my family would just say I was trying to pick faults. Later on, in bed, I was thankful that all Tom wanted to do was cuddle – with my parents and sister and brother-in-law in the surrounding rooms, it would have been unthinkable to do anything else.

'Are you okay?' I asked into the darkness, his breath warm and steady on my cheek.

There was a pause that, looking back, I would have considered too long, but I, like everyone else, had drunk far too much and so I took his silence as preparing himself not to slur his words.

'My sister wanted to be a waitress.'

Tom's words cut through the darkness, and I heard myself say, 'Sister?' very quietly, not wanting to disturb his train of thought, which seemed so random, but I needed to make sure I had heard him right. He had only ever mentioned his family to me once before. I wanted him to keep speaking.

'Yes. She liked to play waitressing when we were kids. She had the whole kit, the fake wooden kitchen, and she would pretend to serve us. We already had several actual household staff when I was growing up. Then, as she got older, she kept talking about it – when we were out in restaurants, she would try to sneak off and help the staff. But my family didn't want that for her. They thought her to be much better than that. She was a rebel, I suppose. She did every-thing she could to mess with them – if they wanted her to play with

Barbies, she would rip all the heads off and play with my Action Men. When they wanted her to study medicine at university, she went travelling to South America. Alone. She liked to play games. With them. And me, sometimes.'

I held my breath for a moment, as I waited for Tom to continue speaking. He didn't for a few seconds and then he whispered, 'You don't know how lucky you are,' then let out a long sigh, and began to softly snore.

8

NOW

Willow Cottage felt cold when I arrived home, even though the day was still warm. Summer was usually my favourite season, but I just couldn't embrace it and was wishing away the warmer months so I could hibernate like a true hermit. Perhaps, just like the trees that lost their leaves in the winter, I would be reborn by spring.

I was just putting my bag on the counter in the kitchen when a loud noise from the garden startled me. I grabbed the nearest object, a hardback cookery book from the counter and, clutching it under my arm, I headed out of the back door to the outbuildings where I thought I had heard the noise come from. I instantly saw that one of the doors was open. I had closed all of them last night. Hadn't I? I had been a little drunk, okay, a lot drunk at the end of the night, but I was sure I'd checked the whole house and garden before it had got dark. My hand tightened on the cookery book and as I gripped it harder, I brought it up to my chest and held it there as a sort of shield-cum-weapon, ready to strike at any moment.

I edged towards the outbuilding, the one I had looked through briefly when I'd arrived yesterday, and I had clocked a few tools through the window but nothing else. Was there something worth stealing in there that I had not spotted before? My curiosity almost overtook my fear of what was lurking in the small concrete room a few feet away from me.

Something made me clear my throat, an unconscious action that was out of my mouth before I'd had time to consider the consequences, that maybe there was a break-in happening right under my nose and I had disturbed them and would be shot on my own land. I could just see the news headlines: *luxury home winner dies protecting prize*. It was not how I had anticipated my friends and family finding out about my win.

Then I heard a deep voice mutter something, and a shadow appeared in the doorway. I clutched the book harder to my chest, ready to thrust it into the face of the intruder. Then a man, tall and broad and wearing heavy-looking workman's boots, stepped into the doorway. For a second, he looked startled, but only to see me there, and I was certainly no threat to him. He looked older than me, perhaps in his late thirties, Scruffy sandy hair fell about his face, and he ran a hand through it, exasperated.

'I am sorry to startle you.' I was surprised to hear a Somerset accent; one I knew well from relatives of my childhood. 'I have a small problem in that one of my pups has escaped and seems to have found sanctuary in the corner of your outbuilding.'

'Oh, I see,' I said, not moving or releasing the grip on my book. I hadn't realised I had any neighbours. My instincts were failing me. I had forgotten what I was supposed to do in such a situation. I tried to focus on his face, to see if it revealed anything to me. After a moment, I realised I was staring blankly at the man.

He shook his head, and swept a hand through his hair again.

'I'm sorry, I'm Blake. I look after the grain store. I live there too. I guess I'm your neighbour, although you can't see my house from here.'

'Grain store?' I said inquisitively, suddenly wishing very much that I had done some research on the surrounding buildings.

'You can't see it from the road; it's down the path and behind the trees. You'd pass the entrance on your drive up here.'

I had seen a turning, but I hadn't considered what it was or where it led to, and I certainly wouldn't have considered driving down it.

Blake looked down towards my chest and I realised he was checking out my weapon of choice.

'Were you thinking of doing some damage with...' Blake leant forward, presumably to read the book title better, but I instinctively edged backwards, '*Slow Cooker Recipes for Beginners*?'

I hadn't considered the book before I grabbed it in the kitchen, and I almost loosened my grip to get a look as I noticed Blake's lips curling at the edges as he tried to suppress a smile. But I corrected myself and pulled my shoulders back.

Blake looked down apologetically.

'Look, I'm sorry for the intrusion, I didn't know anyone had moved in. I just need to move the equipment in this here outbuilding. Do I have your permission?'

'Yes, but please, whatever you move, put straight back,' I heard myself say in a voice that was sterner than I would have liked.

Blake nodded. He didn't know this was not my usual style of delivery and so he turned and walked back into the outbuilding. I wasn't about to follow him, to find it was some sort of trap, so I stood back from the doorway a few feet and listened to the sound of grunting and heavy machinery being lifted and scraped across a concrete floor. Blake emerged a few minutes later, clutching a ball of black and white fluff. I heard myself let out a small gasp. I had always loved dogs, had grown up with them. And I was a sucker for a puppy. Blake remained a few feet away from me, but my grip on the book slackened a little and he moved closer.

'Our rescue bitch Marley managed to get out and mate with the Labrador down the road from us. We ended up with a litter of six crossbreeds. We never knew what Marley was – a proper Heinz 57 variety – and now these pups.' He looked down at the furball in his arms. 'This one seems to be taking after her mother, always looking for the escape route. I had no intention of breeding, see. I managed to give a few away, but I'm still left with three.'

I carefully placed the book on top of a wheelie bin and stood next to Blake. I placed my hand on the puppy's head and she lifted it up and looked at me, then stuck out a little pink tongue and licked my finger. I felt a bolt of something rush through me, and a sudden connection to this living breathing creature. I snatched my hand back. I wasn't even going to entertain the thought that Blake was trying to insert into my head. I was not fit to look after anything. I could barely look after myself.

'You looking for a companion? Living here by yourself, are you?' I glanced past Blake towards the garden. And I could see her again, as though she was actually there, running across the lawn. She would have been exactly the right age to appreciate a puppy like this one. Maybe she would want me to help, to give a dog a home. I heard Blake clear his throat and I looked at him. Should I even trust this man who had just introduced himself as my neighbour?

'I love dogs,' I said quietly, glancing to the lawn again. But she was gone.

'Had much experience?' Blake was being a responsible owner, vetting me first.

'I grew up with dogs. My... parents had Collies.' I found I had almost stuttered before I spoke of my mother and father and a sliver of a memory jabbed at me.

'Ah, Collies are the best. Are you home much? Would she be left at home alone? I wouldn't want anything for her, I just need her to go to a good home.'

'I... I work in a restaurant. I work short lunch shifts or evenings,' I found myself saying and maybe, just maybe, believing that I could do this.

'So, you'd be around to exercise her in the day. I'm not quite sure how big she will grow but I imagine a medium-sized dog.'

I cleared my throat. 'I am all alone out here, so it might be a good idea to have a companion.'

'Well.' Blake smiled. 'That's that then!'

We talked a little more and eventually we began walking around to the back door. We stood in the doorway, and I thought I should invite him in, but I knew that I didn't want to. I knew I would appear rude if I didn't. The idea of making small talk in the kitchen brought on a sudden tightness to my chest. Hospitality was what I did for a living. Surely I could still extend that to my private life too.

Blake handed me the dog and I nuzzled her, and she licked my face.

'I reckon it was fate,' he said, and I noticed, for the first time, the darkness and intensity in his eyes. 'Not something I usually believe in, but she seems to have found her way to you.' He smiled at me this time and instantly I looked down at the floor, unable to hold his gaze for fear he might see something in me that he didn't like.

I suggested I give Blake something in return for the dog, but he brushed away my offer.

'I'll be back to check on you both soon, to see she's settling in all right. That is all I ask for in return. A happy and healthy life for her.' I felt my body deflate a little. I had puffed myself up ready to play host but he had no intention of coming in, and I was thankful for that.

I waved Blake off with his promises to return the following week, and then I turned and went inside the house. Half an hour ago, I was a woman living alone in a huge house, and now I was a dog owner. The whole experience was starting to feel a little surreal. I wondered how my life could have turned around so suddenly, and why I had been chosen to win this house and now be gifted a dog; the perfect accompaniment to the cosy country life. God knows, I knew I didn't deserve it. The image of my parents that had been lurking in the back of my mind now reappeared as bold as if they were standing right in front of me. The look of love on my mother's face was pure and raw. I thought about how long it had been since I had spoken with them. It had been too long.

I wondered if they would be proud of me for what on the surface appeared to be such an achievement. My parents were the kind of people who would be more impressed with the dog than the house, and they would see it as me finally settling and taking some responsibility. Even as I held the dog in my arms, I could feel, not the physical weight, but the weight of the responsibility that came with looking after a creature. One who was so small. She would grow and it would be down to me to make sure she was well fed and cared for. *Of course you can do it.* I heard the voice of my mother. But she would only see a simple act of raising a dog, something she and my father had done for many years. What she didn't know was that I was capable of taking a young life and crushing it.

9

NOW

I woke up with a puppy under my arm and a nose full of fur. She had whined the whole night, so I had brought her into the bed with me. 'A rod for my own back' were the words that were echoing through my mind, but I would deal with that later. I had managed one night. But one night was nothing in the life of a dog. There would be years of being there for her. I felt my heart flutter in panic and the prospect of something being dependent on me. I thought of others who had relied on me, and I had let them down. A life that should have been long, was gone too soon. I glanced around the room to see if she was here with me today, but I felt nothing but the chill of the morning. I looked down at the puppy and she licked my nose again. I had a lunch shift to tackle, and I knew this puppy would soon need to pee.

As I drove out of the gates and along the road that would eventually lead me back to the seafront, I noticed the turn-off Blake had mentioned and I caught a glimpse of a modern-looking barn and beyond that several farm-style cottages that looked a bit battered and run down on the outside. I felt a slight sense of relief that I was no longer a stranger in a new village and that I now had a neighbour, someone I could call on if I needed help.

Whenever I had imagined moving out of my flat into somewhere bigger, I had always envisaged doing it with someone else. That person was always faceless, though. All that time with Tom and I had never really thought about us in that sense. It was as if I always knew something about him would prevent us ever moving on and moving in together. So I didn't feel a loss that he wasn't here, only a slight bereft feeling, that this wasn't exactly how it was supposed to have worked out. But I could never have believed that I would be in the midst of such a tragedy, that the win – which should have seen me celebrating with friends and family – was a mere glint of light amongst the haze of misery.

I pulled into my usual spot, two streets away from the restaurant, where parking was cheaper. A wave of panic gripped me as a car I recognised pulled out of a side road. I clung to the steering wheel as I watched the car edge away slowly, as though they had seen me, and they wanted me to see them. It was inevitable that I would see Tom around from time to time, but still, panic seized me because it had been over a month since we had been near one another. The day I'd left him, I'd left him for good. There was no going back. He had tried calling, coming round, and of course sending me endless gifts, but it was my ability to remove all my feelings and emotions from the situation that got me through the breakup. Nice and clean. No mess. Even now – even though I thought of him most days – I didn't hold any of those emotions with me. It was better this way. I watched his expensive sports car drive away and composed myself as I made my way to Citrus, putting all thoughts of Tom from my mind.

I was mindful of Maisie watching me during the shift. I felt like a school kid. It was ridiculous, because I could leave at any point, walk away and go back to Willow Cottage, live off the winning cash.

I could stay at home with the dog, not worry about bills or food for a year. But then it would be just me, alone with all these thoughts.

I heard a commotion at the front door. My heart began to thud in my chest when I heard the high-pitched sound of a young child. A girl. She was with her parents. Maisie brought them through. She headed towards me, making small talk with them about the weather. The young girl held her dad's hand. Maisie arrived and stood in front of me. 'Table sixteen for this family, please, Kit.' She smiled inanely at me and suddenly I felt as though we were in a play and that was my cue to smile inanely too and then I found I had forgotten my lines. I looked down at the little girl. She was about five or six. I felt my gut twist, and I thought for a second I might run straight out of the restaurant and keep going until I reached the sea. I could see myself at the edge of the ocean, letting out a primal scream.

'Kit?' Maisie's voice cut through, a hint of urgency to it.

I looked up and forced my face into a smile. It was painful.

'Let's get you guys seated,' I blurted, and I could feel the weight of Maisie's stare as I made my way across the restaurant to the booths.

I tended to the family's needs and I tried not to look for too long at the little girl: at the way she twisted strands of her father's hair between her fingers, propped up on her knees, or the way she sucked the tip of her thumb until her mother gently coaxed it from her mouth.

This was torture and I was wondering why I was putting myself through it again. Then I reminded myself that this was what I did, I was a waitress. I had loved my job once. I was sure I could love it again one day.

The restaurant filled up and soon the buzz of the lunch shift distracted me and so, when 4 p.m. arrived, I threw my waiter's cloth and apron into the laundry basket, and picked up my handbag and went to leave. I took a cautionary glance around to see who I could say goodbye to before I left, but it was only Maisie by that point in the restaurant. She bid me farewell in her usual polite manner but I could tell she was onto me. I had to keep this job – if I didn't, I had nothing.

I arrived back at Willow Cottage, looked at the front of the house from where I had parked my car, and heard the words 'welcome home' in my mind. Would I ever be able to believe that this was my home, that I deserved it enough to feel settled? I felt as if I were floating through someone else's life right now. The period between splitting with Tom and winning Willow Cottage had been a time of quiet reflection. I had intentions to do so much more with my life – maybe winning this house was just another sign I should stay here, a short drive from the restaurant, and stay working there for as long as I was supposed to. However long that was. Until there was a sign that I was forgiven, that I could move on. But there were no signs, only more reasons to stay hidden away. I mean, winning a house was a dream come true! For most people. The surroundings were beautiful, the gardens were magical, the house was spacious... too spacious, I had to admit. Walking around the place made me feel a little nervous. My mind was so confused, always in a muddle, panic gripped me at unexpected moments. But I would try to let the nerves settle and make the most of my time here, despite my heavy heart.

Over the last few weeks, my mind had become heightened and tuned in to the external world, noises and even just notions and feelings sometimes. So, when I got out of the car, I noticed that my body had become rigid, stopping me in my tracks as though it was absorbing some sort of invisible force. I had come to recognise this as a feeling that something was wrong. It had happened on that day. The day I wished to forget but could not. Since then, I had experienced it on perhaps three or four occasions when something was not as it should be.

I tried to shake off the feeling, because what could it possibly be? It was almost five in the afternoon; I had left the puppy for longer than I would have wanted to, but I was sure she would be okay. She had water and a toilet mat.

I took myself in through the front door so I could pick up any post on the way. The kitchen was just off from the hallway, a few steps down, and when I took the first step, I could already see what it was that my body was trying to tell me before I had even arrived in the house. There was a large puddle on the floor between the steps and the kitchen door, which I had closed when I left. It was too big to have come from the puppy. Besides, she was on the other side of the door. I thought about her and that she would be soaking wet, so I padded over and swung the door open so I could assess the damage as quickly as possible.

The kitchen floor was flooded and water was spurting from under the sink. The floor resembled a paddling pool. Without thinking, I plunged into it. I exhaled loudly at the shock of the cold around my ankles. I opened the cupboard under the sink to turn the mains off. I could see a long jet of water coming from a pipe. I pulled the lever down and it stopped. Had there been a leak in one of the pipes that could have been dripping consistently since I left, long enough to have filled up the kitchen floor by several inches? I inspected the pipe closer and indeed there was what looked to be a small hole. It had to have happened since I'd gone. Had it eroded?

I looked around and assessed the damage to the kitchen, then gasped as I remembered the puppy. She had been in the corner when I'd left. Her makeshift dog bed – a cardboard box – was sodden in the corner of the kitchen. She was not inside. The door to the utility room was two steps up and was ajar, and I hoped she had thought to hide in there. My heart was racing by now and I realised in the moment of panic how much I cared about the dog. I wanted her to be okay. After so much loss already, I *needed* her to be okay. I pushed the door open further. The floor was empty, and I started to catastrophise, thinking she could have drowned. I opened the first cupboard, and there was nothing but a grimy washcloth. Then I heard a tiny whine and I leant forward and peered into the sink. There she was, dry and curled up in a ball in the centre. She rose when she saw me and rested her paws on the edge of the sink.

'Oh, my God, you're all right.' I picked her up and she started licking my face as I snuggled her as close to me as possible. I checked her over for any signs of injury, then I traced my gaze down the counter side, edge and all around it to look for a way she could have possibly clambered up to safety. She was far too small to jump. I looked around as I felt my body convulse with a shiver. My legs were freezing from the water, but it was something else. It was fear. I had thought I would be safe here, alone where no one knew where I was. But someone must know, because there was only one possibility. Someone had lifted her up there.

10

NOW

I tried to fathom why someone would have found their way into the house at exactly the same time the leak had begun and then decided to lift my puppy to safety, as I oversaw the plumber fixing the pipe. I had managed to make us both a hot drink. But the thoughts of someone coming into the house were still with me.

'Cute pup, what's its name?' He was from Martin's Plumbing Services – presumably Martin himself, or even Mr Martin. He popped up from beneath the sink to take a sip of the tea I had made for him. I was now in dry socks and wellington boots, leaning against the counter with the warm ball of fluff in my arms.

'I, um, well she doesn't have a name yet,' I was ashamed to admit.

'Well, that's no good, is it? You can't have a pup with no name. Especially in a new house. It's bad luck.'

I frowned, wondering if that statement was true and if a lack of name had caused this catastrophe.

'Well, I guess I haven't got around to it yet. Not had time to think.'

'You don't need to think too hard, though, do you? Just think about something that is special to you, like your mother's middle name, or places you've visited or your favourite flower. Something special, you know, something that has meaning.'

I pondered over his words for a few moments. A name kept appearing in my mind, but no matter how hard I tried to push it away, it wouldn't budge. It just wouldn't take leave of my brain.

Eventually, I looked at the plumber and spoke.

'Lucy. She's Lucy.' Heat rushed through my body as the name left my lips and became the air between us.

'Ah, that's pretty. Has it got some sentimental value to it?'

I gulped and I felt my heart race. He wouldn't know, he would never know. So why was I so nervous, as though he could read my thoughts, see straight into my past?

'It does. Yes,' I said eventually.

'Ah, well, there you go then. Welcome home, Lucy.' He walked over and tickled her under her chin. I let the sound of her name settle in the room, spoken by this burly stranger who had no understanding of its association to me and was, thankfully, far too polite to ask. I had been brave to use the name, to bring it back to life. It wasn't easy to hear it, but this was all part of the process. This was what I had to do, because surely one day I would be free. I had to be patient and do what was needed. Just keep following the signs and listening to the clues.

'Well, I think I seem to have managed to fix it for now, but the pipes *are* a little old and rusty. There might be some investment needed in the future. You staying long, or thinking of selling? Only saying, in case you want a quote on any work that might need doing before you put it on the market.'

'So was it an accident?' I said hurriedly.

He frowned. 'The water burst through for sure, there was some weakness there.' He looked at me with an expression of concern on his face. 'Just you out here, is it?'

I nodded. 'For the time being.' I hated admitting the truth, even to a stranger. 'But I think I'll be here for a while.' I looked down at Lucy. And for the first time since I had won the house, I believed what I had said. Maybe for the first time in a long time, this was exactly where I needed to be.

* * *

The plumber left a short while later and Lucy followed me outside. I already felt as though I had a companion in her, and one who would be faithful too. I found myself back at the outbuilding she had been discovered in and began to search for something the tiny dog could use as a bed. Dusk had painted the sky a deep amber and I thought of the rhyme: *red sky at night, shepherd's delight*. That thought led me to Blake. He lived and worked near a grain store. He did something outdoors.

I began sifting through the discarded items in the room when Lucy suddenly darted behind me into a corner. I turned around to see what had startled her.

I was surprised to see a familiar face loitering outside.

'Hello there,' Hendrick said.

'Oh!' My shock at seeing him must have been clear on my face. 'Hello,' I said eventually, righting myself. I was suddenly aware of my heart thudding heavily in my chest. He had startled me.

'I was in the area, and I just wanted to pop in and see if you were...' He paused for a moment. I almost began to speak for him. 'Just checking in on you and the dog. How are you settling in?'

'I'm good, thanks.' I turned around to find Lucy, who had scurried under a small table, and as I bent to reach her, my hands met something. I pulled her gently out and popped her under one arm then went back in with the other hand and retrieved a medium-sized square basket, the sort used for putting hamper goodies in.

'Oh, this is perfect!' I pushed myself back up to standing. Hendrick was looking at me with a strange expression.

'Are you okay?' he asked and I almost laughed; he sounded so sincere.

'Yes, I'm fine. I have this dog now, Lucy, and I needed to get her something to sleep in until the morning when hopefully Amazon will deliver her a brand spanking new deluxe doggy bed.'

'Oh, right. I can see. And she's yours is she, not on loan or anything?' He looked perplexed, clearly troubled by something. Perhaps he was allergic to dogs or plain didn't like them. 'Were you, I mean, are you feeling unsafe? Is that why you got a dog?' I thought about his question for a second and realised I did feel a small amount of contentment now that Lucy was here.

I explained to Hendrick how she turned up here from Blake's farm.

Hendrick nodded.

'Would you like to come in, for some tea or something? But you'll probably need wellies.' As soon as I said it, I regretted it. It was odd that Hendrick was here, and me inviting him in would only prolong this uncomfortable feeling between us.

'I won't, thanks.'

'Okay,' I said and almost sighed in relief. 'Is this something you always do, check on the winners? Is it some sort of follow up?'

'I... yes. Yes, we usually like to give it a day or two and then pop back and make sure you have everything, that the house is okay and all that.'

'We had a leak,' I said.

'Really?' Hendrick was checking out his surroundings, his concentration elsewhere.

'Yes, this afternoon. The plumber just left.'

'Oh right, let me, erm... I shall look into that for you, at the office. Make sure you're covered for it or if it's under a guarantee or something.'

'Really?' I felt my heart lift. 'That would be good if it was. I mean, it could work out to be quite expensive. All those hidden things like pipes and wires usually are. My dad was a plumber, you see. Hey, you didn't happen to pop by earlier, did you?' I had been thinking about Lucy being in the utility sink and trying to fathom who could have sabotaged the pipe. Would it have been the same person who had lifted her into the sink? The only other person who might have a key was Hendrick. I shuddered at the prospect. It was too obscene.

He shook his head. 'I just said I was passing. I didn't mean to intrude. I hope you're okay.'

I frowned openly at him this time. 'Are you sure you don't need some tea?'

'No, I'm fine, really. I'll let you get on with your evening.' He started to walk away and I followed him to the front of the house, where his car was parked right at the end of the drive. That was odd, why hadn't he brought it right up to the top of the drive? That way, I would have heard him arriving.

He began to speed up as he walked towards his blue saloon. He turned around before he reached it.

'Call me if you need anything. I'll look into that plumbing issue for you.'

'Thank you.' I waved and then bent to pick up Lucy, who had followed me onto the drive.

'What a funny man,' I said to her and realised how lucky I was to have her with me here. I turned back to the house. The sky had become darker since Hendrick had been here, and I felt a sudden sense of doubt at having to go back to the house. What had the person who had been there come for? All I could console myself with was the fact that picking Lucy up and putting her in the sink was a kind thing to do and whoever did it was obviously a lover of animals; they hadn't wanted to see her suffer, yet they had wanted me to suffer. Had someone really tried to cause damage to Willow Cottage? Had they done it as some sort of warning? As I turned to walk back to the house, a thought entered my mind. I rewound to how Hendrick had shown up here this evening. When he arrived, he said he was checking up on me and Lucy. I was tired and now overthinking things, but there was no way he could have known I had a dog before today. After I had collected the basket for Lucy from the back of the house, I went inside and double-locked every door and window.

11

THEN

We had eaten dinner out three times already in one week and I craved a night in front of the TV, a bottle of wine and a cheese board. I could not be bothered to get dressed up and drive up to London or wherever Tom wanted to go to try out some new restaurant that had just opened.

'Do you mind?' I asked him.

'Of course not. I fancy a night of trashy TV. I have a brand-new pair of sweatpants I need to cut the tags off.'

I sniggered and Tom looked at me.

'What?'

'Did you just call them sweatpants?'

Tom pulled a funny expression. 'Is that bad?'

'I don't know, Tom – it depends if you really want to call them sweatpaaants?' I said in an American accent.

Tom smirked. 'Very good, you should do voice overs, or acting or something.'

I smiled and shook my head.

He took my hand. 'No, Kit, really, you're great at so many things, I sometimes think you're wasted just waitressing in that place.'

I looked up at him with a hardened expression.

'Waitressing is a good job. We all need waitresses. You met me there, don't forget.' I tried to keep the tension from my voice. This wasn't the first time that Tom had suggested I forge a new career path during these last few months since we had begun dating. Tom could read the frustration in my face, yet he continued to challenge me on the one thing he knew I was 100 per cent sure about. I felt myself deflate every time a conversation evolved to this point. Tom talked often of us in the future, but it was moments like these when I could not see us getting beyond six months.

'I'll never forget,' he said and slipped his arms around my waist and pulled me closer to him. 'I had my eye on you from the moment I stepped through that door, and I said to myself, that girl will be mine by the end of the day.'

'And I was,' I murmured. This was his way of winning me back. And it worked every time.

'And. You. Are.' He kissed my neck between words.

I let him because it felt good, but it also meant that there would be no more talk of me leaving my job. I loved it there, I loved the banter at Mirabelle with the chefs, the buzz after a great shift, the sense of satisfaction when I remembered an entire table's order without writing it down and the look on their faces as though I had just answered the most difficult question on *University Challenge*. To me, waitressing wasn't just a job that people did because there was nothing else for them to do or they were unqualified to do anything else – some people were really good at it. *I* did it because *I* was good at it. Customers liked me, the management liked me, the kitchen staff liked me. I liked working the evening shifts and I loved the late-night chats at the bar when the customers had all gone home and it was just a handful of us playing cards and drinking rum. The only dark cloud over the whole experience was Courtney.

'There's that girl there, do you remember me mentioning her? Courtney,' I said as she popped into my mind.

Tom stopped kissing my neck and stepped back. He shook his head. 'I don't think so, there are so many of you that work there.'

That was true, but I was almost certain that Tom had seen Courtney at least once. He had come in to meet me after my shift and was having a drink at the bar. Courtney had been collecting some water glasses and I saw her look right at him and he at her. Of course, he might not have known her name, but her face was so distinctive. Her cheek bones so defined, her hair a mass of bleached blonde. Courtney was not the sort of girl you looked at and forgot about in an instant.

'Well, it's just her, really, that makes the job annoying. Everything else about it I love.'

'Well, there's always going to be someone you don't get on with in work, in life, really. You should be thankful that at any point you can walk away from her.'

He edged closer to me again.

'And you can – walk away whenever you want to.' He clocked my taut expression. 'Besides, you won't do it forever, will you?'

'Won't I?' I had never really considered what my life would look like if I wasn't working in a restaurant.

'Well, maybe one day you won't be able to,' he said, pulling away from me and holding me at arm's length. I could see he was looking at my stomach.

'Meaning?'

'Meaning you might want to take a break from work in order to... you know?' He gestured to my stomach with his head this time.

'You're talking about me leaving my job to have a baby?' My voice became high and stretched.

Tom laughed.

'Well, unless you had plans to carry the baby on your back around the restaurant whilst you worked?'

I pulled myself out of his grip. I was thirty-one. I wanted to excel in my career, become more financially stable. I didn't have time for a baby. Tom's presumptions were way off my radar. I felt the usual flutter of annoyance that flooded my body whenever Tom made references to us accelerating to the next stage of our relationship. Why was he in such a rush?

'No, because I don't have any plans to have a baby at all!' My voice was more strained.

Tom looked sheepish. 'Okay, calm down.'

'I... I... isn't this something we should discuss? Doesn't it usually come after buying a house together or getting married?'

Tom smirked. 'Are you proposing?' I looked at Tom's cute face, and suddenly I was back in the pull of his charm. I felt the plush surroundings around me, I thought about his big business brain, how much he knew about so many things. I knew I would be forever financially stable with Tom; a life with him would be exhilarating.

Yet I shoved him away. He couldn't keep bringing up marriage and babies and think that was going to win him any points. Tom pretended to look hurt.

'Kit, all I'm saying is that one day you might like to settle down and have kids. And maybe you might like to do that with me. You're thirty-one. I'm thirty-seven.'

'Yes, thank you for that reminder of my age. I am well aware that the proverbial biological clock is ticking. But thirty-one is no age and...' I heard my voice breaking. How had this happened, how had we ended up talking like this? We were just having fun and now this! Talking about the future, making plans for when I would leave work to have a baby.

Tom put his hands up. 'Okay, calm down. It was just a weird way of me letting you know I'm in this for the long haul.'

I let out a long sigh and moved closer to him, one inch at a time, until I was wrapped up back in his arms.

* * *

Later that night, in bed, I knew a seed of doubt had been planted in my mind. Tom was everything – funny, good-looking, successful – but being with someone like Tom made me realise how important it was to me to maintain a sense of independence. Both of my parents had worked hard for a living to get to where they were now. I wanted to do the same. It was ingrained into my very core; I could not and would not let someone just take over my life because they had enough money to do so. I would always need my own space, somewhere to call my own. How could I see myself staying with someone when I had already had 'that feeling' about them? The one where you suddenly realise they are human and full of flaws, and not just this perfect specimen sent to make each day a little brighter and to keep making you feel good. I would need to push away those feelings, return to the goodness of just being with him, because Tom and I were great together. But I could see beyond what we were right now and because I knew nothing about his family and what his life had been like growing up, it was difficult for me to see a future with him. I was determined to unearth whatever secrets he was hiding.

12

NOW

I decided to acquaint myself with the local shop and so I walked the mile down to the village I had driven through a handful of times. There was a pub, a little village hall, and a small school as well as the shop. I thought it would be a good idea to introduce myself to anyone working there – perhaps I would need to advertise for a lodger at some point. Once I had learnt to live with myself and my mistakes first. I couldn't let anyone in when I was such a mess. I longed for conversations about anything, without this weight of guilt hanging over me. I had been such a social butterfly before. Now I felt the flutters in my stomach that would rise through my body and labour my breathing whenever I had to do anything as simple as walk into the village.

The shop door made a loud sucking noise as I opened it. There was one man behind a small counter that doubled up as a post office. He looked up as the door closed behind me and gave me a small smile before continuing to look through a pile of paperwork. I suddenly felt awkward and exposed in this small quiet room and so I shuffled slowly along the first of only two aisles, feigning interest in a packet of chocolate macaroons. In the end, I picked up a jar of decaff coffee and took it to the counter. The man took another few seconds before he looked up at me. Then he smiled as though he had only just seen me there.

'Hello,' he said. 'Just that, is it?'

'Yes.'

He rang it through the till.

'Two eighty-five,' he said. I stood for a moment, then suddenly remembered my purse in my handbag. I took out a card and held it to the machine until it beeped. Worried the transaction was almost over and I had only said one word, I began to think of something else to say.

'It's a lovely shop. Is it yours?' I said, putting my card away.

'It is. Mine and my wife's. Been here for, oooh, nearly ten years now.'

'Oh wow, that amazing,' I said, although I wasn't entirely sure my delivery mirrored my words. 'I've just moved in. To Willow Cottage.'

I thought I saw a look flash across his face. One of concern. Confusion, maybe?

'Willow Cottage, eh? So, you've got it now, have you? Well, I hope you got it for a good price.'

'I, um, yes I did,' I mumbled. I hated lying but I didn't feel ready to disclose how the house had come into my possession. I still felt a stab of guilt. I clenched my fists, hoping he wouldn't expect me to divulge any further.

'Good, good. Is it just you, do you have any family? Pets?'

I hadn't expected to be asked that, but of course it was a perfectly natural question to want to ask a new resident to the area.

'It's just me. And a dog.'

He gazed at me for a moment, as though he was trying to work many things out about me at once.

'Well, I hope you stay for a while; that house deserves someone to love it. It's such a pretty place.'

'It is,' I said, suddenly feeling I owed the house a little more, as I was hearing it described by another.

'Are you Kit Lowman?'

'Yes,' I answered with worry in my voice. How would he know my name already?

He bent down behind the counter. 'There's a package here for you. It got dropped off yesterday. Needed signing for, by the looks of it.'

I let out sigh of relief. Of course he would know my name if it was on a parcel with Willow Cottage on it. He bent down and then stood up, holding a neat brown package about the size of a loaf of bread.

I hadn't been expecting anything and I grabbed at it through the hatch. I suddenly became hot from the interaction. The shop felt imposing, and I felt as though I could barely catch my breath. I thanked him before darting from the store. Outside, I took big lungfuls of warm humid air. My whole body was sticky and all I wanted to do was get home and close the door.

I felt the weight of the parcel in my hand and looked down at it as my breathing began to return to normal. I peered at it, searching for a postmark or some clue to say where it had been sent from. I raised my head and found myself face to face with Blake. 'Oh, it's you,' I said, feeling unprepared to be so close to him.

'It is me,' he said with an amused expression.

'I popped down to the shop; just checking out the area.' The second the words were out of my mouth, I felt conscious of them. I didn't need to tell him what I was doing. I had lost the ability to converse normally, and it pained me to admit it.

Blake nodded his head, his hands in his pockets. He was

wearing a green and black checked shirt and jeans, the shirt sleeves rolled up to his biceps, exposing golden hairs on tanned arms.

'There's a fish van here on a Friday. The chips are pretty awesome.'

'I'll have to try them.'

'Decaff drinker?' he said questioningly as he spotted the jar of coffee.

'I struggle to sleep.' The words were out before I could stop them. I cursed myself. Why had I said that? The questioning that could come from such a statement.

'I'm the opposite. I struggle to stay awake past nine. I'm up so early for my job, you see. That's the trouble with agriculture. Say, how is the little pup?'

'Lucy,' I said with a sigh of relief that Blake was someone who knew when not to ask any more questions.

'Ah, you named her.'

'I did.'

'Is she okay?'

'She's settling in fine. She follows me wherever I go, including upstairs, which I'm sure is not best dog owner practice, but it's just us in that house.' I stopped myself before I said any more, and I wondered if Blake had noticed that I'd ended the sentence abruptly.

'Great, that's great. I should pop in, say hello.'

'Yes, you should,' I said, trying to sound light-hearted, but I was just being polite. I felt the sweat prickle under my arms at the prospect of playing host at home.

'Great, my car is just there. It's open. Hop in, I'll drive us back. I just need to pop in and grab a few bits first.' Blake gave me a winning smile and headed past me into the shop. I looked where he had pointed at an old green Land Rover that looked as if it was about thirty years old.

I had not been expecting him to offer to take me home and I was worried I was unprepared for visitors. At least the house was in good shape, even if the kitchen might be a little messy after the flood. I slipped into the passenger seat, my mind going into overdrive worrying about it all.

We were back at Willow Cottage within a few minutes, and I slowly climbed out of the car, my feet hitting the ground with a thump. I walked with him up the drive and went in through the back door, so that Blake would be greeted by Lucy straight away. She climbed from her bed, did a small stretch then promptly did a small wee on the kitchen floor.

'Well, there's a nice greeting.' Blake walked over to her and lifted her up. He held her away from him as though he were assessing her for any damage, then he tucked her into the crook of his arm and stroked her head.

'I'll put the kettle on.' As I filled the kettle, I looked at the package on the side. I did a quick mental check of who could know I lived here. Hendrick's face flashed in front of me, but a deeper fear was buried in my gut. A fear that someone else other than Hendrick knew where I was. And if they did, there was a reason they wanted me to know that they knew I was here. I had thought I could just walk away, but maybe someone else had other ideas. I opened a cupboard door and noticed my hand was shaking. I took a deep breath and I shoved the package in there. I would think about it later when Blake wasn't here. I could be worrying about nothing. It was just as likely that it was something from the competition company. But there it was again, the pitter patter of fear that always launched in my gut before advancing through my body.

'Did you move far?' Blake spoke, interrupting my thoughts.

I felt my body become hot. Would this be the beginning of a string of lies that would need to keep evolving? I swallowed.

'No, just from Bournemouth. I had a flat by the sea.'

'Upgraded to a forest view.'

I laughed, a stark hollow sound because I could no longer emit normal reactions; my emotions were hardened. I turned back to finish making the coffee.

I walked over to Blake with the two mugs, then placed a plastic bottle of milk and a bag of sugar in the centre of the table. It looked messy and I knew my former self would have put the milk in a jug, the sugar in a bowl. I held my hands out to take Lucy.

I watched as Blake filled his mug with so much milk it almost spilt over the sides, then loaded it with two heaped teaspoons of sugar.

'I've lived here for almost five years now. Moved with a woman who couldn't hack the country life and so she left me. Now it's just me and the dogs. The hours suit me, nice and early starts, I get most of the afternoons off, plus I get the accommodation, which saves me a fortune. But it's nothing like this place.' Blake paused for a moment to look around the spacious kitchen. I was glad I had managed to get all the water up and there were no signs of any damage. Just a few wads of kitchen roll and screwed up towels. There were also some dirty plates and cups in the sink, waiting to be washed. I noted how Blake had managed to slip in the information about his ex and move past it quickly. I wasn't sure if I was supposed to react to it.

'How about you?' He took a sip of his coffee, and it was so casual and led straight on from talking about himself that I almost missed what he had said. He looked at me and I fought to find the words to explain my situation and why I was here. But no words would come. They remained a muddle inside my mouth, and I was terrified if I spoke they would all fall out and it would be too much for even me to comprehend, let alone Blake, someone I barely knew.

I touched my forehead and took a deep breath, turned away from him and reached above the sink for a glass.

'Are you okay?' Blake asked.

'I feel a little...' I poured water into the glass from the tap.

'It's a hot day. Maybe that walk to the shop took it out of you.'

'You make me sound like a weak woman in a Jane Austen novel,' I said sharply, and I felt Blake physically recoil. I glanced sideways and saw his eyes flicker up and rest on me for a second before he looked back down at his coffee.

'I wouldn't know, I haven't read any Jane Austen. I know *of* her, of course.'

I felt foolish for speaking that way to Blake; of course he didn't sit and read Jane Austen in his spare time, and why did I blurt out that ridiculous reference? I glanced uncomfortably at him, too afraid to say any more, even an attempt at an apology for my silly outburst. I was sure he was just trying to be perfectly pleasant, except I seemed to have forgotten how to converse in pleasantries.

'You're right,' I said after I had taken a few sips of water and Blake waited expectantly but also glanced awkwardly around the room. 'I think I've been overdoing it, with the move and working a lot. I haven't slept much over the last few days.' The last month was more accurate, but I didn't want to share that with anyone, not my own family or friends and not Blake. My reasoning sounded feeble, even though Blake had been the one to suggest it. I sensed the atmosphere change in the room; Blake had been chatty and happy to spend a little time getting to know me and now I could feel him shifting about, trying to take long sips of his hot coffee until he stood up, poured what was left in the sink and gave the cup a quick rinse.

'I'd better be off then, glad to see little Lucy is settling in. You know where I am if you need me.' He made his way out of the back door, and I thought he couldn't have gone any quicker if he had tried. I felt a wave of despondency wash over me. Was this how it was to be from now on? I had lost a fundamental part of who I was, someone who used to be able to talk to people freely without prejudice or fear of offending them. Was I doomed to spend the rest of my life living alone, destined to become some sort of hermit, unable to converse spontaneously without fear of tripping on my words and revealing a part of me that was too dark even for me to comprehend?

I felt the emptiness in the kitchen once Blake had left. His presence had filled up some of the empty spaces. I felt sad, not because he had left, but for what his leaving had exposed. I was still just a woman in a house that was too large for one person. I needed to think about what I was going to do. I longed to speak to the only two people I could think of who would help me, but I hadn't been in contact with my parents for over a month. I had gone from speaking to them every day to zero contact overnight. I knew what I needed to do in order to begin to make any sense of all of this, but revealing the truth to the two people who loved me most in the world would be the biggest tragedy. They had put me on a pedestal for so many years and I would absolutely shatter their illusion and almost certainly break both of their hearts.

13

NOW

Citrus was heaving. Sweat was pouring from the walls, it seemed. My shirt was drenched and sticking to my skin, and I dabbed my face with a napkin when I had a quiet second to myself.

It was only 9 p.m. and there was at least one more hour of this level of intensity before the restaurant would begin to empty out. Maybe it would be a later shift than I had realised.

I thought about little Lucy, who had been alone since 4.30. What had I been thinking when I had accepted her from Blake? I felt the flutter of panic seeping through me, like a drug being pumped through my veins. My arms began to feel numb. I thought about the way I had spoken to Blake a few days ago and how if I had been a little more neighbourly, then he would perhaps return the sentiment and be someone I could call on to ask him to pop round to check on the little dog, who might be lonely and could be whining and yelping for all I knew. It was a mistake to take on Lucy. I was not ready for this level of responsibility when I had yet to sort even the basic logistics of my life out.

But the restaurant was too busy for me to think about her for too long. The bell rang again and there were now six main courses on the hot plate. I grabbed the food and delivered them to a table, before racing back to begin collecting more items. I managed to carry three plates at once and I could feel the sweat trickling down my back. Then before I could stop it, an image of Lucy at home alone flew through my mind again, and I could feel myself beginning to catastrophise. After the water pipe incident, why hadn't I made sure someone was available to check in with her when I was away?

I tried to focus on the next task ahead of me: clearing starters, taking the order of a table that had been sitting for the optimum amount of time – left any longer, they would begin to feel as if they had been neglected. But stopping and allowing myself time to think had taken me from working on automatic to suddenly becoming very present in my life. My conscious self was now a target. I had opened the flood gates for all the other thoughts to come. And they did. They emerged as small sparks, flying through my mind like little fireflies, but soon they were as powerful as the sun, penetrating me and pinning me to the spot so I couldn't move.

It had been just over a month since I had left Mirabelle, and no matter how much I tried to distract myself, the vivid memories were always there, ready and waiting to surge at me with full force should I let my guard down long enough for them to attack. I felt weak with the effort it took to keep fighting them off and so I found myself standing in the middle of a busy restaurant, as waiting staff rushed all around me, and customers talked and laughed loudly. Suddenly, each sound pierced my eardrums and each laugh and clatter of a wine glass or coffee cup cut right through me. I felt each sound as it pulsed through my body.

'Kit... are you okay?' A voice was somewhere nearby. I turned and Maisie was standing next to me. Oh, great, how many more times would she see me locked in a trance and unable to function like the capable person I should be?

'I'm hot, just going to get some air.' I walked quickly away before she could question me further. Outside, I sucked in big lungfuls of air. It was just cool enough to feel the benefit. I looked around at the busy street, where so many people were taking advantage of the warm summer evening. I breathed out a long sigh, as a slight feeling of despair gripped me. How had this become my life? I used to have so much to look forward to and now I couldn't imagine a time I would ever feel normal again. I had never wanted anything more from life than for things to be simple and to feel a general sense of happiness. Some people wanted a great career that took them to exotic countries or three sports cars on their drive or to have 50,000 followers on Instagram. I just wanted my life to be simple. And I'd had that and now it was all gone. I had done something so terrible, so inconceivable that even I could hardly believe it at times. When I really thought about it, when I played out the scenario over and over in my head, it was like watching a TV show on repeat. It began to feel as if it hadn't really happened to me, but to someone else.

I knew I needed to get back inside the restaurant, to feel connected and a part of something. I wished I didn't feel as if I suddenly wanted to hibernate the whole year long.

I took one last long intake of air, and I was about to turn back to the restaurant when I saw him. I hadn't noticed him before because I'd been focusing on breathing and recentring myself. But now I saw him, and he had seen me too. He had probably been sat there for some minutes, maybe he had been sitting in his car with the window wound down and watching me work. I shuddered at the thought. Our eyes locked; the busy road bustled with cars between us. Tom had chosen a safe enough distance away to park up and observe me. I felt the same dread in the pit of my stomach when I thought about him, only for it to be enhanced when I saw him in the flesh. He started the engine and began to slowly pull away. He was looking for closure. I had ended things badly. I owed him more. But I couldn't bring myself to go to him, to explain what had happened. That the woman he had fallen for, was not who he thought she was. How could I explain something so hideous to him, something that was still so unfathomable to me? How could I tell him that the person he knew and trusted was a killer?

14

NOW

The next morning was a Sunday. I had a lunchtime shift that would begin at eleven. I had gone home at 1 a.m. the night before and slept for approximately four hours. I had read that sleep deprivation was a clear-cut path to developing Alzheimer's. I was worried for my health.

I had dreamt about Tom all night. Enigmatic thoughts that spiralled through my mind until I woke, dizzy and disorientated.

I had yet to go for a swim because I had been overwhelmed by the thought of using my own pool. But I wondered if now might be the perfect time to do so because it would energise me for work. Counting lengths could distract me from the image of Tom, sitting outside Citrus, that had been plaguing me all night. Doing some daily exercise would improve my mental health, surely? This was basic knowledge now, but I felt myself go clammy at the prospect. Everything overwhelmed me.

It felt very strange walking from one room to another in just my swimming costume, knowing that I could dunk myself in the pool whenever I wanted. It was something I had once only dreamt of and now I was living it, but I couldn't even appreciate it. I wondered how the normal version of me would react to living like this. I wondered how the normal me would react to a lot of things. But because I was living in the shell of my former self, I would never know.

As I entered the pool room, the tang of warm chlorine hit me. Who would look after the pool? Wasn't that a job that needed doing? I knew nothing about pools and I would need to get someone in to clean it, maintain it. Another thing to add to the list of little things that were nudging me every now and again, reminding me that winning this house came with a huge amount of responsibility. The sort of responsibility I wasn't sure I was capable of. I had thought about owning such a house before, when I was confident and capable. Now here I was, the stark reality of my worthless existence glaring at me from every crevice.

I stood, taking in the length of the pool, which was just long enough to get a good stroke on, something that my former self would have been thrilled by. I sat down and dipped a toe in. It was the perfect temperature. How typical, I thought to myself. Why did this have to happen now, why did I have to be rewarded with something so grand and spectacular a month after being responsible for something so catastrophically life-altering? I didn't deserve to be here, dipping my toe in perfectly warm swimming water, whilst others had lost so much. I sat, torn between wanting and needing to go in the water for my own sanity and walking away, knowing I shouldn't be experiencing any kind of satisfaction.

I thought again about speaking to my parents, how my mum would walk in here and be flabbergasted, how my dad would do his long whistle, his way of showing his appreciation for anything expensive or fancy. I hadn't given them a reason for my radio silence. I was the worst daughter. How would they be able to forgive me for the lack of contact? And that was before I broke the news to them about what a terrible person I was. They would be sure to disown me. No, it was better this way.

But deep down, I knew that both my mother and father would be worrying. Despite how they would react and feel after I had talked them through everything, I knew it was the decent thing to do to at least explain where I was right now and why I was no longer living in the flat in Bournemouth. Once I had stopped accepting their calls, I knew they would have been over to the flat to look for me.

I slipped into the water and allowed my arms to begin a simple stroke. This pool belonged to me, I thought to myself, it's just a swim. Just go with it.

As I swam, it allowed my mind to break free of some of the boundaries I had instilled over the last few weeks. I would allow my parents a little insight into my life, I decided. Purely so they wouldn't be worrying and then that would ease one of my own stresses. Of which there were too many now.

I fell into a flow and counted each length, allowing my mind to roam free, but whenever it tried to dwell on anything too dark, I simply focused on the number of lengths I had done. I pulled myself out of the pool and wrapped the towel around me. I walked through the sunroom and up the stairs, aware of how much water I was dripping everywhere and wishing I had brought my change of clothes to the little shower room. Once I was dry and clothed, I knew what I needed to do.

I just had to work myself up to it.

I arrived at Citrus just before eleven. I had always been good at being on time but since I had left Mirabelle, I had little else going on in my life and there was no such thing as being late in my books. My days were simply eating, sleeping and working. I allowed myself little pleasure in between, because right now, I didn't deserve anything else. Would I ever again?

Maisie greeted me at the restaurant door.

'Kit, hi,' she said. There was a tone to her voice that meant she was about to try to say something that I wasn't going to like, and I already had a feeling I knew what it was going to be about.

'How are you?' she asked. It was sunny outside, and the streets were almost empty. Whatever she was going to say, she felt she could say it here, outside the restaurant.

'I'm good, thank you,' I began with much more vigour than I felt but I mustered it all the same. Maisie cocked her head to one side as though she were really considering my response.

'Uh huh,' she said.

I knew it, I could feel it, and I knew what she was going to suggest, and it would be a pretty slippery slope to outing me.

'Yes, I had a swim this morning and I feel really good. It helps my mental health, you see.'

Maisie looked taken back. 'Your mental health?'

'Yes, I've struggled for years, and this is what helps me. I could sense things were starting to build, so I think I've nipped it in the bud again for now.'

'Oh, okay, well, you never mentioned your mental health when you took the job.'

'That's because I don't have to. But I can assure you at this point I don't need any assistance with anything and I'm coping just fine.'

'Okay. Well, you must come and talk to me if you feel... not fine at all.'

'I will.' I smiled and walked past her through the door. I knew exactly what she'd wanted to say to me when I saw her standing there and it would have involved me getting in the car and driving home again and I didn't want that because I didn't want to lose my job. I needed the distraction, the busyness, and even if it was nothing like the atmosphere I had experienced at Mirabelle, it was something. It was better than sitting at home alone with my dark thoughts all day. Here I was relatively unknown, and I could just get my head down and do a good day's work.

But Maisie had spotted my weaknesses these last few weeks. I had done a good job of disguising them when I had first begun. But now I had let the veil slip and she had interpreted them as laziness, general tiredness or maybe some sort of dependency. And I was on probation here still. I needed to prove I was the best version of myself right now. But when I had seen her standing at the door, she might as well have been wearing a sign around her neck that said, 'I am concerned that you are not quite up to the role; you seem distant, you drift off from time to time and you look unhappy.'

Mentioning my mental health was a sure way to stop her in her tracks. I would try harder because if my mind did continue to spiral, then I wouldn't be able to do this job, I would be a danger to myself and everyone else around me and I had already proved that I could be. I needed to up my game and I would.

I worked the Sunday lunch shift with a smile that could steal a million hearts and it had been painful to wear because of how unnatural it felt. By the end of the shift, I was not only physically exhausted, but my face felt as though it had done a full workout.

* * *

I returned home to a very excited Lucy. I felt something shift and lift inside of me. This was why people had pets, I was suddenly reminded. They give unconditional love. Lucy knew nothing other than that I was a physical presence who came and went each day. I fed her, walked her and cuddled her. She didn't know that I had the potential to harm and maim. That I could end her life in an instant. The thought took hold of me and gripped me so hard that I took a step back from her, as if just by thinking it, I could hurt her. Instead of giving her more affection, I took her straight outside and sat on the lawn at the front of the house. I felt too hot in my work trousers and shirt so, after watching Lucy bound around for a few minutes, I took myself into the house to pour myself a glass of water. When I opened the cupboard where the glasses were kept, I saw it was empty. I had not done any washing up and instead had been putting every dirty piece of crockery into the dishwasher, which I had yet to put on.

I began opening more cupboards and the first door I opened held the package I had been given at the post office. Terror licked at the edges of my mind. Deep breaths, I told myself. It was just something from the competition company. But I could already feel the darkness spread through me like a wave. I could sense all was not well. I had completely forgotten about it, but now it was here in front of me, I knew there was no more ignoring it. I held it between my hands and gave it squeeze, turned it over a few more times, but it wasn't giving anything away. I ripped open the paper and as I did, several chocolate protein bars fell onto the counter. There must have been fifteen or twenty of them. I picked one up and then the memories came flooding back. I knew exactly where these had come from and what they represented. These bars had been sent for a reason. Tom knew I was here, and he knew what I had done. And as much as I was trying to better myself and move forward, he was determined not to let me forget.

15

THEN

There weren't many more conversations about babies, but I knew now this was my destiny, this was the end goal for Tom. He didn't speak directly to me about wanting them, but there were stray comments that flew about. If he saw an advert with a young baby, he'd say something like, 'How cute,' or we would pass a couple pushing a pram and he would say, 'What a lovely image.' I was no expert on babies, but I had watched my sister struggle with Josh and Emily. First post-natal depression, then the endless fights and arguments with Stanley about work and whose turn it was to look after the kids. The constant sleepless nights – that went on for years in Josh's case – and the little time they had left to commit to themselves or their relationship. And the guilt. Jude talked of feeling it every day: if she didn't read the third book Emily had asked for that night in bed or she had barely played with them all day and been cross with them at bedtime.

These were the things I knew Tom wouldn't understand; that he would see as minor problems that could be solved by throwing money at them. But I knew when I became a mother it would be all-consuming. I wanted to experience the highs with the lows, I didn't want everything taken care of for me, so I only got to experience the good bits. I knew that enduring the rocky road some days was what made the path down again so much sweeter. But I couldn't explain this to Tom, he would think I was mad. He had come from money and had also made a lot of his own money. But he had yet to discuss his parents with me in depth. And this was what worried me the most. I had an innate desire to get to the crux of a person when I met them. Tom was holding so much back. I knew if I waited around long enough, snippets would begin to fall out of him; little offcuts of information would become mine for the taking, so that I could sew them all together and create a better picture of who Tom really was. Then maybe I could begin to talk about my hopes and desires for when I had children. His perceptions of raising children could be very different to mine. My sister would tell me I would be mad to turn down an easier version of motherhood. Not that I had mentioned to Jude that Tom had shown any interest in being a father.

We had only been together for a few months and besides the fact I rarely spoke to my sister about personal issues, the thought of becoming a parent with someone I had known for such a short space of time made me feel uneasy. But I was sure that deep down somewhere was a man I could love and trust. Then we could be a family. One day. He only had to let me in.

So, I stuck to my guns and began changing the subject whenever Tom made one of his subtle references. He didn't get to discuss a future that involved bringing a life into the world when I knew so little about his.

About a month after the forest lodge trip, my mother called and invited me and Tom over for dinner.

'I didn't want to ask straight after the break, dear, because we didn't want to seem desperate, did we, Rod?'

Mum spoke the last part away from the receiver, towards my dad.

'No, Maeve, we didn't. Tom is a very nice chap and what he did, paying for that little holiday for us all...' Dad's voice came through loud and clear; I imagined he had moved closer to Mum. 'And so we'd like to do something to repay you both for your kindness and hospitality so we thought—'

'Yes, yes, thank you, Rod,' Mum said, and I heard Dad's protests in the background as if she had just pushed him aside. 'What I was trying to say was that your father and I would like to have you over for dinner next week. Dad was going to make his fajitas.'

Mum pronounced the J in fajitas instead of letting it fall silent and I rolled my eyes at the same time as I felt my gut do that swirly thing it did whenever either of my parents were so endearing. Which was quite often. I was like my parents in many ways, down to earth and not overly aspirational. I had heard on a podcast once that humans weren't born to be successful, only to survive. And that was all I needed to do. I was forever grateful that my parents had – without intention – instilled in me that very ethos.

So, when I mentioned to Tom over dinner – a swanky sushi restaurant in Oxford – that Mum and Dad were inviting us over, I was surprised when his response was stilted and awkward. I was so sure he wished to appease me and getting to know my family was an integral part of moving our relationship forward. He took a long time to finish what was in his mouth and then began fussing with his chopsticks and napkin.

'They really like you,' I added to fill the silence that engulfed the space around us.

'And I think they are perfectly reasonable people too.'

I frowned and almost laughed at Tom's comment. 'Perfectly reasonable?'

'It means they did a good job raising you and they seem... fine people.'

'Okay, now you're talking weird. So, I thought we could go over next Thursday; Dad does a mean fajita – all the accompaniments. Mum tries to mix a margarita but always gets it wrong; maybe we could take some of your mix over, to help her along a bit.'

'You're speaking as though we've already decided we're going,' Tom said with a small nervous laugh.

I studied Tom's face for a second as he began eating again, but his attempt to back away from conversation had not fooled me.

'They would be so pleased to see you,' I said. He made no facial expression. 'And it would make me happy too,' I added without thinking. He stopped eating and put his chopsticks down, wiping his mouth with his napkin.

'It would?'

I nodded. He leant forward and kissed me full on the lips.

'Okay,' he said but it sounded uneasy.

I studied him for a few seconds, then he put down his chopsticks again and took both of my hands in his.

'I will do anything to make you happy. Anything at all. You will never have to want for anything. I will make sure of that.'

I heard his words and realised what I had done. He had jumped upon my request. I hadn't even said it consciously. Tom believed that our relationship was based on me making requests and him fulfilling them, to make me happy. But when did his happiness come into play? Why did the simple act of having dinner with my parents make him recoil? There was nothing for me to argue with him about right now in the middle of the restaurant because he had agreed, and with a smile and a kiss too.

So I beamed at him and thanked him. Then I turned and gazed out of the window at the passers-by in the busy street and took a very long drink of sake.

16

NOW

I threw the protein bars in the bin. I was usually so waste-conscious; they had to go so I didn't have to think about them any more.

But there was a small part of me that thought keeping hold of them might be a good idea. Perhaps I would need to provide them as evidence at some point. I tried not to think too long or too hard about that because it was just a package and he was obviously trying to assert his presence. But what I wanted to know was, if Tom knew I was here, how did he know? I couldn't think of one person who might have any actual knowledge of my whereabouts. But then an image of Courtney crept into my mind. Of the way she had stood there and looked at me outside Citrus. Tom knew where I worked. She would have been the one to tell him and then perhaps he had followed me home one day. That wasn't his style. He would have paid someone to follow me.

When I began to think about that, I then thought about the leak and Lucy in the sink. Was that Tom's doing too?

Maisie, who was obviously now conscious of my mental health, had ordered me to take a day off from the restaurant. And with so much whirring through my mind, it was probably best that I spent a day trying to process what had happened over the last few weeks: from the win to the mysterious package and the flood in the kitchen. But it was only 7 a.m. and I was already anxious about how I would spend the day. Getting up and having a job to go to made everything a little easier. I knew I would take a swim because it was a sure way to tire myself and distract myself at the same time.

I also knew I needed to see Blake so that I could apologise for my behaviour towards him. He had been kind to me, given me a dog, invited himself over to check on her as well as tried to have a friendly cup of tea with me, and I had been nothing less than rude to him.

Not getting ready for a day at the restaurant also gave me extra time to think, and the image of my parents swirled fresh in my mind again.

I needed to make a move. The least I could do was let them know I was okay. I just needed to think how I would do it in a way that wouldn't encourage too much response from them.

I took myself across to the pool and sat on the edge with my toe dipped in the water. This was how I would start off, allowing my mind to come to terms with what was to come, that I would send them a simple text message and that it was a good thing I was doing. I then slipped into the cool water and began the swim, taking care to count each length as I went. The pool room had a floor-to-ceiling window, and I experienced a moment or two of exposure. If someone happened to be wandering around outside, they would see me half naked. I had thought I was anonymous here, but it was now apparent that I wasn't. Tom knew where I was. What I needed to know was what he planned to do now he had found me.

I felt the emptiness of the house and realised how small and insignificant I was here, all alone. Had I done the right thing by insisting on not telling anyone of my whereabouts? I *was* lonely and

I craved a little company. But I could not have Tom here. I instantly thought of Blake and was reminded of my terrible behaviour towards him. He was a small part of my new life now. He and Lucy were the only parts of my life right now. It would be wise to keep a door open for him, if only in the metaphorical sense.

I had a tried and tested brownie recipe up my sleeve that would possibly help me with an apology. All I needed were the ingredients.

* * *

An hour later, dried and dressed, I found myself back at the local shop. The same man who had served me before was there again. At first, he didn't seem to recognise me, but then his face changed as he obviously placed who I was.

'Ah, Willow Cottage, isn't it?' he said.

'Yes, that's me.' A quick smile used to come so easily to me but now I physically felt the muscles pulling on my face and it was as painful as all the emotions I was carrying. How well did he know the house I was living in? I felt I needed to know more, yet he hadn't introduced himself to me, I realised.

'I'm Kit,' I said.

He looked at me. My delivery must have sounded a little out of sync. He hadn't asked for my name. I felt as though my ability to converse with strangers was getting more and more difficult and appeared forced and unnatural. I had been a waitress for years and had been able to jump into any conversation, completely unfazed. It felt so unnatural not being able to do the one thing I had done for so long.

'It's nice to meet you. I'm Arthur. My wife is Lyndsay. But she tends to stick to the back of the shop. I like to be out here, where I can keep abreast of what's what. I like to know what's going on, you see. It's a small village. Nothing goes unnoticed.' He held my gaze, and I felt my body tense. I tried to swallow so I could reply, but I found I could do neither. Why had this man suddenly put me on edge? He looked back down at his papers as though he hadn't just spoken, and I finally found I could speak.

'Good, I like to know I am in safe hands.' I marched over to the shelves. I could feel Arthur's gaze on me as I picked out some dark chocolate, eggs, flour and sugar.

'Just these,' I said; they hit the counter harder than I had anticipated. Arthur eyed me for a second.

'Doing a spot of baking?' he said as he began to ring them through the till.

'For a good friend,' I said plainly as I held my debit card over the machine.

I began placing all the items inside the bag I had brought with me.

'Well, enjoy your baking!' he said, and he sounded much brighter. I wondered if I had imagined an ominous tone to his voice.

I left the shop with adrenaline racing through my veins, my mind awash with confusion. I had not imagined how he had looked at me; how he had seemed as though he had wanted me to feel threatened, somehow. It made me think about Willow Cottage and the history of the place. Arthur had seemed to have an avid interest in the property. What did he know that I didn't? If I was feeling even half the person I used to be, then I would be inclined to do some research to discover what the old place had once been or who might have lived there before me. But already I was tired. The swim this morning and now the walk to the shop had robbed me of energy. Funny how I kept going when I was at the restaurant, yet take me away from the hustle and bustle of Citrus and I found it hard to function. It was as if working in the restaurant was my lifeline now – my only real link to the outside world and people.

Back at home in the kitchen, I found a mixing bowl and set to work. There was comfort in the pouring, melting and stirring and I used the task as a base to bring my thoughts back to when they began to wander towards places of a less happy nature. Which they often did.

Forty-five minutes later, I had a batch of brownies cooling by the window, even though it was now mid-morning and the air was thick with the warmth of the day.

I sat at the kitchen table and waited for them to cool, but I was slowly losing confidence about heading to Blake's now. What would I say? How would I be? He was clearly a busy man, and I was someone who no longer knew how to have a conversation. Perhaps, I thought, I would just leave it on his doorstep with a note. He was bound to be out at work, doing whatever it was he did with grain.

But I had to apologise or at least try, so I popped Lucy on her lead and set off up the road. It soon became obvious as I began walking that Lucy was nervous and skittish and with every car that sped past, I was forced up onto the grass verge, an uneven and uncomfortable makeshift path. We arrived unscathed at the entrance to the lane, and I hesitantly began the descent along the narrow private road. The grain store stood large and looming to my right. One hatch was open, displaying a mound of grain so high it looked like a mountain of gold coins from a children's fairy-tale. A younger, less affected version of myself would have gone over to inspect it, but I pulled tighter on Lucy's lead, worried she would slip free and run straight into the grain and be suffocated.

At last, I arrived at the cottages. Three together, but I wasn't sure which one belonged to Blake or if he would even be in. What a calamity. I hadn't thought to check or ask. And I didn't have his number to call him.

I approached the first door and rapped loudly with my knuckles. A few moments later, the door swung open and a lady who was in her sixties answered the door.

'Can I help you?'

She looked flushed, as though I had dragged her away from a task.

'Oh, sorry to disturb you, I was looking for Blake.'

'Were you now? He lives there in the middle one.' She pointed to the house next door. 'But he'll be out on the field.' She had closed the door before I had even constructed a reply. I felt a stab of rejection and took a step backwards, trying not to take it personally but wondering if I was emitting negative energy.

I pulled at Lucy's lead, and we walked to the middle house. I took the Tupperware out of the tote bag and held it in my hand. Then I realised that I didn't have a pen and paper and that Blake would come home and not know who they were from. The day was getting warmer. A spasm gripped my chest. It was hotter now than it had been when I had left the house and I was starting to sweat profusely.

I crouched down and put the Tupperware on the corner of the doorstep, where it was most shaded, but then realised the sun would come around and then heat the box up like a greenhouse, resulting in sweaty melted brownies. Another blunder on my part. I felt despair and decided I was going to just go back home. I stood up then stepped back suddenly as the door swung open. There, with a towel wrapped around his waist, exposing a toned and golden-haired chest, was Blake.

'I heard you from my bathroom window.' He sounded breathless, as though he had rushed to get downstairs. 'I got so hot in the field, I had to come and take a cold shower.'

'It is very warm today.' I didn't recognise my own voice. Blake's stature took up most of the small cottage doorway and I felt a heightened focus on the present.

'Ah, little Lucy, is she okay?' He bent to stroke her, and I averted my eyes.

'Yes, she's fine,' I said, looking over towards the grain store. I could feel my cheeks reddening.

'Ooh, what's this? A delivery?' Blake stood up, holding the brownies.

'Yes, from us. Lucy and me. We... I... well, you came the other day, and I was short with you, and I appreciate you giving me the dog, Lucy, and I made you brownies.'

Blake listened intently. 'Do you want to come in? I'm only on my lunch break – I can make you a cold drink?'

'I should get back...' I trailed off. I was doing it again – isolating myself. It was my go-to response. But this time I recognised it and stopped myself. 'But we can pop in for a minute, can't we, Lucy?'

Blake stepped aside to let us in, and Lucy raced ahead, the lead coming loose from my hand. I was greeted moments later in the tiny hallway by a larger dog, presumably Marley, Lucy's mother, and two other puppies of similar size and colours, who began licking her.

'Oh, look,' I said and for a second, I felt all the anxiety and tension melt away as I witnessed a mother and daughter regrouping after a short time apart. I felt my eyes well with tears and shook them away. This was what pure love was. This was, of course, how my own mother would receive me after all this time apart. But there was always that nagging doubt in my mind – how could I ever admit to her and my father what I had done? Blake directed me into the kitchen at the end of the hallway and Lucy jumped straight into a dog bed, followed by her mother.

'She's missed her other pup by the looks of it.'

I sat down quickly at a small circular table. I surreptitiously brushed away a few crumbs as Blake prepared a cold glass of juice and set it down in front of me. We watched Marley and her puppies for a few moments in what felt like a companionable silence until I realised how long we had been sitting without saying anything, and then I shifted in my seat and cleared my throat.

'I'd better get those brownies chilling.' Blake turned suddenly and began to move things around in the fridge to make room.

He then turned around and looked down at himself. 'I should probably put some clothes on too.'

I found I couldn't look at him again and so I took a long welcome drink of the juice and went to stand.

'I should get off, anyway, I have a lot to do. It's a day off for me today, still trying to... do things around the house.' I thought about Willow Cottage, heavily furnished. The only thing that needed to happen was for me to commit to moving in and go and collect all the rest of my things from the flat.

'No, please don't rush off; finish your drink.'

I looked at my drink, picked it up and downed it in one.

Blake let out a loud laugh.

I placed the glass back on the table and found I was smiling, too.

'What a woman!' Blake said, still laughing. 'I should like to see what you're like out on the beers.'

My smile faded and I looked down at my feet. I thought about the few empty bottles of wine back home and how I only seemed to use alcohol as a way to numb the pain. I had forgotten what it felt like to drink when you were happy.

'I won't stay, but now I know where you are, I could pop back again, when—'

'When I'm more suitably dressed,' Blake laughed. I couldn't help but smile.

'Yes.'

We both walked to the door.

I turned at the threshold and faced Blake. 'I just wanted to say sorry, you know, for being a bit weird the last time you were at the house.'

'That's all right,' Blake said brightly and I felt even worse; he really was a lovely guy.

'There's no excuse really, I—'

'I get it. You've just had a massive upheaval. Moving house is stressful. You're trying to settle in. Besides, I wasn't offended. I was worried about you.'

Blake's eyes glimmered with concern and I wished these were different circumstances, that I was the person I was before. Blake seemed interested in this version of me, and I wanted to scream, 'I'm even better than this, this is 10 per cent of who I really am.'

'Thanks for understanding,' I said solemnly as I stepped outside.

'Thank you again for the brownies!' he called after us.

I turned and waved as we headed off along the little private road onto the main road and braced myself for another five minutes of awkward walking along the grass verge.

* * *

I went through into the kitchen and Lucy flopped down on her bed. I watched her for a moment and wondered if she still missed her mother. My eyes prickled with tears again, and I was surprised by their sudden arrival. I had been putting off what I needed to do for too long. I needed to let my parents know I was safe.

I pulled out my phone and held it in my hand for a moment, trying to work out what to say. Then it occurred to me that I could send them a photo of me with a short message. I remembered the day of the handover with Hendrick; I had asked him to take a photo of me outside the house. If they knew I was living somewhere like Willow Cottage, they would be happy, content that I was okay. I didn't have to explain too much to them. I scrolled through my phone until I found the handful of photos that Hendrick had taken of me, looking awkward on the front lawn with the house behind me. As I flicked between numerous photographs, I began to notice that the back left of the photo was changing between shots. I stopped on photo three, scanned the image and saw that everything looked fine.

I flipped to photo two, and yes, my eyes were drawn instantly to the top left corner: the front window of Willow Cottage. I couldn't quite work out what room it was from the front of the house, but the window itself had a dark shadow to the left-hand side. Was there a curtain in that room that had blown across? I specifically remembered it being very hot that day. No wind. I needed to check out the first image, so I scrolled again and this time the window was almost all blacked out. But I could see a shape to the blackness, so I pinched the picture and zoomed in. The dark shadow had arms, a torso and although it was sightly fuzzy, I could clearly make out the figure of someone standing in the window. Watching me.

17

NOW

I dropped my phone on the floor as a cold shudder struck my whole body. I suddenly realised that maybe I wasn't alone in the house. I felt a need to run to every room and check them from top to bottom. But even that terrified me. I needed to calm down. I was being rash. The obvious and most likely explanation was that there had been another staff member from the competition company around that afternoon, checking over the house before it was handed over to me. Perhaps it was them who had put the hamper in the kitchen; perhaps they had overseen finalities, ensuring the house looked 'winner ready' for me. But I hadn't seen anyone else enter or leave the house that day, and the only cars in the driveway had been mine, the photographer's and Hendrick's.

I cursed myself for not seeing that photo before Hendrick popped round the other day. I would have been able to ask him who it was, but then I remembered that he had given me his number. I would call him and he would clear all this up in a second and put my mind at ease.

I scrolled down to his name and hit the call button. The phone rang and rang until eventually it went through to a generic answer machine message.

'Hendrick, hi, it's Kit, from Willow Cottage.' I took a deep breath; my voice was shaky. I cleared my throat. 'Just a quick question about the house... well, about the day I moved in, actually. Could you call me when you have a moment, then I can explain? Thanks.'

I hung up and placed my phone down on the side in the kitchen, then looked up at the ceiling, as if I could sense what had gone on up there the day I had moved in. I walked towards the hallway then suddenly turned back and grabbed my phone. Just in case, I thought. I climbed the stairs and looked at the three doors to the rooms that faced the front of the house. One was the main bathroom, the other two were spare rooms. The image of the person in the window had been on the far left, which could only mean that the room I needed to look in was the one on my right. I had been in there once since I had arrived.

I clutched my phone, took the door handle in my hand and eased the door open. I wasn't sure what I was expecting to see, but it was as I remembered it from the first time. One double bed, plain white sheets, a wooden bedside table. I took a few tentative steps into the room and over to the window. I was standing where the person had been in the picture. My skin tingled but I remained where I was, as though I needed to prove to myself that I wasn't scared. But my whole body was tense; sweat gathered on the palm of my hand where I was holding my phone too tightly. I looked out of the window at the view of the front garden. Trees and shrubs lined the outskirts. Not only did no one know I was here, but the framework of trees ensured I was also well hidden. If there was ever a time to feel alone, it was now.

There was a crash; something had fallen. I swung around, my heart pounding in my throat. I ran to the landing as though I could ascertain where it had come from. I could only imagine it had come from downstairs. I raced down the steps into the hallway, an image of Lucy in my mind, squashed under a heavy piece of furniture. But when I arrived in the kitchen where I had left her, she was lying on the floor, hot and exhausted from the walk to Blake's.

I turned and headed back to the hallway. I opened the room to the study, a tiny room with just a desk and chair; nothing untoward in there. Then I turned and I was facing the formal sitting room. I felt my mouth go dry as I looked at the door, which was ajar. I had kept all of the doors closed in the house. I had been overwhelmed by the size of the place and open doors made me feel uneasy. I did not recall coming back into this room for anything. In fact, I only had a memory of being in here once when I looked around on the first day. Was this where the crash had come from?

I pushed open the door and stepped into the room. To my right were two long sofas facing each other. Between the sofas were the remains of a black glass coffee table. I glanced upwards and saw there was a large part of the crystal chandelier missing – it was now lying amongst the shards of black glass. My ears pricked up to the sound of a car engine revving loudly and I dashed to the front door and ran down the driveway. As I arrived at the end and looked to the right, I caught a glimpse of a silver sports car in the distance as it accelerated away down the lane.

I walked back up to the house. When I had first met Blake, he had mentioned something about people taking the wrong exit into this lane from time to time or using it as turning point. There was no way that whoever had been in that car could have been in the house moments earlier without me realising it. It was a big house, and I still hadn't got used to the spontaneous groans of the old place. But I couldn't allow myself to think like that.

I paced the kitchen and hallway for a little while, wondering what I should do. I couldn't face going back into the sitting room and clearing up the broken glass, nor could I relax.

It was only lunchtime, and I had such a lot of the day left. I was having more and more moments of wondering what I was doing here and whether it would be easier and safer to head back to my small one-bedroom flat.

I would have to go for another swim and try to rid my belly of the tension that was creeping in and would soon invade my chest and begin to tighten around my neck. That was the only way I could explain it if anyone cared to ask. But I wouldn't be speaking to any counsellors or psychologists. This was something I had to endure on my own until the very end.

Before I took myself off to the pool for my second swim of the day, I sent the image of me in front of the house to my parents, taking care not to choose the one with the face at the window. I added some text to both of them.

All is well with me. Have some nice digs for the foreseeable. xx

I tried to force myself not to go back and look at the second and first photo, the ones where the shadow crept in at the window and then exposed the figure of someone, but I couldn't help myself. I took another look, moving between the two images to try to ascertain any striking features. What were they wearing? It looked as if they had on a hoodie in the first photo, but by the second photo, I couldn't be sure. I pinched the first photo again and scanned around the head area. It looked very much as though they were wearing a hat, perhaps a baseball cap, and there was a smattering of light hair underneath.

Perhaps the person was some sort of runner/PA and they'd slipped out of the back and into the car of the photographer when I had been talking with Hendrick. What was holding my attention the most about the photos was that the figure did not look like Tom. They were too short. Tom was tall and slim, and I was sure he would have had to stoop to look through the window, whereas this person's face, albeit pixilated and fuzzy, was perfectly framed within the centre. I thought back to the strange conversation with Arthur at the shop. Were the people who had lived here before me not done with the place? Perhaps they came back to visit from time to time, unable to come to terms with their loss. I decided I would make some enquiries into getting all the locks changed, just to be sure. It had never occurred to me before that once someone left a house, they could easily come back if they'd kept a spare key. It seemed an odd thing to do, but highly plausible.

My phone pinged with a message, and I looked at the words from my dad's number.

That's good love. Nice to hear from you. Miss you and love you xx

I felt my heart begin to crumble and I thought I would collapse right there on the floor. How could they love me when I had done so much wrong?

18

NOW

Citrus was dead. One lonely customer – a man in a Panama hat and beach shorts sitting at a table on the front path – had made one coffee last over an hour so far. With the start of the holidays, the beaches were packed with families. From where I stood at the front of the restaurant, I could see a glimpse of the sea and the sand littered with people stripping off, ready to roast their pale skin to a shade of beetroot.

Maisie assured me there would be people here by lunchtime, but as the hands on the clock crept closer to midday, I felt a growing sense of agitation. I needed to be busy. Images of the smashed glass table kept appearing in front of me, and the agitation would overwhelm me. I didn't know where to begin with clearing it up. At least here at Citrus there was order and structure to the day. Everything back at Willow Cottage seemed to be unravelling and getting out of my control. I had thought I would be safe there, but now I was not so sure.

Maisie had stopped me when I began taking things from the shelves to have a clean – my way of distracting myself from the angst that was inching through my body. So I paced the restaurant like a caged animal, wringing my hands then catching myself and folding them under my apron. I walked from table to table, adjusting the cutlery into perfect symmetry, I checked the toilets for a third time, then began a second lap of the restaurant.

I thought of Lucy and how we had walked for miles this morning. She enjoyed me being an early riser, as she was raring to go at six or seven. I hoped she was tired and would snooze away all afternoon until I could get back to feed her and take her out again. I hadn't heard anything back from Blake and it had been several days since I had dropped the brownies off. But he didn't owe me anything. We were even now. He didn't need to take up space in my brain. Except – aside from Lucy – he was the only person who would occasionally creep into my mind. I found myself thinking about him at odd times of the day, wondering what he was doing. He had spoken so openly to me, about little elements of his life already. He was the very antithesis of Tom in that respect. The very thing that I sought in a partner.

The clock crept around to 1 p.m. and a trickle of customers came through the door. I gave my best performance of a waitress who was happy with her life. The tips were poor at the end of the shift but that was understandable with families in the summer – parents were dragged back to the beach by impatient children or tending to hot and cranky toddlers. I was just glad of the distraction, to have a purpose for a few hours. For my mind to be so consumed with information about drinks orders and which table needed new cutlery that I didn't have room to think about anything else.

I finished my shift at 4 p.m. and as I was about to walk out of the door, Maisie approached me, clutching the landline phone.

'Are you able to cover a shift tonight?' she hissed, holding her hand over the receiver.

'Yes,' I said, not needing to think about it. I would have to pop back home first and return after I had tended to Lucy, but I was glad that I would have more work to distract me.

'Great, one waiter thinks he is too ill to come in,' she whispered, then took her hand off the receiver. 'Yes, that's fine. I've got you covered. Get well soon,' she said into the phone, then hung up.

'Thank you, Kit, you're a life saver.' She patted my arm, and I froze at her words. Life saver. I glanced across the room to the empty restaurant. She was sitting at the table this time, drawing. She had loved to draw; she was so creative. I found I was smiling. Because she looked so happy. She would have grown up into a beautiful woman who loved to paint. She faded as quickly as she had appeared, and I felt my smile drop.

'So I'll see you tonight?' Maisie was speaking. I looked at the empty restaurant and then at Maisie. She looked at me curiously for a second.

'Absolutely no worries whatsoever. I'll be back in a few hours.'

Maisie patted my arm again.

'Brilliant. See you soon.'

I rushed out the door and felt my whole body flood with adrenaline. Maisie's compliment flooded my brain, heat rushed through my body, and I had an overwhelming urge to run or be sick. I walked outside quickly and to the back of the restaurant where I had parked my car and when I reached it, I leant one hand against the side of it and threw up.

I pulled up in the driveway and sat still for a few moments. The drive home had calmed me slightly, but I was still playing Maisie's last words to me over and over. I looked to the garden to see if I would see her there, playing. Had she followed me home? Not today; the garden was empty and still. It was just after 4.30 p.m. I would have time for a shower and to give Lucy a walk, then I would need to head back to Citrus. I began walking up the path to the front of the house, but stopped dead in my tracks when I saw someone standing in front of the window, peering in. I stood frozen and watched the figure move across towards the sunroom and then the swimming pool. They suddenly turned as though they had sensed me watching them. Then they began running towards me.

19

THEN

The dinner with my parents was a triumph. Tom was as merry and as amiable as he always was, topping up drinks, giving compliments to my dad about the moistness and flavour of the chicken, even though everyone knew it was a fajita pack and Dad had simply poured and stirred. Tom showed Mum how to mix a margarita and put salt on the rim of the glasses and Mum clapped with glee and took out her phone to photograph the green cocktails lined up on the counter.

When Tom popped out to the loo, Mum and Dad huddled around me like we were in a rugby scrum.

'He's even better than we remember him being, love,' Dad said, and I could smell the alcohol on his breath. We were three margaritas in.

'Yes, and a real hunk too. Do you think this is the one, love? You're thirty-two this year...' Mum let out a small hiccup.

'Yes, I do realise my age. But I'm getting to know him still, Mum.'

'I know, dear, but it would be so nice to have a couple more grandchildren.'

'You still have Josh and Emily, they're not dead,' I said flatly.

'Now, love, leave her be, we've said our piece, she knows how we feel. Things will work themselves out in their own time.' Dad gave me a reassuring look and I smiled.

'I know, but people take so long these days; why are they afraid to have children? Even Jude waited until she was in her late twenties. Not like us, early twenties, we were.'

'Yes, Mum, people like to try other things first, marriage and kids is just not on my radar. Not yet.'

'What's all this then; not talking about me, are you?' Tom came bounding back into the kitchen with as much enthusiasm as he had when he had left, and I wondered how he managed it.

'Only good things, son,' Dad said, and Tom looked at me, his face frozen for a second, apparently shocked at the sentiment. What had he experienced growing up? Had he never been called 'son' by his own father? I prayed Mum and Dad wouldn't continue the conversation now Tom was back in the room. He didn't need any encouragement when it came to discussing having kids.

'Is it time for another cocktail?' I said brightly and walked over to the kitchen counter. I felt Tom arrive next to me. He didn't speak but I felt his energy and I just knew he had overheard the conversation and that I would have to speak to him again. I would need to reiterate how I felt about having children, I would need to be more straight with him and explain that if there was to be a future with us, he needed to open up about his life before me. Because without that openness, I felt as though I would be taking a big risk committing myself to him.

Tom had booked us into a hotel a short taxi ride from Mum and Dad's house. He ordered night caps to be delivered to the room and was unusually quiet.

'Is everything okay?' I asked as I began removing my make-up.

'Hmmm?' Tom said questioningly. But I knew he had heard me.

'Look, Tom, if you're upset about stuff we've talked and not talked about, the whole baby/marriage thing, then please know it's not that I don't ever want to settle down and do all that stuff, it's just—'

'Do you mind if we don't talk tonight? Your parents have wiped me out.'

I was so shocked I didn't know what to say. Tom had been the one who had been over-energetic. He was a charismatic person, no doubt about that, but I felt throughout the whole evening it was *he* who had been trying hard to impress my parents, two people who needed very little impressing.

The next morning, I woke to the door opening and Tom's hushed voice thanking someone. As I came to, I saw Tom approaching the bed with a huge bouquet of flowers, and a trolley laden with a fruit platter, pastries and a pot of coffee. He knew how much I loved a continental breakfast. I felt a swell of love for him. Why couldn't he be this person *and* someone who was not afraid to tell me who he was?

'I say let's settle in for the long run. I've organised an extra-late check-out, and your shift isn't until tonight, so dig in, babes.'

I sat up and took in the flowers and the smell of the coffee and I smiled to myself as I thought about the next few hours ahead of us with nothing to do, nowhere to go. I would take a long shower, read my book, sit out on the balcony and look at the busy street below. Tom always seemed to hit the nail on the head when it came to this sort of stuff. There was so much to like about him. I knew this was his way of apologising for his behaviour when we'd got back here last night, and he didn't want to say it out loud. This was enough for now. I would bask in his attention for the next few hours, enjoy the luxurious hotel suite and try to ignore that nagging doubt at the back of my mind that, even though I was here in the lap of luxury with a man I cared about, it could all soon come to an end.

20

NOW

When she reached me, she threw her arms around me and held me so tight I thought she might never release me.

When she did, she looked me up and down.

'My God, you got skinny.' Jude spat out the words like they disgusted her but we both knew she meant them as a compliment. Then she turned around and faced Willow Cottage. 'And what in God's name is this? How are you affording to live here?' She gestured to the house, then looked at me questioningly.

'I won it,' I said pointedly.

'You what?' she gasped. 'You bloody won it? How in hell did that happen?'

'I entered a competition. And here I am.'

'Just like that? You absolute jammy cow. And look at you, you're so blasé about it, like you always are about everything. Does it not faze you at all that you own this mansion? And why would you not think to tell your own family?'

Jude's voice was ringing out around me, but I wasn't absorbing her words. I was thinking about her being here.

'How did you find me?' I asked.

'Well, let me tell you a little story.' She put her arm through mine, and we began walking to the top of the drive via the path.

'You sent Mum and Dad this photo of you outside this house, which I showed to Stan. The first thing he does is look at the 5G tower in the distance in the background.' I turned to Jude and frowned. She stopped and pulled her phone out of the back pocket of her shorts.

'Look.' She scrolled through her photos until she found the one I'd sent. For the first time, I noticed the tip of a tower in the background.

'Here you are, posing in front of your new digs – I looked at that and thought, she doesn't look happy – and I was telling that to Stan but he was already on his phone looking something up and then, next thing, he's showing me his map and told me he knew exactly where you were. All from that 5G tower, and the fact you can see the house name clear as day. Stan was pretty sure he knew where the most recent 5G tower had just gone up as he'd seen loads of pictures – people kicking off online apparently, they don't want their brains fried – and then the house name confirmed it. Thirty-five minutes it took me to drive here. The air con is bust in the car, so I was hanging out the window like a dog most of the way. I'm parched. Can we go in? Get something cool to drink, then I absolutely want to try the pool out. I brought my bikini because I had a sneaky feeling this place would have a pool. And I was right.'

I thought I would keel over from the heat and Jude talking at me. Jude could never stand me getting one over on her when we were kids, so she must be spewing at me owning Willow Cottage. Yet, at the same time, I felt a faint flutter of relief that she was here. For a moment, I thought about spilling everything to her. But I stopped myself because just her being here and knowing I had won a house was enough. If she knew any more, she would probably leave immediately.

'Willow Cottage is bit of a naff name though, isn't it, I mean, it's hardly a cottage, it's flipping massive. It's more of a manor than a cottage. Can you change it?'

I was searching in my bag for the house key as Jude whittled on.

'Erm, I'm not sure.' I certainly hadn't ever considered it. I had become fond of the name Willow Cottage; it had a certain homeliness to it. I hoped soon I could embrace the house for what it was supposed to be, a comfortable sanctuary. One I would hope to share with someone one day.

I took Jude in through the front door so she could experience the house in all its splendour, from the grand hallway to the staircase. I walked through to the kitchen, and she followed, gasping and commenting on everything she saw. I opened the kitchen door and Lucy ran out, barking. I bent down and scooped her up, letting her lick my face as a way of thanking her for being a good guard dog. It was the first time she had let out a little bark like that. I knew it was because she sensed new energy, and Jude's energy was off the scale.

'Oh, my days, a puppy as well!' Jude took Lucy from my arms and nuzzled her face into her fur.

'This guy down the road had one spare; he gave her to me.'

'For nothing? You got a house and a dog... for nothing?'

I nodded, thinking about the twenty grand sitting in my bank account and wondered if I should mention it to Jude.

'No frigging way.'

I noticed Jude had dropped a bag by her side when she took Lucy from me, so I pointed to it.

'Are you planning on staying?' I said hopefully. I really could do with the company.

'Well, of course. I didn't drive all this way just for a cup of tea.'

'All this way? You'd drive further for a Nando's,' I said bluntly.

'Hmmm.' Jude put Lucy down and then assessed me. 'You've not lost that sarcastic side of you then.' She shook her head. 'I came here because a month ago you deserted us all. Me, our parents, your niece and nephew. Tom.'

I felt my skin prickle at his name.

Jude nodded. 'Yes, don't think you could get away with that one without us knowing about it. He came to Mum and Dad's house almost in tears. He was so distraught. He doesn't know what he's done wrong, Kit, none of us do.' I felt the heavy weight engulf me again. The effects of one act had spread across so many people.

Jude's forehead wrinkled as she read my expression. She touched my arm. 'Shall we go and have a cold drink and you can tell me all about it?'

* * *

I sat down in the kitchen and Jude poured us two fruit juices, cold from the fridge. She sat down and let out a loud sigh.

'So, you need to tell me, what's going on?'

I shrugged my shoulders and felt like a schoolgirl again, in trouble with my parents. There was no way I could tell Jude, or anyone. No one would understand.

'It's nothing, Jude. You really didn't need to race all the way over here. I'm perfectly fine, as you can see.' The lie felt thick in my throat.

'I can see, but it doesn't make sense. Did you win the house and suddenly decide you were too good for us?'

I snorted. 'No, Jude, I just needed to get away from it all, from everyone. I'd been in that relationship with Tom, and it felt suffocating. I needed to just reset.' This was partly true, of course. I did feel as though I was suffocating. Every. Single. Day.

Jude shook her head in disbelief. 'So, you finish with Tom – the best boyfriend you have ever had, did I tell you that? Yes, I think I did. Then you leave Mirabelle, the restaurant you loooooove so much, then you stop speaking to me, Mum and Dad, and Josh and Emily, and then you move out here to the middle of nowhere to live like some rich hermit.'

'I'm not rich. And I'm not a hermit. I still go to work, to the shops.' I was trying to convince myself more than Jude. There was every possibility that I would turn into a hermit. The situation was not good.

Jude let another loud sigh. I knew she wouldn't get to my core because she never did. Jude had never had that ability to dive into my soul, to get to the heart of matters. She would rant and rave and demand answers, thinking that volume and over-the-top hand gestures would make me open up and speak to her about how dismal I felt from the moment I woke up until the moment I shut my eyes at night. Which only ever lasted for a few hours before I was awake again, staring at the ceiling and replaying that day in my mind over and over. Until I drove myself mad enough with it that I had to get up to distract myself from swallowing enough parac-etamol that the horror film I was living would just fade to black. Jude couldn't handle hearing that from me. We had never had the sort of relationship where I could discuss my deepest, darkest thoughts. But it didn't stop me thinking, imagining even. Jude leaning forward and looking me in the eye and saying to me, 'Tell me all about it, Kit, I can see you are hurting.'

But of course, she didn't, and so I knew I was safe. I knew the secret I was holding close to me was still safe away from my family. But for how long? I wasn't the only keeper of this secret. I had managed to keep it quiet for over a month, saved my family the heartache.

I hadn't expected an easy ride when I'd made the decision to cut myself off from everyone. I knew for certain Tom would come looking for me; he had gone to such lengths to keep me in his sights. Why would he give up now?

21

NOW

'I have to get back to work soon,' I said to Jude as I walked her to the pool.

'I know, you little workaholic. I'll be fine here, just Lucy and me. God, I really need this swim; it's only the beginning of the school holidays and the kids are driving me bloody mental.' She slipped out of her towel to reveal a skimpy bikini and sat down at the side of the pool. I looked at the silver streaks of stretch marks along her waist. She hated them so much and usually covered up, but she obviously felt comfortable next to me.

'Do you need anything else? I haven't got much food in, just bread and cheese and fruit. I can bring you back some food from the restaurant tonight?'

'Yeah, sure,' Jude called. She was already off, swimming to the other side of the pool.

'Okay, so you'll be fine, will you?' I said a little louder. She turned over on to her back.

'Yes, silly. I'll be fine.'

'Where are the kids, anyway?'

'Oh, now you ask.' Jude laughed. 'You're not exactly Mrs Maternal, are you? They are with Stan's mum. Having a sleepover. Stan gets to go to the pub with his mates and I get to be here with you.'

She was treading water as she spoke.

'Well, only I'm going now, so you'll be on your own. And it will be dark.' I thought about the smashed glass table and the car that had gone screeching off along the lane.

Jude laughed. 'I'm not in a *Scream* movie, am I?'

'No, but you used to be terrified, when we were kids, of basically everything.'

'Yeah, well, I've had two kids since then; the only things that terrify me now are nits and nosebleeds.'

'Right.' I stood for another moment. 'Well don't go in the formal sitting room, I had a... slight accident in there.'

'The what? Did you just say formal sitting room?' Jude tilted her head back and laughed again.

'Okay.' I ignored her comment. 'Lucy had a good walk, I've fed her, so you know, just chill. Oh, I don't have Netflix or Sky, just terrestrial TV.'

'What?' Jude protested.

'Sorry, I haven't got round to it; I am barely here for that.'

'Oh, well, good old BBC it is then. Let's hope there's a murder mystery on!' she said with a wickedness to her voice.

'Okay then.' I stood for a moment and watched her. Was it a good idea to leave Jude here alone? Maybe I should tell her what had happened since I had been here, and then she could make an informed decision. Was I doing a terrible thing by holding back? Or had I just been completely paranoid these last few days? Lack of sleep will do that to you.

I finally left my sister to her swim. In the kitchen, Lucy was gnawing away at one of her toys. I picked up my handbag from the back of the chair and as I did, Lucy let out a loud growl.

'Oh, sweetheart, what is it?' As I bent down to give her some fuss, she growled again, and this time I heard a noise from outside the back door. I leapt back up and reached over to the counter. If I had been caught out by someone trying to cause damage to the house on more than one occasion, I wasn't about to be caught out again. This time I was prepared with a large carving knife. I walked up to the back door and pulled it open. Lucy was at my heels now, her hackles slightly raised, and I felt a wave of happiness that she was there.

I pulled the door fully open and there, with his back to me, about to walk away, was Blake.

'Oh, it's you!' My voice bore a pleasant tone that I hadn't expected.

Blake turned around. 'Yes, it's me again. Sorry. Hope I didn't scare you.'

'No, you didn't.' I saw Blake looking at the knife in my hand. 'I was, erm, chopping something.'

'Okay, right.' Blake didn't sound too convinced. 'I brought your Tupperware back. I ate all the brownies, and I am not even sorry.' He laughed.

'Why would you be sorry? I made them for you.'

'And they were absolutely delicious. You should be a baker. Is that your job?'

'I... I, no, I work in hospitality, though.' I stalled, still not ready to explain about my life. About how I had won a house, but went to work as a waitress every day. I could hear Tom's voice, challenging me about my job. Perhaps Blake wouldn't be so quick to judge.

'Nice. Well, there's your tub, and I also brought a bottle of cider for you. My brother makes it in Somerset. I have to say, it is pretty good.'

I looked down by the door and there was a bottle filled with an amber liquid.

'I can't wait to try it. Thank you. Thank your brother.'

'I will,' Blake said with a glint in his eye and a wry smile. He bent down and stroked Lucy, then stood up again, eyeing the knife.

I looked at it and dropped it to my side.

'I have to get to work, so I'll see you.'

'Oh, yes, absolutely, I didn't mean to bother you.'

'Oh, you didn't. I'll let you know how the cider goes down.'

Blake smiled and waved and disappeared around the side of the house. He would walk past the swimming pool to get to the drive, and I thought about what Jude would say if she saw him. Then I surprised myself when I realised I was more concerned with what Blake would think if he saw my sister standing in a bikini.

I made it back into work just before seven. The restaurant was starting to fill up and it made a change from the day, which had started off so quiet. I knew the next four hours would fly by. But there was a nagging in my mind. I was worried about Jude at the house by herself. With the few incidents that had happened recently, it was unnerving for me that I had made the decision to leave Jude alone and not tell her what had been happening at the house. Would she have just laughed it off? Oh, how the tables had turned, and it was now me fretting about everything. As much as Jude had tried to make out to me that she was no longer the scaredy cat that I grew up with, I was sure she would get spooked out there alone at night if something or someone... I tried not to think about it.

I had texted her before I got out of the car, and she had told me she was curled up watching a BBC documentary about plastic in our food and had opened a bottle of prosecco that she had brought with her. But I was still baffled about how Lucy had ended up in the sink. I was certain Tom had sent me the package, yet the other stuff just felt a little beneath him. He wasn't the sort of person to take revenge and seek to sabotage my property. I hoped that the incidents with the pipe and then the smashed table were just down to bad luck. Or if there had been someone hanging about the property these last few days, I hoped that now they were keeping their distance and things would settle down and maybe, just maybe, I might begin to start to feel at home. I would see about getting the locks changed and then I would feel a lot safer. Jude arriving today had been a shock initially, but now I knew she was there, I felt as though the house was getting the proper use it deserved.

Once I had my apron on and my waiting cloth tucked in the side, I set about making sure the tables were as they should be for the evening sitting. Maisie approached me, looking a little flustered. 'I have to take a phone call; can you hold the fort for five minutes?'

'I...' I went to protest, but an excuse didn't come quick enough. Maisie had disappeared out the back of the restaurant before I'd had time to speak. And just as she disappeared, the customers began to arrive. I approached the door as a young family came in. I felt my heart race at the sight of them. I looked around to see if Maisie was back, so that I didn't have to greet them. I could handle them once they were seated, where I could give them what they needed with little interaction, but the initial greet felt too overwhelming. My mouth was dry as I went to speak to them. They were a mum, dad and two young children, a boy who looked about six or seven and a girl who looked about four. I gazed at them and saw how happy they looked, fresh from the beach, the kids with their tousled hair and freckled cheeks. I felt my gut twist. I wasn't sure if I would be able to go through with serving them; they were putting their trust in me, after all. I had too much power.

I seated the family with a pain in my gut that almost crippled me. I went back to the ottoman and took a long sip of water. I was about to go into my usual speed mode, which would eventually morph into autopilot, but I stopped myself. That was when mistakes could happen. I glanced over at the family and watched the little girl take her thin jacket off and lay it carefully across the back of her chair. Her father touched her lightly on the head and the boy crawled closer to his mother with a handful of Lego.

I knew for the rest of the shift I would be going slower; each action would take me longer as I pondered my choices and wondered whether they were the right ones to make. The next four hours that I had anticipated flying by would now be slow and enduring. Usually, every move I made was swift because I didn't need to think. I might have lost the ability to converse as easily with the customers as I once could, but I was an experienced waitress, and from time to time, I needed to slow down and remember. Today was one of those shifts. And I would spend the whole time remembering.

By eleven o'clock, I was mentally and physically exhausted. I sent a quick text to Jude, checking she was okay. She replied she was still up and was looking forward to me coming home. I asked the chef to box me up a meal and carried it out to the car. I felt weary on the journey back and I realised that now I lived further away, I should maybe consider a job closer to Willow Cottage. There was the pub in the village, which ran a table service. I was sure I could get a job there if I wanted to.

Thirty minutes later, I pulled up in the driveway and noticed all the lights were off. Not even the security light came on as I got out of the car and walked up the driveway. My legs felt weak as I approached the door and I used my phone light to help me guide my key through, but my hand had begun to shake, and I struggled to get it in the lock. Eventually I turned the key and stepped into a pitch-black hallway. I fumbled for the switch and was surprised when the light came on. I had been convinced there had been a power cut.

I walked through into the kitchen. Again, the light was off. I couldn't see or hear Lucy and she didn't come up to greet me the way she normally did when I arrived home. I moved around the kitchen, looking for her. My already shaky body – exhausted from work and lack of food – was now practically convulsing. I dropped the warm box of food on the counter. I trotted through to the sitting room where Jude had said she would be and saw no sign of her or her belongings, although her car was still in the driveway. I felt my heart thumping through my chest. Where the hell was she? This was all my fault. I was stupid to have left Jude alone. I should have told her what had been happening, at least, so she could have made her own mind up. But telling her those things would have meant I had to reveal more to her – about why I was here alone. About what I had done.

I ran up the stairs and into the spare room, where I had set her up before I had left. Her bag was there, but the bed was still made. I ran back downstairs, the panic now flooding my veins. What if someone had been in the house all those times? What if that person at the window in my photo was a crazed person who used to live here and they still had a key? Or worse still, the one thing I had not wanted to contemplate, what if this was revenge? Was my time finally up? Had they come for me? Why hadn't I changed the locks already and installed security cameras and alarms? I had twenty grand in my account, I could have paid someone to come and do the whole house. I went through to the sunroom, and then the pool room. All the lights were off, and she was nowhere to be seen. I went back to the kitchen and took my phone out of my bag and called Jude's phone. It rang out and then went to answerphone.

'Shit,' I said as I hung up. I was not prepared for this. I'd gone against my instincts and left Jude here alone, despite her macho words that made her seem stronger than I knew she was. She didn't know the full story, she didn't know that I had done something so terrible that there was a chance someone needed to even things out. That I was potentially a target and that Jude's life too could be in danger.

I carefully opened the back door and switched the porch light on. I stepped outside and tripped over something hard that was shin-height and right outside the doorway.

'What the hell?' I turned around and rubbed at my shin as I bent down to get a look at what was in front of me.

It was a large plastic tub of peanuts.

Was this something from Blake again? I noticed a flash of white and next to the tub, a piece of card, face down. It must have been on the tub when I tripped over it. I picked it up and turned it over and read:

Don't forget to feed the birds.

I felt my stomach lurch at the cryptic words, but the sight of the tub of bird food alone was enough for me to want to retch. I let out a small choking sound. This was it. I was right. I was a wanted woman and they had found me.

Then I heard a noise from the kitchen, and I stood up and faced the open door.

22

NOW

'Jude!' I gasped. 'You're here.'

'Of course I'm here, where else am I going to be?' Jude was still fully clothed but rubbing her eyes, as though she had just woken up.

'I looked around the whole house; I couldn't find you anywhere.' The relief ran through me, flooding my body as though I had been injected with it.

Lucy trotted in behind Jude, and I bent down to stroke her.

'Is Lucy okay?' I said, trying to control my breath.

'She's fine. I'm fine, everyone is okay, why are you acting so weird?' Jude stretched and reached into the cupboard for a glass to pour herself some water.

I stopped before I said anything. I couldn't even begin to try to explain the inner workings of my mind to Jude. It was for my head only. 'I don't usually turn all the lights off before bed, I always keep the security lights on at least.'

Jude waved her hand about. 'Well, I don't know which is which, I just switched everything off. This house is massive, Kit, if you keep leaving all the lights on, you'll have a huge electric bill. You need to be careful; you may have won this house but it still costs a lot to run it... hey, are you okay?' Jude sipped her water then handed it to me.

I felt lightheaded and slumped into a chair at the kitchen table and sipped slowly. 'I haven't eaten, that's all.'

'Why not, you silly thing, is this why you are so skinny, because you're skipping meals? What can I get you?' Jude looked around the kitchen.

'I brought back food, it's in that box.'

Jude brought it over to the table with two forks and sat down opposite me.

She opened the box to reveal butter chicken and rice, one of tonight's specials.

'Ooh, that smells lovely. I had Nutella and banana on toast earlier.'

I took a forkful and before I put it in my mouth, I asked, 'Where were you? I looked everywhere.'

'I was in your room. I went to check out the bed, which looked way comfier than mine, and I'd had a few glasses of prosecco and Lucy followed me and we both lay down for five minutes and well, that was it, I was out like a light. Except Lucy must have heard you come home as she was up and off the bed and scratching at the door to get out. Were you looking for me outside?' Jude gestured to the open kitchen door. I felt my stomach lurch again as I thought of the tub of peanuts.

'No, I... not really. I was just turning on the security light.'

'And what's that?' She pointed with her fork to the massive tub of bird nuts.

'Bird food,' I murmured.

'Ah, it must be so nice living here. You must love watching the birds; do you remember you loved feeding them as a kid? You hated the thought of them not having any food. You used to cry when the feeders were empty.' Jude dug her fork into the chicken.

I looked her, amazed that she'd remembered that.

I thought about our lives as children. I had always felt as if I were the big sister. That was how I had remembered it. Jude was always lagging behind, too scared to do the things I wanted to do.

'I remember things differently,' I said quietly.

Jude looked at me. 'So, what are your plans with this place? I mean, you can't afford to live here permanently, can you? Not unless you change your job. I know you love your waitressing, but the wage can't sustain a property this size. Hey, maybe Stan and me and the kids should move in? It's six bedrooms, right? Still plenty of room for us all.' She chuckled but I knew she was being semi-serious.

I looked up at Jude and then straight back down at my food. I didn't need to say anything else in response to what she knew was a ludicrous comment. I could never live with my sister as an adult.

'Okay, so what do you plan to do, then?'

I put my fork down. I'd had two mouthfuls and I felt my stomach begin to churn.

'I don't know, Jude. I am just existing now. I can't think about anything else.' I could feel my mind swirling with dark thoughts. If only I could share them.

Jude let out a loud sigh. Then she said brightly, 'Who was that hunk earlier? He walked around the side of the house.'

I let out a half laugh, glad of the comic relief. 'That was Blake, the guy who gave me the dog.'

'Oh, and he often pops round, does he?' Jude sniggered.

'No actually, he doesn't, he just brought back some Tupperware. I made him brownies to say tha—'

'Wait, you made him brownies? You didn't even make me a cake on my birthday, and I know you can bake 'cos you did it all the time when you were a kid.'

I shook my head. 'It was a one-off impulsive thing; the man had just given me a dog.'

Jude shook her head. 'You are so jammy, you know. I cannot believe you have managed to get all this.' I left her to her own thoughts as I tried one more mouthful of food before giving up.

Jude let out a loud yawn.

'I'm so tired, I might just head back up to bed.'

I looked up at her. 'The spare room, obviously, this time.'

Then she touched my hand. 'Unless you need me to sleep with you this evening. You know, you seemed a bit spooked earlier with all the lights being off.' There was a sarcastic tone to Jude's voice and so I instantly shook my head.

'No, of course not,' I said defensively. Jude stood up and kissed me lightly on the head.

'Okay, night, then.' And she walked out of the kitchen, Lucy following at her heels until Jude reached the kitchen door, then Lucy turned around and came back and settled next to me.

I thought back to Jude's last words, and her half-hearted offer of company in bed. Had she offered in a more serious tone, I probably would have accepted. I didn't want to have to ask, and I didn't want to appear weak and scared, which Jude had already begun to see that I was. But the truth was I could have done with the company of someone in bed with me tonight. Things had spiralled out of control so quickly I no longer knew which way was up. I was convinced that someone had been in the house, more than once. And I was sure it was Tom who had sent me the protein bars. I would probably sleep easier with someone by my side. But I couldn't take the risk of Jude wanting to know more. So I stood up, closed and locked the back door, leaving the bird nuts where they were. Then I turned and looked at Lucy, who was already in her bed. She knew the routine now and I almost wished she wasn't such a good dog who had trained so easily in a few days.

'Night, then.' I bent down and gave her a big fuss before I turned and assessed the kitchen once more before turning off the light and heading upstairs. Alone.

23

THEN

'Tickets to Ibiza?' I was standing in Tom's kitchen in his riverside apartment in Bath. We had come for the weekend. Tom said he felt we needed to spend some quality time together. I wondered if he had sensed something was wrong after the evening we had spent at my parents' house, how my behaviour had maybe revealed my deepest thoughts, ones I had been grappling with and trying to hide away for fear they were the truest ones.

And now, a trip. I had never been to Ibiza before. The thought of it instantly grabbed me and I began to imagine myself there. It was April, it was pretty cold, and the thought of sun made me feel instantly warm.

'We could celebrate our three-month anniversary,' Tom said as he straightened a tea towel on the oven door so the bottom of it was the same length as the oven cloth on the other side. I watched with interest. He was nervous and I could hear a slight jitter in his voice. Was it because he had remembered our anniversary before me? I was the kind of girl who was down with a year's anniversary, maybe even six months. But three months?

I was slicing peppers to go in the stir fry we were having for dinner. Tom suggested we cook together but he had followed me around the kitchen, wiping down the sides and sweeping up the bits I had dropped on the floor. He had just finished washing and drying up the chopping board I had used to cut the chicken on. A red one, from a set of four other colours for specific food groups. It reminded me of being in the restaurant kitchen. Except it was even tidier in Tom's.

'I don't know if I could get time off work.'

'I spoke to Denim already.' He scooped the pepper debris up with a kitchen towel and deposited it in the bin. I put my knife down and turned to face him.

'You spoke to Denim?'

Tom nodded. 'Yep. He was fine about it.'

'But it's not up to you to ask my manager if I can take time off work!' My voice was louder than I would have liked it to be, and Tom looked at me, his eyes slightly wide.

'I know Denim, I've been dining in that restaurant for years, way before you were working there. He's cool.'

I cleared my throat, to give myself a moment so I didn't say the wrong thing. Tom had good intentions. I had to remember that.

'I know, but it is kind of my responsibility to organise my own time off. It feels a bit like a dad thing to do.'

Tom looked at me and blinked hard and then edged closer to me.

'And are you mad with your daddy?' Tom said in a funny voice that made me want to laugh and retch in equal amounts.

'Okay, you're officially sick.'

'Yes, but you love it.' Tom took my hand and started pulling me out of the kitchen. 'I think I fancy a little starter before our main course.'

We left the immaculate-looking kitchen and I let myself be taken to the bedroom by Tom.

* * *

Tom went back to finish the stir fry and I stayed in bed. I thought about the Denim situation and how it must make me look like some little girl who couldn't sort her own days off at her job and had to send her boyfriend to do it for her. Tom had laughed it off and I'd melted into his embrace. And that was that. My opinion did not matter. The same way he had wanted me to quit my job and the same way he had spoken of us starting a family. And the hundred other little things in between that I had picked up on and pondered over. But then there was the spontaneous sex, the great apartments and houses, the ability to take a trip whenever we wanted. My parents were smitten. But I wasn't sure they could see the blurred line between Tom the human and Tom the money-making tycoon. They just saw security for me for the rest of my life and there was a part of me that wanted that for me, just for them alone. Of course, the prospect of lifelong financial security was a good prospect for anyone. I had begun making notes on my phone. 'Tom's pros and cons' in the subject line. I pulled out my phone and added another line:

Interferes with my job.

I clicked my phone to blank and laid it on the bedside table. I closed my eyes, thinking I would just doze for a second.

* * *

I opened my eyes and Tom was standing next to the bed. There was a sweet garlicky smell filling the room and it took me a few seconds to remember what day it was and what had been happening before

I fell asleep. Tom was holding my phone and I held my hand out towards it.

'What are you doing with my phone?' I took it and cradled it to my chest. I couldn't fathom why he would need to be holding it.

'I just put in the date for our holiday on your calendar.'

'You could have sent it to me from your calendar,' I said croakily.

'Well, I wanted you to have it your calendar straight away. Dinner is ready, by the way.' He sounded monotone, not the same perky person he had been only moments earlier.

I sat up in bed and swiped my phone into action. I had never liked using a passcode on my phone, it took too much time and effort. It was open on my calendar. The weekend at the end of the month was marked with 'Tom and Kit's trip to Ibiza'. He'd added the flight times. We would leave Friday morning and head back Monday night. Three days of sun in the middle of a pretty chilly April. I suddenly began to feel as if it was possibly the best decision that Tom had made since we'd got together and tried to discard the nagging feeling in my stomach, knowing Tom's despondency could be due to my own ungrateful behaviour. He wanted to book a lovely trip and I hadn't even shown any form of thanks.

I threw my legs over the side of the bed to start getting dressed. I would head straight to the kitchen and put my arms around him, give him one of those long deep kisses he loved so much and thank him for a sweet and thoughtful gesture. It was as I was pulling my T-shirt over my head that my brain and my gut finally connected and told me it was not that I hadn't thanked Tom for the gesture, it was because the last page I had left my phone open on was the notes section, and the last note I had made was another con on my list. The con had brought the total of negative points to seven against six positives. I felt my stomach sink. I was disappointed with myself for such churlish behaviour. Why couldn't I just feel satisfied with what I had? A happy-go-lucky man, with a good income, who wanted to make babies with me and look after me forever. I knew a lot of girls who would have been more than happy with that offer. But they didn't see the side to him that I did. Tom was a bright light shining amongst my friends and family, but when we were alone, he couldn't maintain the brightness. I saw through those cracks in the light and there was a whole cavern of darkness that needed exploring. And I would need to explore it before I could let us go any further.

I found Tom in the kitchen, stirring the vegetables in the wok.

'Are you okay?' I whispered. He shrugged. It made him seem younger than he was. He was usually so certain and confident. I had managed to drain him of all of that with a silly list on my phone. 'I didn't mean to write those things.'

Tom looked up at me, the accusation written plainly across his face.

'I mean, obviously I did write them, but only so I could be sure.'

'There are more cons than pros, Kit,' he said.

'I know, but the aim was for the pros to overtake the cons. I just...'

'...you just hadn't found them yet. After three months? You should know what you like about me the most and that should stand out more than the negative stuff. Surely?'

'Yes,' I mumbled. I felt silly.

Tom stopped stirring and put his spoon down.

'Kit, you need to make a decision. I am in this for the long haul. I adore you. You know I am good for you. You need to stop looking for reasons not to be with me.'

'Okay,' I said. I felt a wave of panic at things ending based on what he had discovered. I didn't want things to end this way. I liked Tom a lot. I was sure that I could get him to open up more about his past and his family.

'Really?' Tom moved closer to me.

'Yes. I want to be with you, I really do.'

Tom pulled me into an embrace. 'Then you will always have me. I will look after you forever, you will never have to worry about anything for the rest of your life.'

I allowed myself to relax into Tom's arms, hearing his words but wishing for a miracle. Did I really have to rely on Tom to support me forever? I let him hold me tight and whisper his words of reassurance in my ear, but all the while I was wishing that I could get to the crux of who he was. I was sure that Tom was holding onto a part of his past that he was too scared to share with me. I liked Tom a lot, but at some point soon, I would need to admit defeat and stop clinging onto the other elements that were holding us together: the sex, the adventure. What I needed was for something to happen so I would no longer be in control of my future with Tom. Someone or something needed to take the decision out of my hands.

24

NOW

Jude stayed for three nights in the end. On her fourth and final day, I walked her to her car to say goodbye. A tight pang hit my stomach at the sight of her leaving. I had relished the company, even though I had not been much of a host.

'Now listen you, make sure you text Mum and Dad and tell them you're okay. They are seriously worried.' Jude threw her overnight bag into the back seat.

'Well, I'm sure you've filled them in a little bit, let them know that everything is okay this end,' I said hopefully, not wanting to weigh them down with worry any more. If Jude had spoken on my behalf, then that would appease them for a while.

'I have done no such thing. And I am not entirely convinced things are okay this end. All I've witnessed during the last few days is a woman shacked up in a mansion, keeping herself away from her family but going to work every day.' Jude shut the car door and folded her arms. 'And you're not yourself. I'm worried about you, Kit.'

I shuffled my feet and tried to retain eye contact with Jude.

'As I said, just taking some time out, that's all. I'll be back firing on all cylinders again soon.'

Jude narrowed her eyes at me. 'Hmm, I'm not sure. But I will pass that on to Mum and Dad if you so wish, give them something to cling onto, at least. Just don't do anything silly, eh?'

Jude frowned again.

'I'm not suicidal, Jude.' It was true. I wanted nothing more than to feel like my old self. I had fleeting moments of becoming terrified that this feeling would last forever, that there was no other way out for me, but they passed as soon as they arrived and I always had my work to focus on. As long as I stayed busy on my feet in the restaurant, I was going to be okay.

We kissed and hugged goodbye and I promised to call and speak to Mum and Dad soon. But it was a half-promise because I was still not sure how I would begin the conversation, because then that would mean admitting the truth about why I was hiding away to all of them.

'I will be back, though, soon. Okay? I'm not letting you have all this to yourself. Plus, the kids need a holiday.'

'Fine,' I said. I could do with the distraction of having other people here. As long as she didn't bring Mum and Dad with her, though, because as soon as I saw their faces, I would crumble. It seemed easier to lie to Jude; she and I were good at doing the general sisterly thing but there was still enough space between us that I didn't need to be entirely authentic with her. She still had her suspicions, but she was going to let it lie. Mum and Dad would see straight through me and there would be nothing I could do to stop them.

Once she was gone, I sat on my own in the sunroom and closed my eyes and thought about my sister's visit. When I opened them a good ten minutes later, I came face to face with someone peering in through the window. I gasped, pushed my weight back into the sofa, hoping it would engulf me. The person at the window began to wave their hands and mouth apologies. It was Hendrick. I stood up and walked to the front door and he arrived there just as I did.

'I'm sorry, I didn't mean to startle you.' His face was etched with worry.

My heart was thumping through my chest. 'It's fine,' I lied. 'In the area again, were you?' I said with some sarcasm.

'I was, and I wanted to say sorry for not getting back to you.' I looked down at his hands. He was gripping one tightly with the other.

I frowned.

'When you called a few days ago. You said you had a question.' His voice definitely wavered.

I had completely forgotten that I had called Hendrick. 'Oh, my gosh, yes, sorry. Come in, come in.' I opened the door further and he came into the hallway. I suddenly felt sorry for the guy.

Lucy was standing behind me and instantly began barking. Her hackles were raised and she shot between my legs, trying to protect herself and me at the same time.

'Lucy, stop,' I said. 'Quiet.' I used the command I had been training her with and she ceased barking and hung about my side, her lips raised in a slight snarl.

'I'm sorry, I had completely forgotten I'd called you,' I said. Jude had arrived and her being here had distracted me enough to forget about it.

I now felt guilty, though, because this was the third time Hendrick had been here. I pushed him towards the kitchen.

'Let me make you a tea or coffee. How's the weather out there today? It looks as though it's clouded over. We could do with a bit of rain.' I chatted away as I walked us through to the kitchen and gestured to the table for him to sit down. I noticed he was wearing slightly more casual clothes than the last few times I had seen him. He was in jeans and a shirt, but he was wearing trainers.

'Coffee, please. Milk, two sugars.' Hendrick scraped a chair out and sat down and I winced at the noise. I was trying hard to play the host, but my nerves were frayed.

I filled the kettle and flicked the switch.

'Dress down day at work, is it?' I eyed his clothes.

Hendrick looked down at his jeans and trainers.

'I'm not at work today.'

'So, you drove out here just to see me?'

'I did.' Hendrick looked at me, unwavering. Is that what people did these days? Did they not just pick up the phone and call? I turned back to lift down two mugs then I turned to face him. 'And where did you say you lived again?'

'I didn't,' Hendrick answered quickly. I felt my hackles rise the same way Lucy's had when Hendrick arrived.

'Oh.' I was sure I had asked him this before. It seemed a basic question to ask someone when you had just met them.

'But I can tell you, I live near Pebble Beach.'

'That's nice,' I retorted.

The kettle reached boiling point behind me and I turned to prepare the drinks. I didn't ask any more questions whilst I worked, and I could hear Hendrick tapping his fingers on the table. There was an edginess to the atmosphere.

I placed two coffees on the table between us.

'Are you working today?' He moved his mug closer to him.

'I am doing a dinner shift. I start at five.' I took a quick sip of my coffee.

'I saw someone leave when I arrived,' Hendrick said without question. I thought I had closed my eyes for at least ten minutes, but it could only have been a minute if Hendrick had arrived when Jude had been leaving. Had he been watching us the whole time?

My body made an involuntary shudder and I pulled on the cardigan that was hanging on the back of my chair for security. I looked at Hendrick, searched his face for those honest qualities that I had recognised instantly in Blake. But he was a blank canvas to me, a stranger. And he always had been.

Hendrick was looking at me and then darting his eyes around the kitchen. It was no wonder Lucy had barked at him; he couldn't seem to relax.

'So, you wanted to ask me something?' he said eventually. I realised I could no longer say anything to him. I felt I had made a big mistake calling him in the first place and then inviting him in. He had put me on edge each time he had been here, I finally admitted to myself. To ask him about the person in the window in the photo on my phone would be to admit I was feeling vulnerable here. And I didn't want to admit my vulnerability to Hendrick or anyone else. I needed to stay on my guard. I was all alone out here.

I had to think quickly. Hendrick would want to know why I had called him. He had come all this way to check on me.

'I wondered who the hamper company was that left all the goodies. It's my sister's birthday soon and I wanted to send her a gift.'

Hendrick looked puzzled. 'I wouldn't know about that. Sorry. I'm just the admin guy.' He picked up his coffee and took a sip as he looked around the kitchen again.

'It's a nice place,' he said. 'Do you think you will stay here?'

I shrugged my shoulders. 'I don't really know. I mean, it is nice, but it's a big place for one person. I'm not sure I could manage the upkeep.'

'Money isn't everything, is it?' he said and it sounded out of context in our conversation.

I thought about his comment as an image of Tom came into my

head. I had enjoyed the trips and the lifestyle with Tom. But I knew it was only superficial. 'You're right,' I said after a moment.

He nodded. 'I know, you seem like that sort of person. You seem like a very nice girl... woman.' He cradled his coffee cup for security. 'I would recommend selling, though. And you might want to make that decision sooner rather than later.' His tone was off, it sounded too serious. 'You know, I think the market is pretty hot right now. You would get a good deal.' He shifted in his seat and rubbed at his face, looking anywhere but at me. 'Yeah, sooner rather later,' he said again.

Hendrick took a few more minutes to finish his coffee but the second he took the last sip, I scraped my chair back loudly and Lucy shot up out of her bed.

'Right, I have to take this one for a walk. It was lovely of you to drop by. Again.' I feigned a smile.

Hendrick slowly stood up.

'I'll walk you to the front door.' Even though I could have just opened the kitchen door and sent him out the back way, I wanted him to understand that I needed him to leave now.

Hendrick turned and faced me at the front door.

'Take care, Kit.' He put one hand on my shoulder and I looked down at his spindly fingers. Was this a come-on? Did he have some sort of crush on me? Should I put him in his place? It was obvious to Hendrick I was all alone here.

'Call me if you need anything,' he said in that bright way he did each time he left. What could I possibly need him for? As he had told me, he was just the admin guy. He could have just called me back instead of showing up. I was sure that whatever it was he was doing went beyond the usual level of customer care.

I watched him walk down the drive and get into his car. I closed the door and listened to the engine fade away. I walked back to the kitchen and pulled open a drawer, taking out the card Hendrick had given me when I'd accepted the house. It had his name, his mobile number and the name of the company ABC Wins. There was a web address, the same website I had viewed the prizes on before. I typed the address into my phone and when I did, the familiar images appeared in front of me. Several houses, and a few cars. I flicked through them, saw an image of Willow Cottage. I put my phone down. Should I make some sort of complaint about Hendrick? Was his behaviour bordering on stalkerish? Was he allowed to just keep turning up like that?

I wasn't sure I had the energy to do anything about Hendrick right now, but I knew I would not be contacting him again. My senses were now fully attuned and there was something about him that just didn't feel right.

25

NOW

At the end of my evening shift, Maisie asked me if I would be available for two split shifts in a row this week. The first thing I thought about was Lucy. I would have to make sure there was someone to let her out. I hadn't considered the logistics of dog care around a waiting job when I'd accepted her as a gift from Blake. But I thought I might ask him if he would swing by when I was at work and check on her. I arrived home and it was almost midnight. Lucy jumped out of her bed to greet me as I let myself in through the back door. I got down onto the floor and played with her for a while, then I took her to the back door, grabbed the torch and headed outside.

Beyond the borders of trees was an open driveway that led onto the lane, which worried me for two reasons. Firstly, Lucy might wander out to the road at the bottom, but I didn't necessarily need to panic too much as the roads were quiet at this time of night. And secondly, there was the worry about people wandering in, especially at this late hour. I followed Lucy around with the torch as she explored every bush and flower bed. I thought about how they would need weeding at some point and made a mental note to make an afternoon of it when I had a day off. A short sharp sound stopped me in my tracks and alerted Lucy to a nearby bush. I froze. The rate my heart had suddenly leapt to was almost audible. I held the torch very still, pointing it at the area Lucy had just dived into. I heard a rustle and the sound of her collar tinkling. I waited and waited some more. Then I heard Lucy let out a yelp. I lunged forward to the bush and bent down, holding the torch as close as possible.

'Lucy,' I called quietly. I waited. I couldn't hear anything. 'Lucy,' I called again, this time more sternly, but still nothing. I pushed my hand against a piece of the bush to set it aside so I could shine the torch through, but all I could see was more shrubbery. I stood up and walked along the perimeter of the bush, calling Lucy's name. I began to feel the chill of the evening air on my skin, which was tacky from a shift in the hot restaurant.

'Lucy!' I said, louder this time. 'Where are you?' I wailed. This was really happening. I should have been more careful, used a long lead for the front lawn. The regret clawed at me. I walked back along the border, then went to the other side of the lawn across the bridge, in case she had run that way without me seeing her. I walked the whole way around the lawn, frantically calling her, and then went back across the bridge. I stood in the middle of the lawn and rubbed my head, letting out long loud sighs, feeling powerless.

I strode over to the front door and sat on the doorstep. Where was she, where the hell was she, why would she leave me like this, didn't she know I needed her? I raised my head up as high as I could then called loudly, '*Lucy!*'

I heard the tinkle of her collar and then she burst from the bushes and ran towards me.

'What? Where were you, you little rascal?' I leant down to grab hold of her and pulled her in close to me, saying a silent thanks to the universe for bringing her back as the relief washed over me. I stood up with her still in my arms and marched back to the kitchen door to find it closed. I was sure I had left it open. It was a still night, no wind. I tucked Lucy under one arm, and I opened the door. I assessed the kitchen before I walked in, then I put Lucy on the floor. She began to sniff about, looking for a treat after her garden exploration. I bent down under the sink and pulled out a handful of dog treats then began to feed them to her one by one as she sat patiently accepting them.

I stood and listened. My racing heart rate was back and pounding at my chest. Could there be someone in the house? In the time I had been outside and distracted with Lucy? I knew I needed to check the house and so, with Lucy tucked under one arm and my phone in the other hand, I went from room to room, kicking the doors open with my foot as I did. The formal sitting room was still a mess, with smashed glass on the carpet, I glanced at it and then shut the door, not wanting to think about it. I went back to the kitchen and stood there for a moment, tears pricking at the corners of my eyes. What was wrong with me? I just wanted to feel normal, not scared and paranoid. I suddenly felt so very alone. I locked the kitchen door and bolted it along the top and took myself to bed.

* * *

I woke with thoughts of Blake floating through my mind. I had slept for less than four hours, and I knew I needed to get to the grain store early to ask Blake if he could see to Lucy whilst I worked split shifts later today.

I showered and dressed and sat at the kitchen table and watched the sun rise. I would take a walk with Lucy in the next hour and give Blake a knock. I knew he would be up and getting ready for work round about now. I made myself some coffee and sat in the sunroom, trying to absorb some energy for the day.

Blake was outside one of the grain buildings, attaching a trailer to a tractor when I turned into the lane a short while later. I was almost upon him when he looked up and noticed me.

'To what do I owe this pleasure at such a fine hour?' Blake sounded chirpy, as though it were eleven in the morning and not just after six.

'I've come for a favour, actually.'

'Go on.' Blake continued with his task.

'I have to work a couple of split shifts this week and I'm a bit worried about Lucy being alone for such a long time. I might make it back in between, but it would be a bit of squeeze.'

'No worries. Why don't you leave her with me? I'm always popping in and out all day and I'm done by three-ish usually. Her mum and sister and brother are in there, she'll be grand.'

'Oh.' I hadn't expected him to offer that, but it made perfect sense, we were neighbours with just a ten-minute walk in between. It would save him several trips to my cottage. Plus, I expected Blake would feel more comfortable if he didn't have to let himself into my house.

'Great, I mean, thank you, that would be really helpful. I'm still feeding her the same puppy food you gave me.'

'That's good as I have loads of it in the back building.'

'Great.' I stood for a few seconds and waited for Blake to finish what he was doing before he stood up, wiped his hands on his shorts and walked around beside me. He held out his hand and I looked at it for a second, confused as to what he was doing, then I looked down at Lucy.

'Oh, sorry, here you go.' I handed the lead to Blake, and he bent down to give her a stroke.

'She'll be fine with me, don't worry.'

'Oh, I'm not worried. I'll just miss her, that's all.'

He looked up at me. 'Bit lonely up at the old house, is it?'

I wished I could just say it out loud, admit how I was feeling.

'No, I love it up there. Peace and quiet is exactly what I was looking for,' I lied.

'So, you'll be staying, will you?'

'I will be, yes.' I thought about the stresses the house had brought so far and how selling up would be the easiest option.

'Strange, 'cos I wasn't even aware the last owner had sold.'

I homed in on Blake's words. 'You knew the previous owner?'

'I wouldn't say knew her, just knew of her. She was never around a lot. She would pop up from time to time. Asked me for the odd favour once or twice like helping her with her horse. I didn't warm to her. Don't think anyone did.'

'Oh, what was her name?' I said, suddenly curious about my predecessor.

'Annalise.' He made a strangled sound as he said it. 'Sounds like a one, doesn't she?'

I laughed. 'Yes, she does.'

'Anyway, she's gone and you're here. All is well.' He and I stood for a few seconds and I found a smile had reached my eyes, all by itself, without force. Blake shifted first. 'I'll get this one settled and see you in a few days.'

'Oh, would you mind if I took your number so I can check in on her?'

'Of course, if it will put your mind at rest,' Blake said as I opened my phone on the contacts and typed his name in. I handed him the phone.

'Here, it's probably easier if you put your own number in.'

He handed me Lucy's lead whilst he tapped away, then we swapped again.

'And I am sure she will be fine, as I said, I've just become used to her company,' I said, already feeling the pull of leaving her.

'Of course you have, they're like our best friends. Once we're attached to them, that's it, we can't live without them. I know I can't.'

I felt a sudden surge of panic at Blake's words. I had grown very fond of Lucy and when she disappeared for just a second, I felt my stomach drop. I had only lost Lucy for a few minutes. There were people dealing with bigger losses because of me. How they felt was something I wondered daily. When she had come trotting back over to me, the relief had been like a tonic. But they would never get back what they had lost. Because of me.

'Are you okay?' Blake asked. 'You were away somewhere for a second there. These early mornings not good for you?'

'No, I... I didn't sleep well last night.'

'Well, you'll need your sleep with two split shifts, did you say?'

'Yes.'

'What are you, a manager of a fancy hotel or something?' Blake tried to sound disinterested by looking down at Lucy, but he was clearly fishing for some more information. And why not, I was a stranger in a new village, and I was starting to know a lot more about Blake than he knew about me.

'Yeah, something like that.' I laughed. How would I explain living in a house like Willow Cottage on only a waitressing wage? 'So, I'll let you get on and I need to... yes, I need to go now, so have fun and see you, well, in a couple of days. Thank you.' I pulled my set of keys out of my bag and pulled off the spare key for the back door. 'Look, just take this in case you think you need anything; she is a bit of a chewer, and I didn't bring any of her toys.' I held the key out to Blake, and as I did, I felt doubtful for a moment. Should I really be handing out keys to people I hardly knew? Blake had to be a good man. He had done so much for me already. I felt a pain sear in my chest, the constant battle of my contrasting thoughts. I wished I knew what to do.

'Okay.' Blake took the key, and I began to walk slowly backwards. 'I'll text you an update,' he said brightly.

'Thanks!' I called before I turned and hurried down the path. It was only when I reached the main road that I realised I hadn't said goodbye to Lucy.

26

NOW

Time sped up like it hadn't done for a long time. I was thankful to Blake that I was able to rely on him to take care of Lucy, as I didn't have the energy to return home during those shifts; I was flat out. The holiday makers were well and truly in full flow as Maisie had suspected, and many of the part-time temporary staff called in sick because the sun was shining. I got it; I wouldn't want to waste my youth in a stuffy restaurant when I could be basking in the sun. But that was then. This was now. I was grateful that it was busy. I didn't have to think about anything or anyone.

On the afternoon of the second split, I was sitting in the corner of the restaurant. It had quietened down, and I sat picking at a salad and bread. I found it difficult to eat when I was hot, and the adrenaline was still racing through my body. My phone beeped with a message from Blake.

Hi. All is well. I've had an invitation to go out for a few drinks with a friend. I will be going out about seven and staying out pretty late. I'll give Lucy a big walk and then drop her off at yours before I go out. Then she should just sleep until you get back after your shift this evening. Hope that suits.

I felt a happy pang in my gut as I thought about seeing her again. I had presumed I wouldn't pick her up until tomorrow, but to know she would be there waiting for me when I got home made my heart swell. I texted back straight away.

Yes, that's perfect. Thank you. Enjoy your night.

I almost added *you deserve it* or *don't drink too much* but restrained myself. I didn't know Blake well enough to add friendly banter, and besides, his text had been professional and to the point, so I left it as it was.

The evening shift felt a little lighter on my soul as I allowed myself to look forward to seeing Lucy again and then having twenty-four hours off. I planned to be out in the garden, tending to some of those weeds; even if I had no immediate plans to sell Willow Cottage, it would be good practice to keep it looking in the best condition.

The last customers filtered out into the warm evening night, and I stripped the tables bare. A part of me almost began to pull out linen and cutlery to set up for the morning, as it was only 11.30, but I told myself no, I deserved to go home after two days of non-stop working. I should. I had to rest; I couldn't just keep going the way I was, or I'd collapse. I was barely surviving on enough sleep as it was.

Maisie distributed the tips between me and the other staff members, and I headed out to my car at the back of the restaurant. At first, I could sense something wasn't quite right, and as I approached even closer, my heart sank at the sight. Shattered glass was scattered all around my car and almost the entirety of the windscreen was gone.

Two hours later, I was sitting in my car with a new windscreen. It was now almost two in the morning, and I wanted to rip myself out of my own skin. I'd paced the restaurant as I'd waited for the windscreen company to arrive, and eventually I'd gone outside and tried to clear up as much glass from the driver's seat as I could. I discovered a slate from a tile roof and after discussing with the technician, it was agreed this was the culprit. But I couldn't stop the doubt that was nagging at me. What if it wasn't an accident? It seemed far too similar to the chandelier and glass table incident. Could I really have been so unlucky?

The drive home was miserable. I thought about the tiny shards of glass that were all around. Discontent was growing within me. I knew I was out of my depth, and it felt to me that there was a stronger force at work here. The work of one person, maybe more. Perhaps everyone was in it together. The thought of going back to Willow Cottage and being alone again brought tears to my eyes and I let out a loud sob. The spark of light I'd felt towards the end of the second shift had now gone. The only thing I had to look forward to was seeing Lucy and falling asleep for a few hours. I would even let her come and share the bed with me, I decided, because I had missed her so much.

I pulled up in the driveway and heaved my weary body from the car. I picked up the box filled with a few leftovers that would see me through tomorrow's meals. I was already thinking of a message to send out to Blake to thank him for looking after Lucy and, despite this evening's setback with my windscreen, I felt a pull of hope –

perhaps we could become friends as well as neighbours? Perhaps I was ready for something more. I needed company.

I opened the door and as I fumbled for the light switch, I wondered why I couldn't hear Lucy jump up and run to greet me like she normally would. Immediately I thought Blake must have changed his mind and kept her with him instead. But then the smell hit me. Hot and acidic. Even when I switched on the light, I still didn't believe what my eyes were seeing. Lucy, in a pool of her own faeces and vomit, laying on the kitchen floor, not moving.

27

THEN

My sister Jude arrived at Tom's seafront apartment at five to nine in the morning on a Saturday. Her two children, Emily and Josh, looked bored and tired.

'I had to get them out of the house, Kit, they were driving me to distraction.'

I was still wearing my pyjamas. Tom was up and dressed in loungewear. He had turned the coffee machine on and was pottering around the kitchen, looking for something to make for the kids to eat. Jude had brought an energy into the house that was not compatible with the lazy Saturday morning Tom and I had been having just before she arrived with barely a few minutes' notice.

She looked and sounded stressed, and the kids were clearly not happy about being dragged into Tom's apartment so early in the morning. Tom heated up some croissants. Emily and Josh brightened at the sight of food and busied themselves layering condiments into the buttery pastry. Jude edged closer to me in the sitting room.

'He is rather good with them, isn't he?' she said wistfully. 'I can barely get Stan to lift a finger and it's driving me nuts.'

'Is that why you're here then, because Stan is being Stan?'

'Nooooooo,' she said exaggeratedly. 'I missed you, the kids missed you.'

I glanced into the kitchen at the children tucking into their food, having barely greeted me since they arrived.

'But he's great, isn't he? Tom?'

I nodded. 'Uh huh.'

'Oh, come on, Kit, for the love of God. How can you be so blasé about all of this? This is the best boyfriend you could ever have; this *is* the best boyfriend you've ever had. In fact, he's the best boyfriend anyone could have! Why are you stalling?'

'Okay, first of all, I'm not stalling.' I peered into the kitchen, Tom had taken out a deck of cards and was showing them an old magic trick I had already seen a hundred times, but it was holding their attention. 'I'm dating. I'm not rushing into anything. We've only been together a few months—'

'But look, look at these.' Jude pointed to the basket of nutritional chocolate bars. 'He's always making you juices and buying you these healthy protein bar things. What is not perfect boyfriend material about that? I just don't understand, Kit.'

'No, you wouldn't,' I mumbled.

She squinted her eyes at me and shook her head. 'What don't I understand? That you have a handsome, rich, attentive and kind boyfriend who wants to have babies with you, and you are clearly having doubts, perhaps trying to find faults with him, the way you did with the seven or eight boyfriends before him? You're no spring chicken, Kit; you need to accept that you have an amazing guy here, and you will not get any better than this. He wants to spend the rest of his life with you and as much as we all know you're the golden child and Mum and Dad will keep on looking out for you until the end of their days, I think they would be much happier going into retirement if you just settled down with someone.'

I looked at my sister. Of course that was how she would see it. She had been with Stanley for ten-ish years now, and had two children. I knew things were tough between her and Stan. They argued constantly, and she thought him not good enough. I thought he was okay: he earned a decent wage; he just wasn't what you would consider 'a modern man'. He was more meat and two veg, feet up in front of the football with a can of lager. Which was fine. But Jude had opened her eyes a little more in the last decade and realised she should have done a bit more window shopping before her final purchase.

'I mean, if you don't want him, you should just let him go, there are plenty of women who would snap him up in a nanosecond.' I felt my body tense at the prospect. I was not ready to give Tom up. But I was not willing to let him rule our relationship on his terms. I needed more. I needed to dig deeper into his soul. But he just refused to give even an inch.

I visibly shook my head this time. It was impossible trying to explain to my sister how Tom would go quiet after spending time with my family, how he spoke so little of his own family, how he clammed up when I asked him about his. How he wanted a family of his own so badly that it unnerved me; it didn't feel as though we were heading through a natural transition, it felt as if he were on a road ahead of me, trying to get to an end goal, and I was just his vessel, the one that would help him become part of that family unit he so desired. I didn't know much about the inner workings of a brain, but I was convinced that Tom had shown me enough signs to suggest that some damage had been done when he was a child. Something that he could not undo. And I was almost certain that it would follow us into our future and hold him hostage. And that any child I had with him could end up damaged as a result too. I just didn't want to take that chance. Not without Tom talking to me and telling me everything so I could understand and maybe between us we could make sense of it.

But Jude would not see this. She only saw the material possessions and how he acted for a short period of time. Her model of the world was very different to mine. She was seeking something better than what she had, but I was just starting out. I had no reason to rush into settling down with Tom when I felt there was something fundamental missing.

'Why are you here?' I asked Jude. She looked at me, confused, because I was no longer connected to her line of thought.

'I just needed to get out of the house. Bloody kids driving me mad. I can park easily here and then take them for a run around on the beach without having to take out a mortgage to park.'

Just then, Tom appeared and leant against the doorframe. I looked up at him and gave him an apologetic smile. He gave a very subtle squint of his eyes and a slight head shake back at me. Jude was over at the floor-to-ceiling window, taking in the sea view.

It was easy, I supposed, if I viewed him from the perspective of others. Of course, he appeared the perfect option. But this was my mind and my future. And I wasn't willing to take any chances. Tom was keen for me to stop waitressing, he felt it would have some adverse effect on my life, and the fact he felt so strongly about this made me want to stay working as a waitress even more, because I needed to prove to him and myself that I didn't need to be rescued and looked after for the rest of my days. I wanted to work, and working at Mirabelle made me feel content. Tom just didn't understand the connection I had to the place and how it gave me such job satisfaction. It would have to take something huge to drive me away from my work family. And I was confident that no matter how much Tom pleaded, that was never going to happen.

28

NOW

I had called Blake's phone over and over; I had lost count how many times. It went straight through to answerphone every time. Whatever had happened had to involve Blake, or he would at the very least be able to answer some of my questions. He had a key to the property; he was the last person to have been with Lucy. He had said he was going to take her for a walk; what if she had eaten something she shouldn't have whilst walking? Blake seemed a bit more carefree than I was; he might have let her off her lead and she might have picked up some poison. I couldn't stop shaking, and I walked around the kitchen, not knowing what to do or who to call. Lucy was dead. She probably had been for a few hours; her little body had already begun to stiffen. Eventually, I ran upstairs and fetched a towel from the bathroom. I laid it over Lucy and sat as the tears heaved themselves out of me.

How long had she been like this? Had she died in pain? She had been alone, and I hadn't been here with her, and that was all I would remember. It was so late, and I didn't know what to do with her. This felt like the final nail in the coffin. The face in the window, chandelier and glass table, the bird seeds, the constant fear that someone was in the house with me. And now Lucy, dead on the floor. I had to wonder if I was going to be next. Would I find out the cause of death if I took her to a vet? But what was the point if she was already dead? Why wasn't Blake picking up? I needed answers. Instinctively, and without much thought, I went into the living room and collected as many cushions as I could carry, wrapped a throw around my shoulders and went back into the kitchen. I arranged the cushions into a makeshift bed next to Lucy's covered body, then I lay down next to her and pulled the throw up to my chin and closed my eyes.

* * *

The phone rang through loud into my dreams and pulled me out of sleep. I went to move and yelled out in pain. My leg had gone into a spasm. I tried to stand but it was in full cramp. As I lay there in pain, unable to stand and reach the phone, I turned and looked at the blue towel, where I had laid it over Lucy's lifeless body last night. I hadn't pulled it fully over her. Her small black and white paw peeked out from under the towel, and I surprised myself that I was still crying as hard as I had been last night. Light was coming through the kitchen window, and I hazarded a guess that it was already 6 a.m. based on the sky.

The phone stopped ringing. I wondered if it had been Blake trying to get through to me. I felt as though I was stuck to the floor. I could feel a draught coming in from under the kitchen door. Was this what it was like to be a dog, had Lucy been cold at night all those evenings I went to bed and left her here alone? I was a terrible person who didn't deserve a small puppy, let alone a house like this. I knew it was time. I couldn't live like this. I didn't deserve any of it. Nothing was ever going work out in my favour, that was for sure. Lucy dying was just another way of the universe telling me that I should give up. If I just lay here, eventually, I would die too. I didn't need to get up or do anything, I could just decompose like Lucy would. So, I closed my eyes and tried to drift off again.

Someone was trying to kick the door in. Or they were banging it very hard. I sat up and the sun was hitting the window at a different angle this time, so maybe I had slept again. I went to stand, wary that my legs might cramp. I stumbled to the counter where my phone told me the time was 8.03 a.m.

I opened the door and Blake was standing there. His hair was standing up on end, his face was tinged pink, and the smell of alcohol coming from him was potent.

'Kit, are you okay?'

He tried to look through into the kitchen, but I blocked his way.

'What did you do?' I hissed.

'I got your voicemails, I tried to call, I was on my way home, you didn't answer. What's happened?'

'What. Did. You. Do?' I asked again. This time I could feel the heat rising in my chest and my face was getting redder, rivalling Blake's hungover tone.

'I don't know, Kit. I don't know unless you tell me what has happened. Please?'

I searched Blake's face for any indication that he was lying, or that he was now a threat to me. All I could see was a man as desperate for answers as I was. I stood aside so that Blake could see into the kitchen.

He put his hand to his mouth. 'Is that Lucy?' His voice was muffled through his fingers.

My face crumpled and I couldn't speak. I couldn't feel anger any more, I just felt so terribly sad. Blake didn't hesitate for a second. He grabbed my arm and pulled me into him. My head became pressed against his chest, and I could hear his heart beating rapidly. I was in two places in my mind: I wanted to tear myself away from him and hit him hard, but I was also exhausted, and grief had begun to numb me.

I had so many questions, so many questions.

Eventually, what seemed like a long time later, Blake released me and helped me get seated at the kitchen table. He filled the kettle, then bent down and lifted the towel to have a peek at Lucy. I heard myself let out a groan and then I looked away.

Out of the corner of my eye, I saw Blake stand up and walk over to the counter. He pressed his hands in the wood and bent his head down. I wondered for a moment if he was crying. A few minutes later, Blake put a cup of coffee in front of me. He sat down opposite; the scraping of his chair sounded so loud amongst the deathly silence.

He cleared his throat. 'She was poisoned.'

I looked up at him. Was he telling me this because he guessed, or he knew? Or because he did it.

'I've seen it before. Rat poison, most likely. She was only small, so it wouldn't have taken much, and from what she had thrown up, I could see there was some dried food of some sort. I only gave her the raw stuff, like you said.'

'Dry food?' My words came out weak and hollow.

'Yes, like dried dog biscuits, it looks like. She's eaten them somewhere, maybe that had the poison on. It would have had to have been on something that was tasty, that she would have been tempted by.'

I felt my eyes fill with tears again. She loved her food so much. Now she would never get to eat ever again.

'You seem to be quite knowledgeable,' I said with a sting in my words.

Blake looked at me but didn't flinch.

'I am. I've seen it before. With other dogs. Especially around here. But this wasn't me, Kit. I did not do this.'

'Then who?' I shouted as my mug came down too hard onto the table. I had imagined that this could be comeuppance for my terrible act, but even this felt a step too far.

Blake blinked slowly and shook his head.

'I don't know. I dropped her back around seven before I went out, and she was fine. We'd been for a walk, but she was never once out of my sight for more than few seconds. I didn't see her eat anything. She was starving when we got back, and I'd defrosted some of her food and she wolfed it down. She was fine when I left. Absolutely fine.' Blake looked at me with pleading eyes, whilst his voice remained calm.

I let out a deep breath I felt I had been holding in for a long time.

'So the most likely explanation is that this happened sometime after I dropped her off. Did you leave any biscuits lying around, could she have got hold of any poison, maybe spilt it on them? Do you want me to check?'

'No!' I snapped at Blake as he went to stand. He fell back down into his chair. I didn't want him to check because I knew that I hadn't left anything lying around. There were no dog biscuits anywhere that Lucy could have got hold of by herself and this house was immaculate when I moved in, with nothing like rat poison lying around. I knew deep down that this wasn't an accident, that Lucy hadn't managed to eat something that she should not have when Blake wasn't looking.

I felt very weak and suddenly everything seemed to dim. Blake was talking to me, but his voice sounded far away. I felt my body jerk to the side, then everything went black.

29

NOW

I was lying on the floor and Blake was leaning over me. I felt something soft under my head and his hand was on mine.

'Kit, are you okay?' he said quietly. I was amazed at how calmly he spoke. He really was a nice man, I thought, as I began to come round.

'Just lie still and I'll get you some water,' Blake said and was back by my side within seconds. He helped me sit up, held the glass to my mouth, and I took a few small sips.

I looked at him, unable to say what I wanted to say. For a moment, everything else seemed to have melted away and it was just us. I wanted to say it, to tell him that I hadn't felt so content in the moment for so long. And that he was the one who had made me feel that way. But I held my tongue whilst he helped me into the snug and onto the sofa.

* * *

Blake assured me there was no need for us to go to the vet. They would only charge me a fortune to tell me what we already knew.

So, he brewed coffee, and set cups outside on the garden table and I sat and watched as Blake dug a hole underneath the willow tree.

He asked if I wanted to see Lucy once more before he buried her, but I couldn't face it. So much death in such a short space of time. I had seen the pained expression in the open eyes of my dog this morning when I arrived home. That image would never leave me. Blake took her with the towel and laid her in the hole, then began covering her with soil. Again, I couldn't watch, and then I felt as though I had let her and everyone else down all over again.

It was now getting on for ten o'clock in the morning and I realised Blake must be famished. I hadn't eaten anything either, but I had some eggs and bread in the kitchen, so I insisted on feeding him before he went. But he insisted on doing it and so because I had no appetite, I followed Blake into the kitchen, where he prepared himself some eggs and then ate hungrily.

I had thought he was to blame when I'd found Lucy, but now I'd had time to absorb the timeline of events, it made sense that Blake couldn't have known nor prevented what had happened. He was an animal lover. He cared for Lucy as much as I did. I knew that I wouldn't be able to keep living this way and getting off scott-free for everything I had done. I knew I had been responsible for the death of not one but two small helpless beings. And I knew now that I had to get prepared. Staying at Willow Cottage was no longer an option. I would have to sell. I would buy myself a smaller place and then give some of the money away to a charity in an attempt to make amends for my mistakes and also offset the massive burden of guilt I felt constantly.

I would call Hendrick for some advice; he must have seen people sell properties within days of winning them. I should have been one of those people, but I had been swept up in the idea that Willow Cottage would be a sanctuary, somewhere for me to come to terms with the horrors of the last few months without anyone disturbing me. But I wasn't sure they would ever give up. Perhaps they had seen me living this life here and realised, as I did, that I didn't deserve it. I needed to get one step ahead, just in case they decided to up their game and take things one step further. I could stay here and take the punishment, but I was sure once I had sold up and moved on, they would give up. I would go back to living a humble existence. They would see that. They would have done what they needed to do, run me out of my own home. And even that wouldn't match what I had done to them.

'Can I do anything else for you before I go?' Blake asked as he hovered by the kitchen door. He looked as though he needed to sleep for a day. I shook my head and walked to the threshold. He surprised me by taking my hand in his. He gave it a small, gentle squeeze.

'Take care of yourself. Eat some food.' Even after he had let go of my hand, I could still feel the weight of his touch. I watched him walk solemnly down the driveway. I wanted to call out after him not to go. To stay with me, because there was every chance that I would need his help now.

* * *

I took a long bath. Those few hours on the kitchen floor had made my bones ache. I lay there in the hot water as images of the last few weeks with Lucy played out before me through tear-filled eyes. I stayed in the bath until the water was cold, then I hauled myself out and dressed slowly and with great effort.

Then I pulled out the paperwork that Hendrick had given me from under the bed.

I began to lift each page. There were so many of them, but I wasn't sure which piece of documentation referred to my complete ownership. I presumed this was what I would need when I came to sell Willow Cottage.

My head began to hurt after thirty seconds of reading through the documentation that was as thick as a novella. The best thing I could do was to find myself a solicitor who could deal with all of this for me. I could afford to part with a small percentage of my winnings to relieve me of the strains associated with selling a home.

I was loath to call Hendrick's number again after the way I had felt the last time he was here, but he was my first port of call. I was certain that he would be able to advise me of the steps I needed to take and assure me that a solicitor was the next and fastest route to a sale.

Hendrick's number rang out this time. It didn't even go to answerphone. I hung up and went to the ABC Wins website to see if his contact details were on there, but the site was down for construction. I imagined all the other beautiful houses they were busy uploading and the other lucky future winners who sat living out their mundane lives, completely unaware that they were about to be changed forever.

Without Hendrick to advise me, the next step was to contact a solicitor. At the first solicitors I called, I was put through to someone immediately. Derek was keen to help me and asked me to send over all paperwork and correspondence. I attached the emails, the signed documents, and he gave me the address and told me to send all the physical admin by recorded delivery. I put the documents in a tote bag, then I took myself to the kitchen. The house felt so empty without Lucy scuttling around and following me from room to room. I poured myself a large glass of water. I still couldn't bring myself to eat anything. The day was warming up and the walk to the post office felt longer than before. I had very little energy.

I walked through into the post office and approached the desk. Arthur appeared from a door behind the counter and came onto the shop floor. He looked at me, perplexed, as though he was trying to place my face, and I realised he was taller than he seemed from behind the counter.

'Hi. It's me again.' I tried to sound jovial, but it hurt my whole body to go against my heart's natural desire to crawl onto the counter and cry.

Arthur looked at me, his expression blank.

'Willow Cottage,' I said to jog his memory.

'Willow Cottage,' he repeated. Then his face morphed into one of frustration. 'You're her, that woman. Why are you here?' He had begun to raise his voice. I took a step backwards, startled by his response. There had been something odd the first time I had spoken with him.

'I just came to post this...' I looked around the shop, but I was aware that he was looking more agitated. He began to move towards the hatch, and I heard it click. He had let himself out from behind the counter and was on the shop floor.

As I turned to leave, Arthur lunged at me and grabbed my arm.

'It is you. Why are you here?' I tried to tug my arm away, but his grip was strong. He was a tall man and even for his age, he was still strong.

'Let go of my arm, please.' I could feel tears pricking behind my eyes.

'I said why are you here? I told you never to come back.'

'I think you may have me confused with someone else... I've just moved here to Willow Cottage.'

'That's right. Willow Cottage. It is you. I told you not to come in here.'

'I can assure you, Arthur, we met before and you gave me a package, I'm not who you th—'

'You're a fucking little bitch.' Arthur leant in close and spat the words in my ear.

'Oh, my God, let go!' I began to turn my whole body to release myself from his grip, but panic flooded my throat and I felt unable to breathe. 'Please,' I squeaked.

Suddenly the back door that Arthur had come out of before swung open again, and this time a tall slim woman in her fifties came out. She looked at us, then burst through onto the shop floor. She grabbed Arthur's other arm and began tugging him hard. He was strong and managed to keep pushing the woman away whilst clinging tightly to my arm. Eventually, after what felt like an age, the shop door opened, and a postman wandered in. He had an armful of packages, but they all dropped to the ground as he launched himself at Arthur, rugby tackled him and took him straight down.

* * *

I sat in the back room of the post office. A cup of sweet tea was cooling on the table in front of me. Lyndsay, the lady who had tried to pull Arthur off me, was upstairs settling her husband into bed. She arrived downstairs and took out a box of biscuits. I shook my head.

'What's wrong with him?' I asked to be polite and to take the emphasis off feeding me. But I was already sure I knew what she was going to say.

'Dementia. Feels so early. It's got a bit worse recently, but today was the first time I've seen him go at someone like that. '

'He seemed to think I was someone else,' I said.

'He's done that a few times.'

'But he knew I lived at Willow Cottage; could he have mistaken me for the person who lived there before? I believe it was a woman.'

Lyndsay looked at me, assessing my features.

'That's right, a woman. About your age, she was. You don't look a thing like her, mind. But I remember now, there was some to do between her and Arthur; we had a dog, little Jack Russell. He barked a bit from time to time – but I think it was only at people who didn't like him. Arthur was outside one day with Dennis – that was his name – and that woman, I can't remember her name, Dennis barked at her. Well, she went ballistic, lunged at Dennis, tried to grab him, terrified the poor little thing. The last thing she said was that she would have Dennis's guts for garters. And she said it menacingly, not as a joke. Arthur was really shaken up. The next time she tried to come in, Arthur told her she was barred. That did not go down well. Anyway, there was a path around the back of her house, well, it's your house now, leads out into the forest.'

'Is there?' I was genuinely surprised by this.

'Yeah, she didn't use it, mind, 'cos she didn't own a dog. But someone reported their dog getting really sick from something they had eaten in the forest. Arthur stopped walking Dennis in the forest after that; he was convinced she had poisoned that owner's dog and that Dennis would be next.'

'Poison?' I spoke. I felt my stomach drop. If there had been any food in it, I would have thrown up.

'Is Dennis okay?' I asked, an image of Lucy looming in front of me.

'Oh, he died just over a year ago. Cancer. But Arthur never forgot that woman. She wasn't here that long. This place wasn't for her. I heard she liked to move around a lot, got bored easily. Well, this place will do that to you if you're not careful.' Lyndsay slurped her tea loudly.

'What's a young girl like you doing living in a big old place like that alone anyway?' She laughed. 'You'll end up like her, what's-her-face. I wish I could remember her name.'

I thought of Blake, how he knew her name and how he had done a bit of work for her. He hadn't mentioned that she had built a bad reputation for trying to poison dogs. This was the sort of information I could have done with knowing. But Blake wouldn't have known that. He didn't know what I was going through and what I was keeping from him.

30

NOW

It felt strange coming back to an empty house. My time at Willow Cottage had been mostly spent with Lucy in tow, and now I would have to navigate the long and lonely days without her.

I had a day off, and my intentions to spend time in the garden, tending to the weeds with Lucy running around my feet, were now well and truly spoilt. I couldn't bear the thought of being out there without her. It was coming up to lunchtime and I still hadn't eaten a thing. I spied the bottle of cider that Blake had dropped around the other day and so I opened it and poured myself a glass. I drank it down like fizzy pop and then poured myself another glass. The second batch hit my stomach and I felt my mouth fill with saliva and then I ran to the sink and was sick.

I thought about how this house was making me feel, what it was doing to me, and I craved my old flat. I realised my tenancy would soon be up and I still hadn't taken everything from there. It would need to come here, and my car wouldn't be able to contain all of it, so I would need to get a van. The thought overwhelmed me. All I wanted to do was sleep and so, taking one look at Lucy's empty bed, I carried myself upstairs in the hope of getting some.

* * *

I woke suddenly. I was drenched in sweat. The thin curtains in my bedroom couldn't keep the strength of the afternoon sun out of the room and I felt as if I had woken up in a sauna. The window had been closed and I hadn't opened it when I came upstairs. I finally felt as though I needed to eat something; my stomach was beginning to cramp. I took myself downstairs and stopped at the last step. I thought I heard Lucy for a second. I closed my eyes and imagined her trotting up to greet me. As I stood there, I was certain I heard her collar tinkle again. I had heard people discuss their deceased pets and how for months afterwards, they would hear them from time to time. The pitter patter of their feet, the clinking of metal from their collars or even the physical weight of their bodies on their owners where they used to lie next to them. I had decided to bury Lucy's collar with her. Now, hearing the phantom sounds, I wished I had kept it.

I knew this place was going to start to haunt me now after losing Lucy in such a horrible and violent way, and so I thought about everything I needed to do. It made my head spin and panic swirled in my gut. I wish I had someone I could consult with, someone who understood my needs. But that would mean disclosing everything and that wasn't an option.

There were messages on my phone from my sister and both of my parents. All checking in on me. There was a backlog of messages from a WhatsApp group I was part of, all girls I went to high school with.

I ignored all of them and thought about the heat of the day and how a dip in the pool might refresh me. My swimming costume was upstairs and so I padded through the sunroom and into the pool room and slipped all of my clothes off. The cool water soothed my baking skin and I thought of how I wouldn't be able to do this soon.

Once I had sold Willow Cottage, I would give at least half of the profits away to charity. I had to live a modest life. Residing at Willow Cottage presented me as a woman who was living a life that was far removed from the one I knew I deserved. Besides, I was drawing attention to myself here. I turned over in the water and lay on my back. I became entranced by the flickering silver reflection of the water on the ceiling and tried to empty my mind of intrusive thoughts. I turned back over again and began a simple breaststroke until I reached the side. Then I turned my head and let out an almighty scream. Hendrick was standing outside, his head pressed slightly to the window, his hand raised in a half-wave.

* * *

I stood in the kitchen in a bath robe, my hair damp against my neck. I waited for the kettle, the crescendo of its boil matching the rage building inside me.

'I'm sorry again for startling you. I'm terrible at returning calls. I knew I'd be passing through, so I just wanted to check on you.'

'I'm selling Willow Cottage.'

Hendrick blinked slowly. 'Okay.'

'You're not surprised,' I said.

He shook his head.

'People often sell then, I guess.'

'Yes. Why did you call me?'

'To ask your advice, if you had been through this with someone before.'

'I just hand the prizes over,' Hendrick said. 'I don't know anything about sales or mortgages. But I'm glad you've decided to get out and move on. You look as though you deserve a happy life, and this place isn't doing it for you.'

I let out a small laugh. Hendrick had no idea about what I did or didn't deserve. But I was curious why he had managed to make that assumption about me.

'Why do you say that? Do I not look as if I am enjoying the winner's life?' I asked bitterly. Hendrick looked at me and didn't speak for a second.

'I don't know you very well, but I think just from what I can gauge from the outside, you might be better off somewhere else. Not here. This place, it's...' Hendrick stopped, and I thought he might not finish his sentence. 'It's no place for a woman like you. You shouldn't be out here alone.' For the first time, Hendrick was actually speaking my language, and I felt as though there was some genuine concern there.

'You're right. It is too much, this big house. Just me living here.'

Hendrick nodded. 'Well, I'm sorry I can't help you with the sale side of things. I just wish you all the best with it. I know you'll be fine, once you leave.'

I sighed. He was right, of course; I should never have accepted the house in the first place. I had been in a strange place in my life; I still was, of course, but at least I had some idea of what I wanted to do next.

We drank our coffees and I told him about Lucy.

'Dead? My God, really?' Hendrick looked visibly shocked. 'Okay, that is bad, that is really bad.'

'I know,' I said quietly.

'You don't deserve that, Kit. You really don't.'

'I know,' I said again.

'Will you be okay, you know, until you move? I mean, are you scared or anything?'

I shook my head. Of course I was scared. But I was making my plans to get out. The fear I felt living here could not compare to the terror that beat through my body each day when I replayed the horrors from that one day.

'I mean, I could stay the night if you like. Oh God, Kit, don't look at me like that, it's nothing like that, I just thought with the dog, and now you're selling... It's fine. Forget I said anything.'

I looked curiously at Hendrick.

'How are things with your girlfriend? Did you ever finish that book?'

'Book?' Hendrick shifted in his seat.

'*Women Who Run with the Wolves*,' I said questioningly.

'Oh, no. She dumped me anyway. I don't like to be tied down, I work too much, I'm travelling around all over the place, you know?'

I nodded. Although I didn't know. I didn't know what he was referring to, nor did I know who Hendrick really was. He was an admin guy who seemed to keep showing up. If it wasn't for the fact that I felt a little sorry for him, I would have booted him out each time.

'Well, I'm sure you'll find someone else.'

Hendrick looked down.

'And thank you for the offer of staying, that was very chivalrous of you. I'll walk you out to your car.' I stood up and Hendrick did the same. I opened the front door and was greeted by a strong warm breeze. The sky had clouded over.

'There's a storm coming. Are you sure you'll be okay?' Hendrick asked again.

'I think I can manage. I have a couple of torches charged and my Kindle.'

Hendrick nodded. 'Okay, well, good luck.'

'Thank you.' I looked down the driveway and saw a flash of bright silver. A sports car of some sort. I thought about the car I had seen speeding off down the lane that day.

'Hendrick, is that your car?' I could tell it was expensive; I had seen Tom drive enough cars of a similar calibre.

'Er, yeah.' He sounded embarrassed.

'They must be paying you too much.'

Hendrick looked down at his feet. 'Maybe.'

'No, seriously, that's a Porsche 911.'

Hendrick looked at me. 'You know your cars?'

I thought of the exact car I had driven around for a while that had belonged to Tom. The one he had wanted me to have, just before we split.

I walked quickly down the driveway and examined the car. Tom's had had a black stripe across the passenger door. This one was stripe-free. Hendrick had caught up with me.

'All right?' he said. 'I could give you a spin if you want, but you might need to get dressed first.'

I looked down at the robe I was wearing. I felt very aware of myself.

'I, yes, I should. But I don't want to go a for a spin. I was just admiring the car.'

Admiring and remembering. The pure materialism of being with Tom had been overwhelming at times, like living in a perfume shop and forever breathing in the scents.

I was suddenly aware of the two separate bits of my life becoming parallel here in the driveway of this house.

'Well, I'll let you get on.' I could feel my body going light, as though there was no ground beneath me.

Hendrick slipped into his expensive car and leant out of the window.

'Be careful tonight,' he said.

The wind blew at the same time as he spoke, and I frowned at him, as I had missed a part of what he had just said.

'The storm. Have your wits about you.'

I shook my head. 'I'll be fine,' I said and waved him off.

The wind blew again and whipped my almost dry hair across my face. I pushed it behind my ear and watched Hendrick drive away. I thought of all the tasks I had to do, like get those papers to the post office. In all the drama with Arthur, I hadn't managed to post them. I would drive to the main one in town. Anything to stop myself from overthinking about Hendrick in a sports car that was so similar to one that had belonged to the man I had just removed from my life and was trying hard to forget.

31

THEN

Ibiza was amazing. I couldn't have asked for a more perfect holiday. Tom and I sunbathed, danced, walked, talked. It was as if everything in my mind just stood still for four days. All the doubts, all the thoughts, they just disappeared. I was in the moment with Tom, and I had never felt so happy. I chastised myself for ever not believing that I could make it work with Tom.

So, as we flew back on the plane, first class, I tried to push away the familiar feeling that was creeping in.

I spoke before I had time to think about what I was saying or why.

'I think I'll go back to my flat tonight, unpack, get an early night.'

Tom looked at me with a look of concern etched across his face.

'But you have everything you need at my place. Several of my places, and whatever you don't have, I can get it for you.'

I took a deep breath. 'I know you do, but my "stuff stuff" is at my house, all my comforts, things I don't bring to yours, it's just—'

'Kit. Let me look after you.' He leant in closer. 'If this is going to work, you are going to have to let me look after you a little. Okay?'

I thought of the weekend we'd had, of the laughs, the endless hours just sitting in each other's company; it was much like it had been in those first few weeks together before I had started over-thinking everything. Surely all I had to do was just let it be. All he wanted to do was look after me; was that such a hardship?

But there was something different in Tom's tone this time, as though he had finally had enough. He had just given us a wonderful holiday, and all I was trying to do was run away. But I was craving more. I needed him to open up a little more, for him to let me in and see who he really was. The money was a massive front for something that was festering away deeper inside. I decided to give him the benefit of the doubt this time. He seemed to be trying to reach out to me, despite the lack of something truly wholesome and real between us.

'Okay,' I said finally. I would give it one more try. Maybe the trip away had filled a void between us and he might feel as if he could tell me more about himself.

Tom sat back and let out a sigh. 'Good,' he said and then he closed his eyes and slept for the remainder of the flight.

* * *

We went to his flat in Sandbanks. I was almost itching to get into the restaurant and get back to work – away from Tom. But I had one more day before I could return to Mirabelle. He asked me what I needed from the shops, then he called his PA and two hours later, a package arrived in the foyer, and he went to collect it. I was embarrassed to say the least to see underwear, deodorant and sanitary products in there. I could have gone out by myself or, better still, got it from my flat and saved everyone the time, effort and money. But if this was what made Tom feel happy then surely I could be happy too.

* * *

I arrived at the restaurant for a lunch shift two days after my holiday with a golden glow about me. One of the other waitresses, Sara, gave me a big hug and commented on my tan. 'Look at you, so gorgeous.'

Some of the kitchen staff asked about the scene in Ibiza and we had a brief chat about the clubs and bars Tom and I had been to. Matt, the sous chef, was busying himself and when I was finally left alone for five minutes, he came over to me.

'So, it was a good holiday, then?'

I nodded. 'One of the best.' And I meant it; I was glad Tom had made the decision just to book me some time off work; that was what money enabled you to do, be more spontaneous, and spontaneity was something I had lacked before I met him. I didn't relay all this to Matt because he was just being polite, and I wasn't the kind of person who felt comfortable rubbing things into people's faces. It was enough that I had been whisked off on a romantic weekend with my millionaire boyfriend without being a smug cow about it as well.

We stood awkwardly for a second in the kitchen before I walked away, but I didn't hear Matt move from his spot. Was he watching me, I wondered? I felt a sudden surge of paranoia, and it occurred to me that people might not really like me because I was dating a man who was so extravagantly rich.

Courtney was already in the restaurant, setting up, and Denim was with her. When he saw me arrive, he came over to me.

'Hello, don't you look fresh and relaxed after your holiday? I'm calling a meeting in the restaurant. Come and grab a seat.'

I did as Denim said and sat down at one of the unlaid tables. Sara followed suit, then two of the other lunchtime part-timers sat down, and finally Courtney arrived. She looked at me with that same sort of contempt, as if I had wronged her in another life, and pulled out a seat next to Sara.

'Right, I'll get straight to it because we have a busy lunch period coming up, no less than thirty tables booked in, almost to full capacity. But before that, I wanted to talk to you about a job vacancy that has arisen. You all know Bret, our delightful maître d', well, he has sadly handed his notice in, meaning there is now a vacancy for that job. There is a slight pay increase, as well as a little more responsibility. So, if anyone would like to apply, then please ask me for an application form.'

There was a quiet mumbling as Sara and the other two part-timers began discussing. We all knew they wouldn't go for it; they were two friends who worked the exact same shifts each week around their beauty course and had no intention of getting any further in the hospitality industry. Sara was an ideal candidate, but she had three small children and often had to race off when one of them was ill or had a school play or dentist appointment, and she liked being able to have plenty of time off in the school holidays. She was probably not on the radar to have her responsibilities increased, which left just me and Courtney.

Courtney said nothing, but I felt her energy. She had been burning to get ahead of me since the day she began here and I had put her nose out of joint. But she had well and truly got her feet under the table. I knew I would apply for the job. And as much as Denim talked of the job being advertised outside of the restaurant, he knew that he had two very capable and interested parties right under his nose. The only thing left to do was to decide which one of us was going to get the role.

The lunch shift was steady, and I was thrilled to see my favourite little family in. The little girl had her hair in tiny plaits, and I held them between my fingers as we exchanged a few pleas-antries. The parents looked exhausted, as they always did. But I made sure I was there for them and gave them exactly what they needed. They relied on me, and everyone else knew not to bother them as they would only ever ask for me when I was working.

After the lunch shift had ended, we went through the motions of collecting the application forms and filling them in. Courtney took hers to the back of the kitchen under the canopy and I sat in the corner of the restaurant. There was an awkward moment when we both arrived at the small office just outside the back of the restaurant.

'Ah, my two favourite waiting staff,' Denim said as he took Courtney's application first. She walked past me and towards the back of the kitchen, where she had begun to spend an inordinate amount of time with Matt. But just as she reached the fire exit that led out to the back of the restaurant, I heard her say – only loud enough for me to hear – 'May the best woman win.'

I knew I was the best woman, yet whenever Courtney was around, I began to doubt my own abilities. It was as if she had some secret hold over me. I couldn't even put my finger on what it was; it was as though she was automatically above me. It didn't help that she and Matt had formed some sort of alliance. It was always beneficial to make good friendships with the kitchen staff; you were then favoured for tasting food, being let off if you damaged a dish on the way to a table, that sort of thing. Courtney had arrived after me and she had still gained the upper hand. She knew what she was doing, she knew the unwritten rules and had made herself comfortable with the kitchen staff, she was on great terms with Denim and she... she was a really good waitress.

Like me, it was as if she was meant to do this job. I couldn't deny it. She built great rapports with the customers, she was fast and efficient. But I was as fast and efficient. I wasn't perhaps as confident as Courtney, but I was gaining confidence. I wanted this promotion because I wanted to prove to my own family that I was capable of standing up on my own feet. And then there was Tom. He would be happy to have me not work at all, and I knew he felt waitressing was beneath me and there would come a point when me working at the restaurant would cause him embarrassment. But I didn't know what else I wanted to do with my life. I had been waitressing since I was twenty years old; it was all I knew and, if I was honest, all I loved. It made it difficult being with a man who made it obvious that my career choices were not up to scratch. But that was one part of me I was never going to give up, no matter what happened.

'Good luck, Kit,' Denim said. 'You know you're good enough for the role, don't you?'

I nodded.

'Okay. I'll see you next week'.

* * *

Tom was outside the restaurant at the end of my shift. I climbed into the front seat, and he kissed me full of the lips. As I reached around for my seatbelt, I saw Matt watching me from the alleyway at the side of the restaurant which led from the back of the kitchen. He kept his eyes on me until Tom accelerated.

'Good shift?' Tom asked as he drove. Watching Tom drive was one of my favourite things about him. I liked to feel the power of the car. I liked to watch him fiddle with things like the radio or type something into the satnav at the traffic lights. He became an entirely different character when we drove. Carefree, animated. Because he was distracted by the road, his attention wasn't fully on me, and I was just part of his life, not a subject that he needed to study, focus on and worry about. This felt equal, this felt good. I also really enjoyed being in the car with him, it was one of my favourite things. When we were driving, it felt as if we were always going somewhere, not just geographically, but as a couple, together, on the move, even if in reality, we were just two people sitting side by side in a metal box. So I was always bereft when it was over. That part of the relationship had ended for now and the other part had begun.

'Something healthy to drink? My new juicer arrived today.' Tom went straight to the sink and washed his hands.

'Nah, I need a glass of wine. I've just applied for the maître d' and I think I'm in with a good chance of getting it.'

Tom was quiet. I heard him drying his hands on a paper towel and putting it in the bin that had a sensor on it, so he didn't even have to touch it for it to open.

'Maître d', hey?' he said but even if I had wished for enthusiasm in his voice, I knew it was hopeless. Tom did not want me to work at Mirabelle any longer, and I was pretty sure he was in no way keen for me to start getting promoted.

'Yes, it's going to be between Courtney and me; I'm pretty sure Denim wants to keep it in-house; saves him money on advertising if nothing else.' I heard myself trying to make this into something smaller. Of course, Denim would pay if he had to, but he knew he had two perfectly capable applicants already. I wanted to feel excited because this meant a lot to me; I lived and breathed the restaurant industry.

'Well, this calls for a celebration, surely.' Tom pulled out a bottle of champagne from the wine fridge. Always champagne, never prosecco.

'I haven't got the job yet, Tom, I've just applied.'

He was trying, but his efforts were out of sync with the actual events.

'Well, let's celebrate anyway.'

'Okay.' I accepted the glass he poured for me, and we clinked glasses. He took a long sip.

'I told you about my sister, didn't I?'

'You did.' I felt a bubble of excitement rise up inside me. It felt like such a long time ago that he had opened up to me about anything to do with his family.

'She was such a fucking nightmare. She made everything so bloody difficult all the time. With her incessant need to go against everything that our parents wanted for her. It was bad enough that they hated me as it was, but when she played up, things only got worse. She made it all much worse.' Tom's voice had got louder as he spoke. It was clear these were painful memories. 'Did I tell you I was raised by twelve different nannies?'

I took long gulp of champagne. 'Twelve?' I said after I had swallowed. 'That is a lot.'

'Yes. And only a few of them were nice. One only lasted three months. It was her, you see, my sister. They couldn't stand her. And neither could I, in the end.'

'In the end?'

Tom took a drink of champagne and looked at me, then his face changed into a wide smile.

'Chill out, she's not dead. Although I was tempted once or twice.'

He leant over and kissed me softly on the lips.

'You don't need to be a waitress, Kit. You have me. But if you need to do it, then... what can I say? I can't stop you.'

'But you won't be happy. Just like your parents weren't happy your sister wanted to be a waitress?'

Tom stepped backwards. 'What? No! That's not the reason. I just want you to be happy. And you don't need to work in a minimum-wage job now you have me.'

'Because you're rich,' I said without question.

Tom looked a little smug and drained his glass.

'Did your parents give you money or did you make it all yourself?' I knew I was pushing it now; I wasn't sure he would want to talk any more about his family.

'Both. I have made a lot of money by myself. But yes, I inherited a lot from them too.'

'Inherited?'

Tom nodded.

'So, your parents, are they...'

'They're dead, Kit,' Tom said with such finality that I knew the conversation was over. I hadn't pushed him to speak, yet everything he had said had probably caused him a great amount of pain to say. I didn't want to patronise him by hugging him.

'Thank you for telling me,' I said eventually.

'We should think about food to go with this champagne. Shall I order in?' Tom said brightly, as though the conversation before hadn't just happened.

'Sure.' I pulled open the drawer where he kept all the takeaway leaflets and began thumbing through them. Tom turned and looked out of the window.

There was so much more he could say. Like how had his parents died, where was his sister now, did he still talk to her, when would I meet her? Whether he would or not was another question. I vowed not to think about it for the rest of the evening; for now there was good champagne, and that always managed to take the edge off any problem. I knew the conversation was over, but I knew there was still so much to say. Tom's frustration ran deeper than I had imagined.

32

NOW

The storm arrived. I had just got back from driving to the big post office in town when the wind became stronger, and rain began pelting down. By the time I had got inside the house and locked up, it was illuminated by the first flash of lightning, followed a few seconds later by a deep roll of thunder. I unpacked the bread, salad and juice I had picked up from the supermarket and looked at it on the table. It was a sad sight, really. But one that would be rectified soon. I had hopes of returning to a semi-normal life after Willow Cottage. Despite my expectations of being swallowed up by the landscape and hopes that people would forget about me, it seemed I wasn't forgotten. It seemed I was very much in someone's thoughts and that being here all alone was not the right choice. But I didn't need people like Hendrick turning up and being all macho and trying to offer help, I didn't need my sister turning up and trying to get me to confess all to her, I didn't need the guilt of my parents wondering about me. I needed to return to some sense of normality, where I was around people just enough, but not too much. A smaller house, a smallish existence.

The lights began to flicker and so I sought out some candles and matches. I wasn't sure of the reliability of the electrics here. The house was pretty old, and electricity had a habit of failing in remote locations.

I wasn't going to worry, though; I had made the right steps to the next phase of my life and as much as Willow Cottage had been a bit of an adventure, I knew deep down it would never work out long-term for me.

I found an old playlist on my phone, turned on my boom box and connected the sounds. The beats flowed out around the kitchen, and I tried to immerse myself in the music, a distraction from the repetitive thoughts. Soon I would be gone from Willow Cottage.

It was getting on for 6 p.m., but the sky was almost black. My playlist took me seamlessly to the next song and I sat down and began to nibble at the bread. I had forgotten a drink and stood up and poured myself some orange juice. I sat back down and began to eat the salad. I wondered if the storm would be bad and, if so, if it would cause any damage to Citrus. I could handle the damage here at Willow Cottage, but if it meant that I wouldn't be able to go to work, then that wouldn't be good.

I was just about to take a sip of my orange juice when the kitchen light went out and the music stopped. There was still a smattering of light around as the sun had not yet set, but it was hidden behind a blanket of cloud so thick it might as well have been 9 p.m. I let out a sigh and realised that was probably it for the night. I would finish my food and drink by candlelight and then get into bed.

The storm was loud, and it did not seem to want to pass. I read until my eyes were flickering – skimming over the words, barely taking them in – and then I put the Kindle on the bedside table. I tucked the blankets up to my chin and listened to the waves and pulses of the storm, imagining it playing out in front of me like a piece of art in a theatre. Suddenly a loud crack jolted me from my position. It was part of the storm, surely. It had seemed louder, though, as though it had come from within the house. I looked at my phone – there were messages from my family.

My sister's text:

Don't get blown away tonight sis.

My parents' text:

We love you kitty kat. Sleep tight. M&D xx

I felt the tears well in my eyes and blinked them away. I didn't need any extra emotion added to the evening. I was too tired and needed to sleep, but my body would not let me. Would going downstairs to investigate make things any better, I wondered? I was out here, without electricity, my nearest neighbour was half a mile down the road. I thought about Lucy and how she would have been in the storm. Scared, no doubt, and I would have ended up comforting her.

I pulled on my dressing gown, took the torch from my bedside table and headed downstairs to check each room in turn, but I couldn't see any damage. The wind was fiercer now than it had been so far all night.

I had just finished up in the pool room and was walking back through to the sunroom when a flash of light caught the corner of my eye. I thought for a second that it was another streak of lightning, but it was moving. First past the sunroom and then beyond it until I could not see it any more. I stood still, waiting, and even though my body was frozen with anticipation, I still jumped when there was a loud rap on the door and terror pulsed through my veins as my mind anticipated who would venture out here at such an hour and in this weather. Someone on a mission maybe? I walked slowly to the front door and waited next to it. The rapping came louder this time. I imagined myself opening the door and seeing a light suspended in the air and I would follow it like the story I had read as a child about a will-o'-the-wisp. The rapping came louder again. Had Hendrick returned, adamant to follow through on his offer?

Then I heard my name being spoken, shouted through the door over the storm. And then I recognised the voice. It was Blake. But he sounded anxious and desperate, so I ran to the door and flung it open.

Blake was standing on the doorstep, sodden.

'I came to check on you after the power went out.'

'Thanks,' I said, 'but I'm fine.' The tension in my body had eased at the mere sight of him. But I wasn't about to tell Blake how stressed I had been feeling.

'I'm sure you are, but there is something you should see.'

I pulled on my waterproof jacket that was hanging by the door and pushed my feet into a pair of ankle-high wellies. Blake walked ahead, head down against the wind – his super-powered torch illuminating the entire pathway. We walked around the side of the house until we reached the willow tree where we had buried Lucy. But before we had even approached the tree, I could see what Blake had brought me out here for, and I felt my blood run cold.

33

NOW

I turned back towards the house. I could get back there in a few strides and then lock the doors. I wanted to run, I tried to run, but I felt a hand grab my arm and I turned to face Blake. His face looked grimmer than I had ever seen it before. The rain had drenched him, it was pouring down his face.

'Don't run, Kit,' he called through the wind.

'Let go!' I screamed through the storm.

Blake stepped closer and put his arm around me. 'It's okay, Kit. Just come and see.'

But I didn't want to. There were so many things about living here that terrified me, but looking at where we were headed filled me with a deep sense of dread that I had only felt once before in my life, and I had run away from that as well. He took me to where I had been trying not to look. There, next to the willow tree, was a huge hole, and next to it was Lucy's decomposing body. She was no longer buried as we had left her. She had been dug up.

'How?' I said.

'I'd like to say an animal, but it's too neat. They would have dragged her body away or tried to eat it.' Blake looked at me. 'Kit, this wasn't done by a something, it was done by a someone.'

I hung mine and Blake's coats on the back of the utility room door. The water dripped off them, falling out of sync with the rain battering against the windows.

We sat down at the table. Blake shone his torch whilst I busied myself lighting candles.

'Shall I make tea?' I asked. Even though I didn't really drink it, it seemed an appropriate thing to do at a moment like this. The electricity was off, but there was still the gas hob to boil water.

'Got anything stronger?' Blake wiped his dripping face with the sleeves of his sweatshirt.

I looked across at the kitchen cupboards, trying to think what I had there. I stood up and pulled open one cupboard. There was the rest of the cider that Blake had brought round the other day. I poured a tall glass for Blake and a small one for me and took them back to the table.

Blake took a long drink.

'Is there something you're not telling me?' he asked, placing his almost empty glass down in front of me.

Everything hit me at once, all the goings-on that I couldn't explain, the notion that someone was here, watching me, and the biggest secret of all. The thing I was hiding from everyone. I still didn't feel that I could explain any of this to Blake and so I deflected the attention from me and onto him.

'I might ask you the same thing?' I said. Blake looked at me, confusion etching its way across his face.

'I mean, you seem to know everything about the woman who

owned the property before me, but you neglected to tell me that she had a reputation for poisoning dogs.'

'No one knew that for sure,' Blake said and then finished his cider. I stood up and brought the rest of the bottle to the table and Blake poured himself some more, offering me some, but I shook my head. I hadn't even taken a sip of my first glass yet.

'I don't go around telling tales of people if I don't have any proof. She was an odd woman, agreed, but Arthur had a bee in his bonnet about her. It was their feud. Him and Annalise, if that is what you are referring to, which I presume it is. I guess you've spoken to Lyndsay at the shop. Arthur isn't well now.'

'Yes, but you agreed, this Annalise, she was an odd woman.'

'Yes. But she's long gone. I've not seen her around these parts in a long time. This place was not her scene. She seemed like a party girl. Someone who wanted a bit more action. She seemed as though she liked to have fun.'

'Fun, as in the killing dogs kind of fun.'

'Kit, we don't know that. You can't accuse people—'

'I'm not accusing anyone, because I don't know who she is, so how can I be accusing her?' I knew I was clutching at straws, knew that the person who was doing these things had a vendetta against me personally. Not the house. But my emotions were running so high and my nerves were so fraught I desperately needed to pin the blame somewhere. I needed to know. I needed it to stop. The room fell quiet, all except the sound of Blake breathing heavily and the rain hitting the window.

'Will she be okay in the outbuilding?' I said quietly after a while.

Blake looked at me and gave me a small empathetic smile. 'Yes, until you decide what you want to do with her. Have you thought about getting her cremated?' he said softly. ''No chance of anyone digging her up again. You could take the ashes somewhere else, scatter them somewhere that is special to you.'

He looked down at the table. 'Because it's not here, is it?'

I felt my body start to deflate where I had been holding it so taut. Was I so transparent? No matter how much I tried to hide the pain, some people managed to see past the façade. But now was not the time to lay it all bare. There was something endearing about Blake, but right now, I still felt I couldn't admit it all to anyone.

Blake left just after eleven and instructed me to lock all the doors before he gave me that look of concern again, as though he was willing me to open up, and walked away in the stormy night. All I could think was how I had spent months with Tom trying to get him to open up to me and now here was someone who wanted me to do the same and I just couldn't. I could feel Blake's frustration and yet there was nothing I could do.

34

NOW

The next morning, the day was bright and calm. A few broken branches scattered across the lawn were the only evidence that there had been a storm last night.

I had managed to stay in bed all night, knowing that there was nothing else for me to do. I was fully awake by six and took a swim. I wanted to call Citrus as soon as I could to find out if it would be open today. I couldn't bear the thought of another day wandering around Willow Cottage.

Blake texted just after nine and asked if I was okay. I replied I was fine and asked if he knew of anywhere that would cremate Lucy. He said he did and sent me a link. I started the day by calling them first. The receptionist was a very sweet lady with a tone that suggested she felt my pain. I arranged to have Lucy dropped off later today before I headed to work. Blake had wrapped her in a several old blankets and towels; I couldn't bear the thought of one part of her body being exposed. She had been through enough. I wished her a peaceful rest from here on in. I had not been good enough for her, but hopefully she could be at peace now.

The cremation place was a slight detour from work and after a shower, I got the go-ahead from Citrus that they were opening today. I walked out of the kitchen door and locked it behind me.

I heard the sound before I saw it. It had been haunting my dreams these last few nights. But maybe, I realised as I turned around, the sound I had been hearing hadn't been in my imagination. Because there, hanging from a high branch, was Lucy's little collar. There was a light breeze that moved the branch and with each sway, I heard the light tinkling I had become accustomed to over the last few days. Perhaps it hadn't been in my mind all that time. I hadn't noticed it before because of the storm and losing Lucy, but now, there it was, as though it had been there all the time.

Or not. I was sure Lucy had been wearing her collar when Blake had dug the hole and we had buried her. But then I was slowly losing my grip on what was real. I felt more tired today than I had for a long time. Was that grief? Lucy had been my opportunity to have a fresh start and I couldn't protect her. It was the name. Of course it was. When the plumber asked me to think of a name, hers was the one that had been plaguing my thoughts for so long. I thought it was the right thing to do, but instead, all I had done was put a curse on her. It was all my fault.

I felt sick as I looked up at the collar there. There was no way the storm could have whipped it into the tree was there? But this was just one more incident amongst so many that I was no longer shocked. I was just sad for Lucy. Tears pricked at my eyes as I prepared myself for the arduous task of lifting her dead body into my car.

* * *

By the time I made it into work, I was weary, but I needed to hold it together, for Maisie still had her eye on me. I beamed a winning smile as I entered the restaurant and Maisie began asking how my day off had been, was the car okay, did I get all of the glass out of it. I wanted to cry and tell her everything that had happened since I had left two days ago, but I couldn't. So I told her about a relaxing swim followed by a spot of gardening before the storm hit.

'Did you lose electric?' she asked.

'Yes, it's pretty remote.'

'Oh, I thought you were in Bournemouth; we didn't have any power cuts there.'

'I was staying with a friend overnight,' I quickly lied. I hadn't changed my address details with HR yet; I didn't want Maisie to Google Earth Willow Cottage and then be hounded by the questions. She eyed me suspiciously. I felt she had done that a lot recently.

'Well, I hope you were okay. It can be a bit tricky out in the sticks without electricity.'

'It was fine. We had alcohol.'

Maisie guffawed and then gave me a list of jobs that needed doing. I felt the orderliness embrace me; this is what I missed when I had days off. If I could just keep working, then everything would be okay.

I would take it slowly, try not to overdo it today, as I wasn't feeling my best.

The day was a little cooler, the storm had done that, and I was grateful as Citrus filled up pretty quickly, and I had plenty to keep me busy. I found I slipped into an easy flow of order taking, delivering drinks. There were a lot of requests for jugs of water and we had many already made up in the walk-in fridge. I received the same shocked response followed by pleasure as customers touched the ice-cold jug handle.

I tried not to think about Lucy and what was happening to her little body as I worked. Every time that negative thought crept in, I stole a glance out of the window.

But it seemed that no matter how much I tried to remove her from my thoughts, she kept coming back, and so I walked over to the front window and took a moment to look outside. The sky was a brilliant blue and the bustle of the restaurant behind me was comforting. I heard the kitchen bell ring and as I went to turn back, a man who had been sitting down at a table outside stood up. He turned to face the window full on. He must have been on his way inside to pay, but in that split second between him turning inwards and my turning away, our eyes locked. His face morphed into that of someone remembering. He would have had seen a lot of faces over the last few months, but there was one that he would never have forgotten, that would have been etched on his brain forever, and that was mine.

I turned and walked quickly away and the first place I thought to go was the toilets. The second I shut myself in the cubicle, I regretted it. There was every chance he would still be out there when I left. I sat down on the toilet and pushed the palms of my hands down my face. How had I thought I could move a few miles along the coast and just blend into a new life and a new restaurant? Of course I was going to be spotted. Courtney knew where I worked, she had walked past and seen me, so there was every possibility that she would have told people. It was a small town, after all. But I didn't want to up sticks and move to a new county. This was my home; I had made it my home when I had left home and began a career in hospitality. I loved the seasons, living by the sea. I would never want to leave. But maybe with everything that had happened at Willow Cottage and now this, seeing him outside the very place I worked, maybe it was time to go somewhere new and start again.

I sat for a few minutes, unlocked the cubicle and splashed cold water on my wrists. I kept my head down as I left the ladies' restroom and after three steps, I made contact with another person. I stepped back, ready to apologise, only to see it was him.

'Kit.' He said my name as though it was one he used every day. It made me shudder. I stepped to the side and hurried past him, with my sights on the back door. I made it outside and then stood and watched as he turned slowly around and headed out of the front door. He didn't look back, but his shoulders hung down as he walked, and I could see the sadness seeping from him. I felt a wretched sickness rip through my body, and I wanted to scream out loud.

There was only half an hour left of my shift, but I couldn't bring myself to spend another second in the restaurant. I didn't care any more. I couldn't do this. I had been trying to hide away for too long. Being at Citrus had been a great distraction, but I was never going to be able to have any kind of life here. It was time to cut and run.

I grabbed my bag from the office and walked out the back and down the side alley to the carpark. I flung my bag on the passenger seat and turned on the engine to bring on the air con.

I pulled my phone out of my bag to check my messages. There were three missed calls from the same number. My solicitor, Derek. I dialled my answerphone and navigated my way to his voice message.

'Hi there, it's Derek from Mullins solicitors. I would like to talk to you about the property you instructed me to help you with. I received the documents by recorded delivery this morning. I'm afraid I need to speak with you quite urgently. It appears there is a very serious problem.'

35

THEN

I walked through the doors of Mirabelle and slung my bag under the dumbwaiter. I stuck my head in the kitchen hatch. I couldn't see Matt anywhere, just a young lad who was looking overwhelmed next to the dishwasher. I gave him what I hoped was a reassuring smile, then I went to finish setting the tables and finishing all the menial jobs such as checking on napkins and topping up the basket of chocolate mints. The mints basket was practically empty, so I went out the back staff exit which housed our one staff toilet and a tiny box room which Denim used for organising staff rotas and health and safety admin. I passed both of these rooms and went out of the fire exit, which was usually open, and into the large outdoor walk-in fridge which adjoined the kitchen. Matt was very particular about waiting staff barging through his kitchen, and I tended to stick to his guidelines of going the long way round. I had my hand on the door handle when I heard the voices of two people talking quietly. I slid my hand off the handle and held my breath so I could hear who was talking. It was Courtney and Matt, and they were under the gazebo outside the kitchen but slightly around the corner, so they couldn't see me, and I couldn't see them.

'I don't know, I just get a little bored sometimes, and she really does annoy me,' Courtney said.

'Does she, or is it because of who she is dating?'

'Please, you're the one who has issues with who she is dating...' Courtney spat.

'Well, what can I d—' Matt suddenly stopped speaking. I took in what he was saying. I'd had an inkling that Matt fancied me. He had never said anything to me. But here he was, confiding in Courtney, of all people. I hadn't realised, but as I had been listening, the fridge door had swung open with its signature creak and one that sounded suddenly deafening. I did the most natural thing and made a run for it, back in through the fire exit and into the single cubicle toilet, where I quietly closed and locked the door. A minute or so later, footsteps outside the door alerted me to the presence of someone. I flushed the toilet and began running the tap, all the while standing there, waiting for the appropriate amount of time to wait before leaving and knowing who would be on the other side of the door. I clicked the lock and stepped out into the tiny corridor. Suddenly the two of us were in close proximity.

'Courtney,' I said, our usual greeting, which was empty and hollow, a mere acknowledgement.

'Have you just got in?' she asked flatly.

'I'm right on time.' I squeezed past Courtney and into the restaurant where she followed closely behind me until we reached the dumbwaiter. 'Ooh, we're out of mints.'

I shook the nearly empty basket that I had already acknowledged minutes before and headed back out towards the fridge. The fridge door was now closed, and I walked inside.

I heard footsteps behind me, and instinctively feeling threatened at being in such an enclosed space, with sparks of adrenaline still coursing through my body, I spun around fast and found Matt in the doorway looking at me.

'Matt, you scared me,' I said lightly, hoping he didn't know it was me who had overheard his conversation. I now felt awkward that he had feelings for me.

'Still got that fear of fridges,' Matt said dryly and I cursed the day I ever shared that fear with him. I laughed.

'Only these ones. Funnily enough, I'm fine at home with my Bosch.'

Matt smiled, but I could see it was forced. Did it bother him that I was dating Tom? I supposed I should have felt flattered. I had never had the attention of two men at once. But he looked now as though he wanted to say so much more, and I felt a surge of panic. I wouldn't know what to say, and even though it was cold in the fridge, I suddenly felt sweat bite at my arm pits.

I picked up the box of mints from the shelf and made my way to the door. Matt didn't move for a second and then edged to the side with what seemed like great effort.

'See you in a bit,' I murmured and I heard him murmur something under his breath back.

'What' – I turned around – 'did you say?'

'Not. If. I. See. You. First,' he said in a staggered dramatic away.

'Have you been drinking the Russian vodka again?' I laughed to make light of the situation but something about Matt felt off. Had Courtney been rubbing off on him?

* * *

Denim sat me and Courtney down at an unset table in the corner of the restaurant. It was Thursday morning, two days after I had put my application in.

Courtney sat extremely upright and engaged Denim with a wide smile. I tried to mirror her behaviour by sitting taller and leaning in towards Denim slightly.

'Now, you two girls have shown great commitment to your jobs here, and I think we all know that it was always going to come down to one of you getting the role.' Courtney shifted in her seat next to me, smiled wider at Denim, but didn't look at me.

'So, what I am proposing is a little challenge. I will put you on the next seven shifts together, some lunch shifts, some evening, and I will be casually observing you in the background. Please don't become overwhelmed and feel you need to be any different to how you normally are; I know you are both great workers and both of you will fill the role brilliantly, but I have to make a decision, and this is the fairest way.'

'That sounds perfectly fair to me, Den, we'll accept the challenge, won't we, Kit?'

Courtney turned and faced me with a wide smile. I was shocked for a second, as she had never looked at me that way before. Had Denim noticed that she was trying a bit too hard? I wanted to laugh at her. But I put on my most professional voice instead.

'Absolutely. I'm really looking forward to it.' Courtney and I locked eyes for a few seconds, then the sound of Denim giving one short sharp clap of his hands drew me away from Courtney.

'Great, great. I am really excited for you both.' He picked up his papers and diary and pen and headed back to his office. Courtney and I both stood slowly, neither of us wanting to make eye contact again.

'Good luck,' I said to her because I knew it was the right thing to say.

Courtney let out a small laugh and wandered away. I wasn't sure what exactly I was supposed to have done to her, but from what I had overheard by the back of the kitchen, she had an issue with me dating Tom. Did she think I thought I was better than her because I dated a millionaire? If she wanted to play games, then I would be sure to beat her at getting the job of maître d' as well. Maybe that might shut her up for a while and stop those snide expressions and prove to her I was as committed to this job as I ever was.

'Bring. It. On,' I said under my breath.

* * *

The sun was shining, spring had sprung, and it was going to be a warm day, so I took the initiative to set up a few tables at the front of the restaurant, where it caught a bit of sun in the afternoon. I could see Denim watching from behind the bar and I set to work, making the tables look at neat as possible and then filling up a large aluminium bowl with water for the customers who brought their dogs. Denim was a dog owner, and I had grown up with dogs. This was one job that I knew Courtney would always forget to do. Here I felt as if I had the upper hand, and I might score a few points towards my application.

Courtney looked unusually relaxed. She was gliding around the restaurant like a swan. Was her brain kicking away like the legs of swan, that part hidden away from the eyes of customers and Denim? I hoped that was how I looked when I was racing around from table to table, but I wasn't sure I ever did. It was funny – how you looked to others was usually so different from the image you had of yourself.

The restaurant looked perfect by 11.30. Customers would be arriving in the next twenty minutes. Families were usually first through the door, and as it was the Easter holidays, I was sure there would be a lot of them today. Denim had timed his challenge to Courtney and me perfectly. This week would pose many different scenarios for us to navigate our way through and for one of us to be the most flexible and calm in any situation.

Let it be me, I repeated over and over in my head like a mantra.

The first customers through the door were two women, in their late fifties or sixties, heavily made up, bringing into the restaurant an array of floral scents from heavily applied perfumes and sprays. Courtney was over to them like a shot. I had no time to consider my approach, which, had I had more time to prepare, would have been casual but confident. I thought Courtney had been a little too bullish if I was going to be picky.

I edged back to the side, away from the front door but still close enough should another customer make their way in soon. I didn't have to wait long and then I was glad I had not pounced on the two ladies. Because it meant I was free to greet my favourite little family. I felt I knew them so well, and even though they had never formally introduced themselves, we were all on first-name terms now. The mum, Ruby, and the dad, Grant. The little girl was six and called Lulu. She skipped through the door first and then I held it open for her parents. Ruby thanked me with a beaming smile.

'It's so good to see you again!' she said to me. 'How are you?'

'Very well,' I said, feeling all warm inside at her genuine greeting.

'It's gorgeous out there, we were tempted to sit outside, but what with Lulu's allergies, that dog would have been a tad too close.'

I looked outside and, indeed, a man had just sat down with a small dog.

'Oh, well, it is just as bright and airy in here. Would you like your usual table?'

Ruby nodded and I walked them through the restaurant to the large table in the corner by the window. I fetched a pack of crayons and a colouring book, and Ruby touched my arm on my return.

'Thanks, but I brought my own. I'm so paranoid about her touching any nut product and there could be a slight risk of contamination. I'm so sorry, I sound such an awful bore.'

'It's fine.' I tucked the colouring book under my arm and put the crayons in my apron pocket. 'We did an allergen course recently, so

I am fully aware of the risks. And we are not allowed to bring any nut products into work either. We're really strict here, we take it all very seriously.'

'Thank you,' Ruby said with gratitude. 'All the laws have changed now, which is good, but we're still so reliant on people like you and hoping that they make the right decisions and take necessary precautions.'

Ruby's face went taut, and I felt as though a small knife had pierced my heart, as though I was feeling her pain, the pain she must feel as a mother trying to protect her daughter from the external forces at work all around her. How hard that must be, I thought, how she must worry every minute of every day.

Without hesitating or even thinking, I rested a hand on her arm. 'It must be so difficult.'

Ruby looked at me, her eyes shiny with tears that she refused to let fall in front of her family. 'It can be,' she said quietly. Lulu edged closer to her mother's side. 'Which is why,' Ruby began with a livelier and lighter tone to her voice, aware of her daughter's presence, 'we come to lovely places like this, where we know we will get the best service and be looked after well.'

I smiled down at Lulu and then back up at Ruby. 'We love having you here.'

The restaurant began filling up quickly and with Denim watching over us, Courtney and I wasted no time in each trying to prove just how efficient we were at our jobs. We could have run the show on our own that first lunch shift, but there were plenty of other waiting staff on. Denim was doing less work than he would normally as his eyes were always on either Courtney or me. He was taking it all very seriously. But I was so swept up in the afternoon shift that I barely noticed as I glided past to collect starters and pick up stray napkins from the floor. When I had a spare minute, I nipped into the ladies' loo and tidied up the paper towels in there and wiped down some of the water spills on the sinks with a paper towel, then pushed all the used paper towels down into the bin so they weren't spilling over the sides. Then I slipped the checklist from the frame on the wall and popped my initials and time on it. There, I thought, I had managed to beat Courtney to the toilet check and Denim would see that I had done it right in the middle of the lunch rush.

Ruby, Grant and Lulu got up to leave after their lunch, an hour and a half after they arrived, and yet again I felt happy that I had managed to give them a good experience and a worry-free one at that, amongst all the worries they must face on a day-to-day basis with a child with so many allergies. I had a good feeling in my chest for the rest of the afternoon.

By 4 p.m. I was tired, but I was still buzzing. Courtney was glowing from the rush of the shift, and she looked relaxed enough that I almost fell into conversation with her, but as I approached her, she clocked me and turned away.

I collected my tips and decided to walk along the seafront to my flat. I needed to pick some things up and as much as Tom tried to convince me that I did not need my place any more when he had so many houses that I could stay in at any point, I loved my little flat.

I arrived home and walked around the small space for a little while, looking at the books on the shelves above the doors that I still needed to read, touching the soft fabric on the small sofa bed that friends had occasionally stayed on, and I felt the presence of the place, and I missed it.

I took a book off the shelf that had been on my radar for ages and walked with it to the bedroom, where I lay down on the double bed. I opened the pages but within seconds, my eyelids were fluttering and I eventually let them close.

36

NOW

I called Derek straight away and the receptionist put me through to his secretary.

'I'll get him to call you as soon as he is free,' she assured me and I drove home, a growing sense of doom creeping over me. What could he mean by 'a very serious problem'?

I arrived back at Willow Cottage and looked up at it from the driveway. What could possibly have gone on with this place now? I was desperate for Derek to call me back and fill me in. I had a growing suspicion that it would have something to do with the woman who had owned it before me. Some financial elements that had been forgotten about that I was now liable for. I hoped that whatever it was, the winning money in my account would cover it.

I got out of the car and was two steps up the driveway when Blake appeared around the side of the house and stood at the top, waiting to greet me.

'Oh, hi.' I stopped in my tracks, and we looked at one another, both smiling. I felt we had a stronger connection now after Lucy and then the storm.

'How did it go?' he asked. We walked together up the driveway to the back door.

I knew he was referring to taking Lucy to get cremated.

'It was sad. I have had a pretty stressful day,' I said, feeling as though I wanted to open up a little. I unlocked the kitchen door and stepped in. Lucy's absence weighed heavy in the room as I glanced at her empty bed. When would I feel ready to move it?

'I thought I had better pop round,' Blake said. There was an edge of urgency to his voice now.

'Oh, right.' I put my bag on the counter.

'Yes. I thought you'd want to know that the lady who used to live here before you, Annalise, has been spotted in the area.'

I put my hand on the side of my cheek. 'Really?' I took myself to the table and sat down. I wasn't sure what to do with the information; I had so many other things bothering me: the run-in outside the toilets at Citrus kept replaying on loop in my mind, I had wanted to just disappear after I had seen him. And I had. Maisie would be wondering where I was. I was now on tenterhooks, waiting for the phone call from Derek, who was undoubtedly going to tell me something serious was going to affect the sale of Willow Cottage. I wasn't sure what I wanted to deal with first. But it seemed the decision was about to be taken out of my hands, as my phone rang.

'Hello,' I answered breathlessly, vaguely recognising the number as belonging to the solicitors. Blake looked at me and I held my hand up, motioning to him that I would be five minutes. He sat down at the kitchen table, and I walked through into the hallway.

'Kit, it's Derek, from Mullins solicitors.'

'Hi, I got your message,' I said quickly.

'Yes, right, well then, you will know that there was something I needed to speak to you about. I would say it was quite urgent, actually. I wondered, are you somewhere comfortable and alone?'

'Yes, I'm in my hallway.'

'Right, well, there is no easy way to say this, but after surveying all the documents that you gave me, it appears that there is a significant problem with Willow Cottage.'

'Okay,' I said, urging him on.

'It appears that you won't be able to sell it.'

'What? Why?'

'Well, you won't be able to sell it because it appears – and I am only going on the documentation you gave me – that the house does not in fact belong to you.'

I waited for Derek to say that although it appeared that way on paper, it was an error, it just needed rectifying.

'It doesn't belong to you and the name that is on the document is Bridely. From the research I have done, it's a business that owns many houses...'

Derek's voice faded away to nothing in my ear as a loud static sound erupted through my body. It was coming from my brain, as though my whole body was being electrocuted.

Bridely. Tom Bridely. How could I have been so stupid? How could I have I not seen through it?

He had wanted to control me. I knew that was what that underlying feeling was. Why he held so much back from me, gave so little away about himself, yet he wanted everything of me.

Derek was still speaking. I tuned back in to his voice.

'... I am not sure I can help you any more, it appears someone has duped you. Although I am sure the house is a lovely one, it does remain that it is not in your name. I suggest you contact the owner direct; would you like their details?'

'No, thank you, Derek. I know where to find them. Thank you for your time.'

I hung up and stood in the hallway, the phone hanging limply in my hand by my side. I instinctively turned to face the doorway and saw Blake standing there. His mouth was moving but I couldn't hear his words. I had left Tom. *I* had left him. But he just couldn't accept that, could he?

'Kit.' Blake's voice filtered through. 'What is it?'

I looked at him; I didn't know what to say. Where would I begin with something like this?

'Kit, come and sit down.' He took me by the arm, and we walked through into the snug. I fell into an armchair and a few minutes later, he was next to me with a glass of water. I took a sip, on autopilot.

'Now, do you want to tell me what is going on?'

I looked at Blake, the hope and anticipation in his eyes. Could I trust him? Would he understand when I told him what I had done? What I was?

'Boring finances and an annoying ex. That is all you need to know,' I said robotically.

Blake looked thoughtful for a moment. 'Okay, if you're sure. I am pretty good with annoying exes; sort of a pro in that area.'

I looked at Blake and suddenly it occurred to me – the ex he had referred to before, she couldn't be the mysterious Annalise, could she? He had been very quick to protect her, and he had said she had been sighted around here again.

I didn't have the energy to get into that now; I would file it away for later in case I needed it. I gave Blake a weary look.

'Honestly, you don't want to get bogged down with my crap. I need to...' I went to stand, and Blake lunged forward and took the glass of water out of my hand.

'Thanks. I am just going to have a lie down, I think; it's been a long shift and I'm pretty tired.'

Blake handed me back the glass of water. 'Okay. Well, just give me a call if you need me.'

We stood by the doorway. Our eyes locked and I wished everything else would just disappear so I could feel whatever it was that was trying to evolve between us.

After he left, I checked the front door was locked before I headed upstairs. My phone began to ring. I looked at the number: it was Citrus. It would be Maisie, wondering where the hell I had got to for the last half an hour of my shift. I didn't have the energy to answer and speak to her. I switched the phone to silent and lay down on the bed.

* * *

I opened my eyes. There was a greyish tint to the room. I had slept until the evening, and it was beginning to get dark. I looked at my phone. There were messages from my family, doing the usual check-in, and then a text message from Maisie's mobile phone. There was also a message from Blake, assuring me he was here if I needed him to be. I didn't know what to think about any of it.

I took the last sip of water from my glass and then began to walk downstairs. I felt the draught as I hit the bottom step and I did a quick recap. Said goodbye to Blake, locked the door, checked the front door, went upstairs to lie down. I walked through the hallway into the kitchen and could see immediately the door was wide open. I froze to the spot, and I felt a cold explosion throughout my entire body and then I couldn't move. Fear had trapped me. The sun had set and there was barely any light left in the house. I wanted to move to the light switch, but I couldn't feel my legs; it was as if they had come away from my body, they were no longer a part of me. The only thing I could feel was my heart thumping at what had to be a thousand times a minute in my chest. I looked down at my leg and willed it to move. I managed one tentative step at a time until I reached the kitchen. Then I sprinted to the door and slammed it shut.

I turned around and a saw the flash of purple out of the corner of my eye. Lucy's collar was in the middle of the table. I pushed my hand over my mouth. Someone had been in the house whilst I had been sleeping. I took a knife from the rack and immediately took myself off around the house.

'Where are you?' I screamed as I headed up the stairs and, one by one, kicked all six bedroom doors open. 'Just get out and show yourself, for Christ's sake.' I ran down the stairs and through the hallway into the dining room, the sitting room, which I still needed to tend to, then the sunroom, the pool room and back again. 'Your game is boring and pretty lame.' I raced through to the kitchen again and looked in the utility room. I swung open the door to the study. There was one chair and a small writing desk in there. No sign of anyone. I opened the door to the toilet. Nothing. I heard a noise behind me; it had come from over by the kitchen. I swung around and headed back to the kitchen, gripping the knife tightly in my hand. I stood by the back door. I could hear a scraping noise coming from right outside. I gripped the knife tighter and swung the door open.

'Hendrick,' I said, letting all the breath I had been holding come out at once. He looked down at the knife.

'I know, Hendrick. I know everything.'

He held his hands up. 'Okay,' he said. 'Can I come in?'

'No, you cannot come in. You are a liar. You conned me. I believed you, I trusted you. I should call the bloody police!'

'I know. And you still can trust me, just let me in, I need to speak to you, it's important.'

'No way, get away from here, or I *will* call the police.'

Hendrick began backing away and I followed him until he was on the driveway. I noted his car again.

'And that.' I pointed with the knife. 'That was your pay-off, I take it. What else did you get from him?'

Hendrick glanced at the Porsche, a look of shame flitting across his face.

'Ah, I thought so. Easily persuaded, then. Do you even have a girlfriend?'

Hendrick shook his head.

'I knew it. And that book, you weren't reading it, were you, it was all part of the trap to lure me in, to get me to like you to buy the tickets from you.'

Hendrick let out a big sigh. 'Yes. It was. But that was then, this is now, look, I know you really hate me right now but—'

'Hate you? I don't even know you, Hendrick. How can I hate someone when I have no idea who the hell they are? You just kept showing up here and now look, at the pivotal moment, here you are again.'

'I'm here to warn you, Kit. I'm on your side. Look, I know you think I'm a bit weird, but the reason I showed up a lot was because I wanted to make sure you were okay. I needed the money, okay, I am... was... in a lot of debt. If someone offered you that much money to get you out of debt, you'd take it.'

'What you did was completely immoral, Hendrick, there was no excuse. I am a real person.'

'I know, that was why I came around, because deep down, I care.'

I snorted loudly. 'You cared about your bank balance.'

'I worried about you; I was here a lot. Checking on you, making sure you were okay.'

I narrowed my eyes at him. 'You did lift Lucy into the sink.'

Hendrick hung his head again, but I caught the nod. 'I'm sorry she died. You did not deserve that.'

'Please tell me you had nothing to do with that.'

Hendrick held his hands up again. 'I had nothing to do with that.'

I felt my grip slacken on the knife and I clocked Hendrick looking down at it.

'Go, now. I have nothing more to say to you.' I lifted the knife up and waved it in his direction.

'Okay. Just listen to me, promise me you will pack up and get out of here as soon as possible. You're not safe here alone.'

'Oh, believe me, Hendrick, I am not about to start taking advice from you, am I? Please go away. Don't come back, okay, I don't want to see you here again.'

Hendrick shook his head. 'Whatever you say, Kit.' He turned and headed down the driveway and slipped into the car. He started the engine then stuck his head out of the window.

'Please just call me if you need me.'

I realised I was shaking as I waited for him to drive away. Then I was crying. I furiously wiped away the tears. I knew what I had to do next, and I was sure he would be expecting me.

39

THEN

Tom was trying to pretend he was okay with me staying a night at my flat, but I could hear and feel the tension in his voice as he walked about the kitchen at Sandbanks. He placed crockery down a little too hard and even the way he brushed past me was a little too brash. But I ignored his petulance and began humming as I made my way around the kitchen. I was preparing a healthy lunch of chicken salad. I wasn't a great cook, even though I watched good food being prepared every day. But grilling chicken was pretty simple, and I had always known how to lay out a nice-looking plate of leaves, having been on salad duty a few times at Mirabelle.

I set the table as neatly as I would if I were working at the restaurant, and Tom and I sat down.

'I can't hang around for long; I want to get to work early. Not too early, don't want to look desperate, but I'm thinking half an hour earlier than usual.' I trailed off. I noticed Tom wasn't really paying attention to what I was saying.

'Have you any plans for today?'

Tom looked up from the kitchen island, where he sat staring at his iPhone.

'I have lots on,' he said frankly.

'Great. Good.' I looked at the neatly set table. 'Oh, water.' I poured two glasses from the filtered tap and beckoned Tom over. 'Come, come and eat.'

He placed his iPhone on the island and hopped down off the stool and sat opposite me.

'Bon appetite!' I said and raised my water glass to him.

He looked down at the food. We had hit a wall again. Since he had told me his parents were dead, he hadn't mentioned anything more about them or his sister. And it seemed my persistence at making maître d' was only vexing him further. If I committed my life to him, I also would also be committing my life to never quite knowing where I stood with him, if something so small as me asserting a little freedom could affect his behaviour in such a way.

I had to admit I was intrigued about his sister. She sounded like an interesting character. But I was scared to ask any more about her. Tom seemed as though he could get very wound up about his family.

'Eat up, then, and I'll drop you at work. I need to pick up a few bits from the supermarket,' he said.

'It's fine, I'd really like to walk; I need the fresh air.'

'Okay,' Tom said flatly. He opened the paper on his iPad and began reading an article.

We finished our lunch, and I quietly went about cleaning the kitchen whilst he returned to his work post at the island.

Then I picked up my bag and was about to head to the door when he called loudly, 'I love you, Kit.' I stopped and my whole body froze as his words hit me. He had never said it before. He had spoken of babies and me moving in with him, but he had never told me that he loved me. Could you love someone after a few months? The seconds ticked past, and I was acutely aware that it was my cue to say something in return, to tell him the same, that I too loved him.

I dropped my bag and walked to the island and wrapped his head into my chest.

Then I kissed his hair, picked up my bag and left the flat.

* * *

I loved the walk to the restaurant from Tom's apartment. The sea breeze always made me feel as if I was inhaling a whole load of nutrients before I arrived at a shift. I felt a particular need to be walking after what Tom had just said to me. It was as if the two of us had been skirting around those three words for months, and now he had finally spoken them, I wasn't sure how I felt. I hadn't even been expecting them or wanting to hear them. But there was a lighter spring in my step as I walked to the restaurant that afternoon. He was beginning to open up to me. It definitely changed things; maybe I could do it, maybe I could settle down with Tom and be a family.

I thought about the little girl, Lulu, and how sweet she was, how Ruby and Grant seemed so relaxed with her, despite the strain they were under to keep her safe. It made me think about how I would be as a mother; would I be that superhuman, be able to put on a brave face to keep my daughter happy? I imagined I would if the daughter was one like Lulu. She was so sweet. My stomach did a flip as I recalled her little face and the way she had asked for extra cucumber with her potato salad the other day. What was that, I thought to myself, some sort of mothering instinct?

Matt was at the front of the restaurant when I arrived. It was between shifts and the restaurant was closed, but the bar was open. He was smoking a cigarette and trying to do it slyly.

'Why don't you just smoke it out the back?' I said to him as I stopped outside the front door.

'I like to see a different view from time to time. Been stuck out the back all lunchtime.'

'Was it a busy shift?'

'Manic. Tonight is looking busy too.'

Matt stubbed out his cigarette on the side of the wall. 'I'd better get back in there.'

'See you in a sec.' I didn't go into the restaurant straight away. Instead, I watched him walk towards the far end of the restaurant but before he turned the corner, Courtney stepped out and grabbed him with both arms. At first, I thought she was just being over-friendly or messing around with him, but then they were both in an embrace and Matt wasn't looking as if he wanted to go anywhere. He was stroking Courtney's hair and whispering something in her ear. After a few seconds, I moved away, conscious I was observing something a bit too intimate.

I felt somewhat perturbed. Now I knew Matt had once had feel-ings towards me, I felt a flutter of annoyance that he and Courtney were an item. It wasn't that I wanted to finish with Tom for Matt, but I would rather not have to see him with Courtney. He could do better than her. I had worked in catering for ten years; the relation-ships were so integrated into the day-to-day job sometimes it was impossible to disentangle the two. The restaurant trade was such a fast-paced and intimate environment that falling for a colleague was something that happened to most staff at some point. Dating someone outside of the restaurant, it suddenly occurred to me that I was no longer one of them, and the fact Tom was wealthy only exposed me as an outsider even more. Courtney had never really taken to me and was clearly ticked off I was dating Tom. Maybe she'd had her eye on him.

Denim was at the bar. He greeted me and I dropped my bag

under the dumbwaiter as I usually did. When I turned around, Denim was behind me.

'Hi,' I said.

'Nice and early, I see.' He smiled.

'Well, it's in my blood, what can I tell you?'

'I know, I can tell. I cannot imagine you working in any other industry.' He looked over his shoulder and saw Courtney coming through the kitchen door. I thought of that embrace I had just witnessed. Courtney looked at me as if she knew I had seen it. 'Ah, Courtney, quick word, please,' Denim said. 'Both of you, whilst you're both here.'

Courtney sidled up next to Denim, looking every inch the class swot, and I wanted to vomit. Maybe it was because I had seen her in that clinch with Matt but something inside me had begun to shift. Perhaps it was the sense of competition that had made me understand I had to be tougher.

'I need you both to be extra vigilant about allergens. You have all done your training, now it is up to you both this week to make sure policy is being adhered to. I want Mirabelle to be renowned for its care towards those with allergies. That means bringing in anything from home too, so no nuts in your bag!' Denim said with a half-smile and Courtney let out a loud laugh at the tiny double entendre, as though that was going to win her extra points.

'Understood,' I said. I knew Denim was tough on this sort of stuff and so it was easy to follow suit when there were such clear guidelines from an employer.

Denim headed back to the bar. Because Courtney had come from the kitchen, I was now standing in front of her, blocking her exit into the restaurant.

She shook her head at me, and I was actually taken back. I felt a slight rage build within me.

'What is your problem?' I hissed at her. She didn't even look shocked that I had finally spoken up and addressed the hostility between us.

'Have I wronged you in some way?' I asked.

Courtney shook her head. 'You really have no idea, do you?' she whispered.

I threw my hands out, exasperated. 'No, Courtney, I do not. I really need you to please explain to me what it is I am supposed to have done. Because if you and I are going to get along in this job we're going to have to get past these issues. Let's be honest, one of us is going to get the maître d' job and the other one will have to suck it up.'

'I think, dear Kit, it will be you who will be sucking it up.' She brushed past me just hard enough for me to stumble slightly. I almost laughed and then I felt a jolt of sadness in the pit of my stomach. I had managed to work as a waitress for years without any relationship hiccups. What was different this time? My mind rewound to what I had been thinking about when I'd seen Matt and Courtney outside. I was not dating anyone in the restaurant, I was dating a millionaire businessman who helped to pay our wages. They no longer saw me as one of them. But it was more than that, Courtney had some sort of vendetta against me. She saw me as competition, regardless of who got promoted. And the only thing I could think it could be was something to do with the man I was dating. Courtney had in it for me over Tom. She was refusing to tell me any more. But I was going to find out.

40

NOW

I pulled up outside Tom's seaside apartment. There were some lights on, but it wasn't clear if he was home. I slipped my hand into my shoulder bag and pulled out a shiny silver key. I had been given keys to all of Tom's houses. And when I had finished things, it had happened so quickly that I hadn't even thought about them. He hadn't texted or called to ask for them back because of course he expected me to come back. He wanted me to come back.

But I couldn't. Not after what had happened.

I parked the car a little way up the road and then walked back to the apartment. With what Tom earned, he could have afforded the entire building, the whole street, but he said he enjoyed the camaraderie of living in an apartment block, it made him feel connected, a part of something that he hadn't been a part of when he was growing up. Another slight insight into his life. But it was never enough. He hadn't gone to university, he was happy to admit; he hadn't needed to when all his money was passed down to him. So much money, he didn't know what to do with it.

Somehow, amongst all of that, he saw me and him, together, making a future.

I tapped in the code on the front door – it had been a while, but I could still remember it – and made my way slowly to the top floor where I would confront Tom. He needed to know that what he had done was not right, it was weird, and it was controlling, all the things I had suspected him to be based on whatever messed-up childhood he had experienced. I wasn't sure if I would ever have truly made a go of it with Tom, but that decision was taken out of my hands in the end. Just as I had wished it to be.

I walked slowly to the top of the stairs. I wasn't sure if he would even be in. He ate out a lot, but it wasn't late enough for him to have headed to a restaurant and he did most of his work from home.

I heard voices before I reached the landing of the apartment, which spread across the entire top floor. The door to the apartment was ajar, and I could hear Tom speaking. No doubt on his phone. Even though he enjoyed a night in, he would always answer his phone, no matter what time of night. The only time I had seen him totally switch off was when we were on holiday in Ibiza. Then I had truly seen him at his best.

I crept a little closer to the door. The entire building was only a few years old, so there was no chance of hitting a creaky floorboard. I managed to get close enough to the door so I could hear his voice clearly, and if he happened to walk out of the door, there was a fire exit right behind me I could dash through.

I pushed my head against the wall just behind the door to help control my ragged breathing.

'I want to help you, but you have to let me,' Tom said, and I held my breath to wait to hear if there would be a reply or if he was talking on the phone.

'I wish it were that easy.'

I almost gasped out loud, because it was Courtney's voice I was hearing.

'It is that easy.' Tom's voice had that softness to it; he sounded the way he used to speak to me when we lay in bed next to one another, discussing our days, before we both fell asleep.

'I know what you're doing.' Courtney's voice coiled as though it were a snake wrapping itself around its prey.

'What?' Tom said almost in a whisper.

'You know what you're doing, what you always do, when you're trying to get your own way. You want me to do what you want to do. As usual.' Courtney dragged the last word out. She sounded drunk. 'But it's not that simple, Tom. You don't get to control things.'

Tom let out a loud sigh.

'You've brought me here, plied me with alcohol. I mean, what was that stuff?'

'No, you're imagining things. Again,' Tom said softly. 'You have a very vivid imagination.'

Courtney choked out a sound in retort to his comment. I heard the sound of feet scuffing as if she was moving away from Tom.

'Come back, for God's sake.' Tom's voice was closer now; they were both at the edge of the doorway.

I heard another scuff, and I knew someone would be out in the hallway soon, so I bolted back along the corridor, and down the stairs. Thoughts pulsed through my mind as I began to make sense of what I had heard. I made it back through the front door and walked as fast as I could along the path to my car, not raising my head once for fear of seeing someone looking out at me from the window.

41

NOW

Tom and Courtney. Courtney and Tom. It made sense now that he wanted me away from Mirabelle. He didn't want the two of us working together, to be near one another. I knew he had been lying when he'd appeared nonchalant when I'd mentioned her. He knew Courtney very well and she him. It all made sense, why Courtney had it in for me; she couldn't stand seeing Tom and me together. But was Tom playing us both off against each other, waiting to see which of us would yield first? Courtney did not seem the settling type. Was this what Tom enjoyed? Trying to tame women who had no interest in being tethered down?

I had arrived back at Willow Cottage last night with the expectation of hearing from Tom, but my phone had been silent for the rest of the evening and so far, all morning too. There were no messages from him and so I was beginning to wonder what his next move was going to be. He had gifted me Willow Cottage under the guise of a prize, and then there was the money, mere pocket change to him. Now what, Tom? Am I supposed to keep living here, am I just a pawn in some stupid little game you have invented? This was very unlike him, he had been someone who had always liked to keep in touch, until I told him unequivocally that he was not to any longer. Well, it wasn't going to happen, because these were my final few hours here. I needed to find alternative accommodation. I called the letting agency on the off chance; perhaps they hadn't had much interest in my flat. But I knew I was kidding myself. The landlord hadn't raised the rent in so long.

'Kit,' the woman at the letting agency said. 'Well, the person we have just referenced has failed the checks. If I give Audrey a ring, she might be interested to know you'd like to continue your tenancy. You've been a good tenant; she was sad to lose you.'

'Oh, that would be great, thank you. But I won't hold my breath. It's a sought-after property.'

'Well, you've left it literally until the last minute, your tenancy runs out in just over a week and there is a long list of interested parties.'

'I know, I know. It would be a miracle. But one I am hoping for right now,' I told her just before I said goodbye and hung up.

My phone immediately rang. It was Maisie. I knew I couldn't keep ignoring her.

I sucked in a deep breath and let out a long one. I quickly prepared what I was going to say to her then I swiped to answer.

'Hi, Maisie.'

'Kit!' she sang. I knew straight away she was trying to sound upbeat because it was the middle of the summer holidays and, despite the signs I had shown of suffering with my mental health, she knew I was the best of them and that I would never let her down unless I absolutely had to. And now I had to.

'Hi, I'm really sorry for just running out at the end of my last shift, but something came up, an emergency; I had to deal with it.'

'Well, I wish you had said, Kit; you know we are here to help you whatever the circumstances. I want you to know that.'

I said yes, knowing she was trying her best to sell herself as a great manager and she was, except I just couldn't bring myself to go back there and keep lying to them and myself every day. I needed a clean break.

'I appreciate that, Maisie. But this is ongoing, and I am not sure I can commit to what you need from me right now, so I think it is best if you look for someone to replace me.'

I heard Maisie take a breath. She was preparing herself to say something that would make me want to keep my job, but my decision had been made. After another few minutes of Maisie trying to persuade me to stay and that she would offer as much flexible working as I needed, I was able to convince her that my situation was serious enough without having to go into detail. She told me that my job would be there whenever I was ready to come back. Which was very touching, as I had no clue what it was I was going to do. But one thing I did know was that I needed to face Tom. I needed him to know that he couldn't control me. I was almost ready to leave Willow Cottage, but I would wait for him. However long that took, I would wait.

42

NOW

I climbed into bed that night with the expectation that tonight would be the night. I wasn't scared of Tom. He had a controlling streak and various issues relating to his childhood, but I could handle him well enough. I imagined he would have to come now; he must know by now that I knew. Hendrick would have surely told him. He would let himself into the house and I would confront him. I had nowhere else to go until I found another place or, by some miracle, the letting agency gave me my flat back. There was no point going back there for the week that I had left on the tenancy. At least, staying here at Willow Cottage, I knew that I had more time. I knew Tom wouldn't see me out on the street, he wanted me here. This was his idea of a happy ending, to have me exactly where he wanted me. I just never imagined he would go to such lengths. It seemed a bit extreme, even for Tom. But I knew how desperately he wanted to settle down and have a family. But now, of course, I was one of potentially many candidates, perhaps he had women up and down the country shacked up in mansions, ready for him to pick which one he would settle with.

So I had decided to wait. But whilst I was waiting, I wondered if there was some way I would be able to lure him to the cottage. To hurry this along. So we could just put an end to it all.

I lay in bed and thought about the time ticking away. I imagined the scenario over and over again. Each time, Tom arrived a different way and I played it all out in my mind, each time, I responded differently to him. Sometimes I was kind, and understanding, other times I lost the plot and shouted at him; getting him to explain exactly what he was thinking. But deep down, I knew I wouldn't stay mad at him, because what he had done did not come even mildly close to the heartbreak and destruction I had caused with one stupid mistake. Tom had set me up in a mansion and given me £20,000. As eerie as it all felt on the surface, if I looked back, it all made sense. Why would someone like me win a house like this? Then it hit me.

I sat up in bed and clawed at my chest. I felt as though I couldn't breathe. I pushed off the thin duvet and took a sip of water. Surely the reason that Tom set me up with this house was because he knew. He knew what I had done, he knew why I couldn't stay with him, why I couldn't commit to being his girlfriend and that I needed time and space on my own.

Courtney was the only person who could have told him. She had been there that day at Mirabelle. She saw it all unfold. She had been waiting for me to mess up the challenge of making maître d', and she had won in the end. Of course, she would have told Tom. But the question was when. If she had told him before, then he had gifted me Willow Cottage to have as a sanctuary; if she had told him recently, once he had already set me up as fake prize winner, then he was so disgusted by me that he couldn't bear to see me. Perhaps he envisioned me rotting here alone for the rest of my life.

Either way, I had to know. I had to speak to him.

I picked up my phone and dialled his number. My heart beat fast in my chest as the anticipation built. I would be speaking to him any minute. It went straight through to answerphone. I heard the familiar recording of his voice and I felt the wrench of nostalgia. I began to leave him a message.

'Tom, it's me. Kit. I am at Willow Cottage. I know it is your house, my solicitor told me. If I had been a bit more compos mentis then I would have read through all the paperwork at the beginning, or at least got a solicitor to look at them then, but I didn't because I have been rather distracted. But I am sure you know all about that too. I know about you and Courtney; I know you have been seeing each other. So, she has probably filled you in, no doubt. Anyway, it's been fun living here, but it's not really me, is it, shacked up here all alone? So why don't you pop over and we can talk? I will be leaving soon, so you need to decide what you are going to do with the place. It would make a good family home, Tom, maybe when you find the right woman...' I drifted off, unsure what to say next, not knowing if what I was saying was the right thing or not. 'Anyway, I'm here, but not for much longer.'

I hung up, then I climbed back into bed, closed my eyes and tried to sleep.

43

THEN

It was a long hard week, but we were getting to the end of it. Sunday lunch was my favourite shift. It was always busy, people were never in a rush, the tips were always great, and the restaurant closed straight after lunch so we would always sit and have a drink together and finish up any of the roast meat that was left over. I woke at Tom's just after 9 a.m. I had been on a dinner shift the night before and Tom had picked me up after midnight. I had told him I was fine to walk; in fact, the fresh sea air would have helped me sleep when we got to the flat. As it was, I couldn't sleep until 2 a.m. Tom drifted off watching a James Bond film on the TV, which I promptly turned off once he was asleep. I felt bad that he had waited up just for me because he'd had a long week and had trained at the gym for a few hours on Saturday. He had been pretty wiped out by the time he'd come to collect me.

Tom was already up and frying bacon in the kitchen. He never stayed in bed past 8 a.m. I was the opposite. With the shift patterns I did, I was either up early or working late, so my body was always trying to catch up with itself.

I met him in the kitchen. I had brought up the 'I love you' incident with Tom when I had returned from my shift that night. He'd tried to brush it off as an in-the-moment thing and I wasn't to worry. He didn't want to pressure me any more. I felt comforted by that, and I felt we had been on the same level this week, despite my aim, which was to get the job as maître d'. But I still found that the three little words whirred around in my head from time, looking for a place to land and settle.

'Do you want eggs before you go?' he asked, and I put my arms around his waist. I felt these little actions were the equivalent of declaring my love for him, which felt like such a cementing of our relationship.

'I do if you're making them,' I said.

Five minutes later, he presented me with two perfectly poached eggs with two slices of sourdough bread with a little butter. He placed the pinch pots of salt and pepper on the table, then, as I ate, I watched him meticulously tidy the kitchen.

'How are you feeling about the job; you know, if you get the position?'

I laid my knife and fork down and looked at him. Was he slowly coming round to the idea that this was the job I wanted to be in? Even though this was something that had been engrained in him from childhood as below him?

'I'm feeling really good about it. It's been a tough week, Courtney has been okay considering, I thought she would try to pull a few sneaky tricks, try to throw me off my game, but she's been pretty quiet.'

Tom looked thoughtful for a moment. 'Has she?'

'Yes, I mean, I know you know who she is, but you don't really know what she is like, she can appear quite devious at times, threatening, almost.'

Tom turned back to the sink and continued cleaning. 'That

doesn't surprise me,' Tom said a bit too quietly and I wasn't sure I had heard him correctly.

'What did you say?'

Tom turned around again. 'I said it doesn't surprise me. She looks the type.'

I picked up my knife and fork. 'Looks it?' I said. 'There's nowt as queer as folk, is there. I'm a reasonable person, likeable, surely.'

Tom stopped cleaning and walked over to me. He put his hand on my shoulder.

'Kit, you are an exquisite individual, you must not ever let anyone try to make you feel second best. No one. Do you understand?'

I looked up at him, at the way his forehead was creased as his face formed into a frown that was steeped in frustration. I felt a rush of warmth through my body. That was better than when he had told me he loved me.

'Okay,' I said because it didn't feel as if there was anything else I could say.

Tom had bought some healthy chocolate bars made with raw cacao and dates instead of sugar. He had purposely left them on the top of the kitchen island, something he had done a few times now, a way to encourage me to eat healthier. Was it because he was prepping me for pregnancy? I wasn't sure any more, but because of what he had just said to me, I took one and popped it in my bag. He would see that one of the three had gone and I knew that would make him happy.

* * *

I walked to work that morning feeling a little lighter, a little more confident about my place in the world and what I was capable of. Of course, I had Mum and Dad telling me all the time how brilliant

I was – their enthusiasm for everything I did in life from singing in the school choir to moving away from Portsmouth to Dorset to begin a job as a waitress and get my first little flat was immense. I couldn't ask for better, more supportive parents. It made me think about Tom and his family and why he found it so difficult to talk about his parents and the sister he no longer saw anything of. How he was sometimes reluctant to spend time with my family, yet when he was with them, he shone like the brightest star, and everyone adored him. I wanted to tell him so many times that he was so good at being in a family, that he should just embrace mine. But he was hiding behind the veil of an experience, and I wasn't sure I wouldn't ever know what it was. I opened his chocolate bar to try a bite. It was pretty good, but I was still full of my breakfast, so I dropped the half-eaten bar back into my bag, thinking I would have it with tea during a lull. Which even I knew wasn't going to happen. There was no such thing as a lull on a Sunday at Mirabelle.

The doors to the restaurant were wide open, letting in the fresh sea breeze. The first thing I noticed was Courtney. She was standing down the side of the restaurant, talking to a man who had parked up in a blue saloon. His arm was resting casually on the edge of the open window. He looked smart, an executive maybe, but his clothes didn't seem to match his run-down car. She was bending down to speak to him, her phone in her hand. She began typing furiously and into the phone. Was this another boyfriend?

The lunch shift began, and I was surprised and happy when some of the first customers through the door were Ruby, Grant and Lulu.

'We just couldn't resist a Sunday lunch. I'm absolutely beat from being with this one all week. She is very demanding,' Ruby said with a smile that said I was not to take her seriously. Lulu grinned up at me.

'I lost a tooth,' she said. She yanked at her lip, and I bent down to inspect the gap she was showing me.

'My, my, that is something, isn't it?' I said, seeming more interested in the inside of a six-year-old's mouth than I really needed to be but enjoying the feeling it gave me as I watched Lulu grin in response.

'Shall I get you seated?' I said to Ruby, and she nodded.

'Oh, yes, please.'

I led them to their usual seats and laid out some specially wipeable laminated menus we had made just for them. She smiled a thank you, which I knew was for my consideration. This was the sort of thing I wished Denim could see, that I was doing my best, that my best came naturally.

I made my way back to the bar with their drinks order. My bag had come out a little from under the dumbwaiter, probably caught on someone's foot, so I kicked it back under. Courtney moved aside to let me get to the till. I punched in their order and heard it coming through the ticket machine in the kitchen. As it was one of the first orders of the day, it was relatively quiet in the restaurant and so I heard Matt rip off the order and start reading it aloud to his brigade of two other chefs.

I cleared my throat. An unnecessary action but one triggered by the awkward silence that had descended on me and Courtney. I thought about speaking, but fortunately a large group entered through the front door and so I took the opportunity to demonstrate my skills as a host, as I knew Denim would be watching me from the bar. As I walked to the front of the restaurant, I was surprised that Courtney didn't try to make it to the customers before I did. Surely she would want to be doing everything she could in these final hours, but she remained very still. I took a moment to turn around before I reached the customers and managed a glance at Courtney. My look was brief but, in that second, I saw a look on her face, not one of stress or worry but of complete and utter satisfaction.

I found that the smile I had put on my face to greet the customers wavered as I approached them. They wouldn't have noticed, and they certainly wouldn't have known that inside my mind, Courtney was going to get the job over me. Then all the positivity I had built up over the last few days suddenly plummeted.

44

NOW

I woke to the sound of my phone ringing. I looked at the time in the corner of the screen. I had somehow managed to sleep until past 9 a.m. This was unheard of. I hadn't been able to stay asleep past 6 a.m. for months. The number calling on my phone was a local one and I thought I recognised it. I answered, still sounding groggy.

'Oh, hi, sorry, did I wake you?' the voice said.

'No, I was awake.' Why did I feel the need to lie to this stranger when they had woken me?

'It's Steph from the lettings agency. Just a quick call to say your flat is still available and your landlady would very much like you to remain the tenant.'

'Really?' This was music to my ears. So much drama had ensued these last few weeks, it had felt like some kind of surreal nightmare. I needed to get back to somewhere that truly felt like home, where I could decide about the next phase of my life.

'Yes, so I will leave the contract as it is, as it is rolling month to month, and just carry on paying your rent each month as you have been.'

I hung up and started crying. I hadn't realised how unhappy I had been here at Willow Cottage. Because I thought I had won the place, I'd felt I needed to live in it. What had happened to Lucy just felt all out of sync with the place that was supposed to offer me sanctuary. Did the woman who owned it before Tom bought it for me really have issues with the place? Did she leave poison around that Lucy had eaten? Or had Tom finally lost the plot? Both were hard to imagine, and I needed to speak to Tom so I would know. Then I wouldn't need to worry about it any more. I could focus on getting better and trying to rebuild my life.

All I had to do now was get my things and start making my way back to my flat. I thought about the money in my account. I no longer had a job, although Maisie said I could come back anytime, but it felt wrong to keep hold of it, as much as I liked to have a healthy-looking bank balance.

It was imperative that I spoke to Tom. But now I knew this was my last night here, I wanted to say goodbye to the place properly.

I wanted to say goodbye to Blake as well. I felt I finally owed him the truth. The truth was always the easier route. I decided to text him and invite him round for lunch. Then I could explain everything.

I dropped him a text, with the notion that if he didn't reply, I would call, but he replied within five minutes and said he would be over at midday. I had to go to the local supermarket and pick up supplies and then, by twelve o'clock, I had laid out a feast of bread and cheese and salad and cold meats.

Blake arrived pink-cheeked just after twelve, and we greeted each other awkwardly. Things had seemed intense between us the last few days with how many times he had been here helping out with Lucy and the storm. But really, I had probably appeared a strange neighbour in his eyes, and now here I was suddenly offering him lunch. Hoping that we could remain friends, maybe?

I let him eat first before I began to explain how my ex-boyfriend had bought a house and tricked me into thinking I had won it.

Blake scratched his head and let out small laughs intermittently.

'I actually can't believe it, I just can't. It's like something you read in *The Sun* newspaper. It really is.'

'Well, yes, I am sure.'

'So, this has been your life. I don't know why you couldn't have told me you had won the house; there's no shame in that.'

I thought back to why I hadn't divulged everything to Blake in the beginning and it was because of the guilt. I had felt so guilty being here after what I had done, but now I knew I didn't need to stay because it wasn't my house, it had lifted a small amount of the guilt. I could go back to living my humble life.

'Okay, so you'll be off then? Soon?'

I nodded. 'Yes.'

'Back to your flash job in hospitality.'

'I'm a waitress,' I confessed. 'I didn't correct you before because, well, I love my job but my ex, he always played it down, he didn't want me to be a waitress. He thought it was beneath me.'

Tom's parents thought waitressing was beneath his sister. Tom had been so affected by his past life our whole relationship, there was so much of it that had seeped through into the everyday, but he would never have noticed. He had simply mirrored what he had heard growing up.

'There is nothing wrong with being a waitress,' Blake said. 'I like waitresses.' He sounded so serious, then he looked at me and laughed and I found I was laughing as well. I was actually laughing, I told myself. 'Are you okay?' Blake said. 'If you need help moving or anything, I can help.'

'No, honestly, I don't have much stuff with me.'

'Okay, if you're sure.'

'I'm sure,' I said, pushing the cheeseboard towards him. 'Here, try the brie. It's delicious.'

Blake only had an hour for lunch and so I walked him down the driveway to his car where he stopped and turned to me suddenly.

'If I were to ask you out, on a proper date, you know, like out-out, would that be okay?'

I felt a small bubble of pleasure, but I wouldn't let it flourish. 'Um.' I hesitated. It felt too soon. I still had so much hanging over me, things that I wasn't ready to share with Blake, and I wasn't going to bring that uncertainty into a relationship.

'I'm not really sure.' I watched as Blake's face fell and he tried to pull it back up again. 'I'd like to keep in touch, though. Maybe once I get settled again and this...' I looked back at the house. 'This mess is all behind me.' Blake nodded. But he didn't know about all the other mess that I had created that I would never be able to make better. Ever.

'I get it. It must have been a bit of a shock and, well, I suppose it means he's not fully out of the picture.'

'Doesn't look that way. But I'm working on it.' I wanted to work on so many things at once and make everything right again. Blake was a good man; someone I could eventually commit to feeling something for one day.

Blake flashed a smile. 'Well, you know where I am when things quieten down.'

I waved Blake off and walked back into the house, fighting the urge not to kick the wall really hard. Why had this become my life? Things had been so very simple once, and in a split second, it had all been taken away.

45

NOW

When I got back into the kitchen, I saw there were messages from my sister insisting I call her, as it was Mum and Dad's wedding anniversary and I simply had to make an appearance.

And there was another message. From Tom.

I'll come to Willow Cottage tonight about 9 o'clock.

I stared at the message for a good minute. I thought about texting back to say something, but what exactly? He had listened to my voice message and now he had replied. He would have seen that I had read the message so that was it, there was nothing else to do but wait.

It turned out to be the longest eight hours of my life. I tried to relax with a swim. I knew I was counting down the hours until I went back to my little flat and so I tried to make the most of the peace and quiet and of having an entire pool to myself. But all I could think about was Tom arriving this evening and how that would pan out. How would I be around him?

After my swim, I began tidying up and getting the few things together that I had brought to Willow Cottage and putting them in a pile. It was amazing how simply I had been able to live these last few weeks with just a few of my belongings. Really, it had been like an extended holiday, and although I missed my own knick-knacks and furniture, it had been interesting to see how I could actually survive without all the extra clutter. If I had been in a better place mentally, I would have thrived in such an environment and found the feng shui of basic furniture soothing.

But none of it was meant to be, and maybe I knew that deep down. That was why I hadn't felt healed since I had arrived here. If Willow Cottage had been some sort of gift from the universe, then I would have felt the benefits. I knew I didn't deserve it and I was right. I hadn't won it; I was given it. But did Tom know everything? This was the question I kept asking myself and the one I would finally get to ask him in a few hours.

Time passed slowly. I moved all of my stuff into the car. Seeing it stacked on the back seat there made it look exactly like I had been on holiday. I would see it as that when I looked back in time, I decided. Nothing more than a holiday. A brief period to look back on and reflect. I was sure that in some small way, my time at Willow Cottage would have served some purpose. I just couldn't tell how yet. Maybe there would be some hidden blessing that would show itself later. I did hope so because it seemed like such a waste other-wise, all this beauty, splendour and tranquillity and nothing to show for it. An image of Blake shot into my mind and for a second, I wondered if all of this was for us to meet. I had stopped thinking and believing in fate, and I had been forcing myself not to feel anything for Blake the entire time I had been here, but I knew he felt something for me and had I been in a better place in my mind, I was sure he could be the type of man I would have happily spent more time with.

When it got to teatime, and my stomach was too much in tatters for me to eat, I thought about what I should wear. What was an appropriate outfit for a meeting with your ex over his frivolous attempt to keep you where he needed you? Despite the market value of Willow Cottage, to buy a house like this would have been easy for him.

Once I had packed the car, I felt a bit redundant, and the nerves were kicking in. I went back into the house and heard my phone beep. I looked at the screen and was surprised to see a text from Matt, the old chef I worked with at Mirabelle. My gut tightened and if I hadn't already been feeling nauseous, I would certainly be now. I hadn't seen or heard from anyone from Mirabelle for months. Courtney was the only one I had seen in all that time. She could have passed information on to anyone about where I worked, especially Matt, who I presumed was getting in touch to see how I was doing. But his message seemed more cryptic than that.

Hope you're okay. Be careful.

Be careful? Why on earth would I need to be careful? Was it just a turn of phrase, as in 'take care'? I hoped so, but for some unfathomable reason, it felt much more ominous than that.

46

NOW

As it reached nine o'clock, the sky turned a deep orange and pink. I felt a wave of panic, followed by a surge of acceptance. This was the end of this drama. I poured myself a glass of wine. I thought I would need some Dutch courage. I took a few long sips and then took myself into the sitting room. I looked again at Matt's message. I wondered if I should reply but I couldn't think what to say, it had been so long.

I held the phone in my hand and was just about to ping a message to him when I saw the bright headlights of a car and froze. Tom was here. I didn't move. I presumed he had a key for the property that he owned. I couldn't imagine meeting him at the door and having some sort of casual chat as I escorted him into his own home. It seemed more fitting that I should be here, waiting for him when he walked in. Like the dutiful wife he had wanted me to be. I almost laughed at the irony.

I heard the car door slam and the sound of footsteps. Tom must be wearing something smart, because his shoes clicked along the driveway. The sound stopped and it was several more minutes before I heard it start again. I was too tense to move. Then, just as I suspected, I heard the key in the lock and the door opened.

I took another long sip of wine and placed it on the coffee table next to me.

I heard footsteps on the stone floor of the hallway, and instinctively, as if he sensed me in here, the sound of his steps ended just outside the door to the sitting room. My heart was in my mouth, all the anticipation exploded within me and morphed into a crippling anxiety, and I wished for this to be over.

The door squeaked as it was nudged an inch. One footstep at the door then another, then a dainty shoe appeared. And that took me by surprise but, before I could question it, a leg, then a torso, then long blonde hair on the head of someone who was clearly not Tom.

'Housekeeping,' Courtney said and the grin she gave me was borderline wicked.

'Courtney,' I said, almost relieved. She had been sent to do his dirty work.

'How have you been holding up in this old place then? Not too shabby, is it.' She walked right into the room and stood opposite me. But she was swaying slightly. And her voice had a slight slur to it. She was drunk, I was sure of it.

I stood up, immediately sensing the power issue building, as it always had done. I needed to be the same height as her, not seated where she could and almost certainly would try to belittle me.

'Why are you here? I was expecting Tom.'

'Of course you were. You always had him wrapped around your little finger; I suppose you thought it was only a matter of time until he came running again.'

'I finished things with Tom, and I haven't had any contact with him since. Since this, actually.' I gestured to the house. 'This is his way of trying to win me back or something. I don't know. I don't care. I'm done. I'm going.'

'Oh, please, as if you have had any control over this; you were put here, for fun, I suppose.'

I shook my head. 'For fun? Woohoo, well, everyone has had their fun and we can all go back to living our lives.'

'Except you won't. Will you, Kit?'

I felt my heart thump hard in my chest. Because she knew. I wiped my palms on my dress, but Courtney looked down towards my hands and laughed.

'Oh, Kit, you're so funny. You were so wrapped up trying to get the grand prize you managed to take your eye off the ball for a while, didn't you?'

I moved awkwardly on the spot, my heart racing, and I wanted to cry. I wanted to cry so much it physically hurt.

'Do you think about her much?' Courtney looked around the room as though she was searching for something, for someone.

I didn't need to tell her that I thought about her every second. The little girl. Lulu. Courtney didn't need to hear me say it either. It wouldn't make any difference if I crawled into a ball on the floor in front of her. Courtney knew what she was saying and the impact her words were having on me.

'Did you feel this place was a bit of a sanctuary, somewhere to hide away from what you had done?'

Courtney turned and spat the last words out at me. I stepped back, physically repulsed by her and feeling slightly on edge. I had never seen this side to Courtney, even when she was drunk after work, she would never let the veil fall. I was shocked by what I was witnessing.

'I'd forgotten what the old place looked like,' Courtney said, and I wondered how many times Tom had brought her here. 'You've done a terrible thing, Kit. You know that, don't you? People's lives are irreparable because of a selfish and thoughtless act.'

'No!' I shouted. 'It was an accident.'

'Oh, yes, of course it was an accident,' she mocked. 'You knew the rules, but you disobeyed them anyway.'

'No, Courtney, I didn't disobey. That's not right, I... I...' I stopped. What had I done? Even I couldn't put it into words. An accident wasn't enough to describe it, for it would live in my mind for the rest of my life. But no matter what I called it, or how I referred to it, it would haunt me forever.

47

THEN

Despite my paranoia over Courtney's expression, I quickly fell into the swing of the shift and found I was no longer thinking about whether she thought she had got the upper hand and had secured the job over me. Ruby, Grant and Lulu had settled in for a while, and were going to order desserts. Ruby was talking passionately to Grant about something, and Lulu looked bored. I approached the table and Ruby stopped talking.

'Hi, I wondered if Lulu would like to see the collection of origami we have over there.' I pointed to the dumbwaiter and a shelf behind it where one of the weekend waitresses – an art student – had fashioned napkins into swans, elephants, cats' faces and even a dinosaur. We displayed them proudly to support her success.

'Would you like to, Lulu?'

Lulu nodded.

'Can you make sure she comes straight back?' Ruby said.

'Of course.'

Lulu slipped out from behind the table, and I held her hand as I took her to the display. She oohed and ahhed and asked to hold one. I let her. Even though Ruby had been a little paranoid about the colouring books and other children's allergy-ridden hands being all over them, these origami figures hadn't ever been touched since they had been made. As Lulu was carefully inspecting the dinosaur origami napkin, Matt shouted from the kitchen. I stuck my head through the hatch that the food came through.

'Yes?'

'Does this salad look limp to you?' He showed me a beautifully vibrant side salad. I inspected it for a second. Then shook my head.

'Has someone complained?' I asked.

'Yup,' he said, looking flummoxed. It might only have been a salad, but Matt took any complaint completely to heart.

'No, it looks perfectly edible. One of your finest, I would go as far as to say.'

'No need for any of that brown-nosing; we all know it's Denim you need to be impressing.'

Matt came closer to the hatch. 'How's it going? Time's nearly up! My money is on you,' he said with a sly grin, and I felt a rush of love for him. For everyone here. They were like my family, and the thought of being able to stay and do this job was the most important thing to me. I knew that if Courtney took the position, my life here would be very different. We tolerated each other under the current set-up but if she was above me, then I knew I wouldn't be able to bear her.

'Just change the leaves at the bottom and send it out again,' I said and backed out of the hatch. When I turned around, Lulu wasn't standing there any more. The dinosaur origami was on the floor. I picked it up and held it for a second as I looked around the restaurant for a sight of her. I let out a sigh of relief when I saw her seated back at the table with her mum and dad. I came over to the table. 'I'm sorry it got a little busy, but your desserts will be with you soon, okay?'

Ruby smiled, still locked in a conversation with Grant about something that needed both of them to use a lot of hand gestures.

Lulu smiled at me from behind the table but didn't move.

'Are you okay?' I asked her.

She nodded. But she looked a little stiff and awkward.

'Chocolate ice cream is on its way, okay?' I was referring to the dairy-free ice cream that we kept in a separate freezer to anything that Lulu was allergic to, including nuts. Lulu pulled a funny smile and shuffled down in her seat. I frowned at her, perplexed for a second. She had gone suddenly quiet. But the bell from the kitchen took my attention away from her. Whatever she was up to, I was sure Ruby could see to it.

I took two soups to a couple of senior citizens who ate here once a month, swung by another table with their bill next to Ruby and Grant's table and noted the chocolate around Lulu's face which meant they must have received their desserts. It was like one fast dance sequence and so, by the time I had slowed down for a second to clear up a spillage next to the bar, I could clearly hear the pained cries of a woman. There was a sudden change in the atmosphere. What had been a busy but placid restaurant was now almost silent as everyone stopped and tried to tune in to the animal sounds coming from the top part of the restaurant. Even though I would never have recognised her from the tone of her scream, I could picture her in my mind's eye.

I began to stand up. The movement jolted my brain to rewind to a few minutes before when I had walked past my favourite family and made a presumption. Lulu had been acting strange when I had seen her safe in her seat. Then I had seen chocolate across her face and instantly felt relief that they had received their desserts, but as I watched it replay, what I then remembered seeing was an empty table, not one laden with freshly delivered desserts. As I made my way around the corner and up the few steps to their table, a scene unfolded before me. Grant with his phone in his hand, bent down, Ruby standing, unable to do anything but keep running her hands through her hair, and between them, with Grant's other hand on his daughter's chest, was Lulu, lying lifeless on the floor.

And Grant repeating, over and over, the name of his daughter – Lucy.

48

NOW

I pushed past Courtney. I needed to get upstairs and collect my pillow and toiletry bag.

'Where are you going?' she said, following me.

'I'm leaving, Courtney. I've had enough of this. I don't even know why you're here. I was expecting Tom.' I turned to face her in the bedroom.

'Ha!' she barked out a laugh. 'Tom! Tom isn't coming, you stupid bitch.'

Her words pinched me, and I quickly scooped up my toiletry bag from the en suite.

'Okay, well, tell him thanks very much for the house, but I'll be going now.'

I went to walk past her, but she grabbed my hand. She took my toiletry bag, which was full of perfumes and jars of creams and threw it, so it hit the window in the bedroom that had steps leading up to it. Of all the things in this house, I loved that window the most; it was like a little room all of its own, with the three steps and its own little seat. It was the sort of place I would have loved to sit for hours in when I was a child. The window smashed like ice. It was a harsh, brittle sound and I looked at the gaping hole.

Courtney wasn't satisfied and ran up the steps and, using her foot, she began kicking out the rest of the windowpane.

Then she turned around and faced me.

'You know they come into the restaurant every day? Her parents, to feel her, where she took her last breath. I have to see them every single day.' Courtney was crying. She was crying. I felt as though I wanted to tell her it was okay, so I took a step towards her, my arm stretched out. She barged past me, and I thought she was going to leave, but she locked the bedroom door, taking the key and putting it in her pocket.

'Only one way out, Kitty Kat. What's it going to be? I can't bear your existence any more. You in this house was a game, a game that was a good distraction for a while, but it wasn't enough. I need you gone.'

What game? Were she and Tom in this together?

A bright light in the driveway seemed to distract her for a moment and I too wondered who had just arrived. I heard car doors slam and hurried steps to the front door, but I was too far away from the window to see or hear who it was. Courtney looked uneasy, unsure which way to look or what to do. Then I heard thundering footsteps up the stairs and a loud male voice calling my name.

'Kit, Kit! Are you in there?'

'Matt,' I screamed. 'I'm in here!' I banged on the locked door.

'They will never get through that door, Kit.' And then suddenly I could smell burning. I turned and saw that Courtney had a lit rag in her hand. She dropped it on the carpet, and it began to catch and burn. I ran over to it and started to stamp on it, but it was spreading fast; was that petrol I could smell as well?

'You made me do it,' Courtney said suddenly. Her voice had changed. She sounded panicked.

'What?' I screamed.

'You and your need to become the best. I was never much good at losing when I was a kid. Just ask my brother. So, you forced me to do it; that wasn't me. I'm not a murderer. I thought I was just going to get you fired.'

'What?' I felt the heat from the fire all around me. Then I heard shouting from outside. There were more bright lights and then a siren.

'You, Kit. You were so perfect. He no longer noticed me. After our parents died, we had no one except each other. Oh, and millions each. He promised them he would look out for me. But he didn't.' Courtney was crying harder. I stepped closer to the edge of the window. There was quite a crowd forming it the garden and I could see there were flames on the other side of the house. Had Courtney set that alight too before she came into the house?

I edged back again and took a step towards Courtney, but she stepped further away.

'This was a game,' she said with a half laugh. 'I put you in this house for a laugh. I thought I could have some fun. But then the bloody thing with Lucy happened. I only moved the chocolate bar to the top of your bag where it was visible because I wanted you to get fired. Not because I wanted a child to eat it and fucking die!'

I felt my heart stand still and I gasped for air. The room was heating up fast, but I felt a massive chill run through my body and a sense that the room was spinning. With the crackling noise from the carpet and Courtney's contorted expression, I felt as though I was trapped in a nightmare. The room was thickening with smoke, and I began to cough. Everything that I had believed for the last few months had been a lie. I had left Mirabelle because I'd thought I had done something that I hadn't.

'It was you?' I finally said. 'You set me up?'

'It was a game, Kit; it was all a fucking game. You took my brother from me. He was all I had left. I didn't mean for it to end badly, I never meant for any of the games to end badly, just like I didn't mean for this to end badly, but here we are. And I am about to burn my house down with you and me still in it!' She let out a hysterical laugh and I realised she must be on something else as well as the drink. Maybe she always had been. But she did just say *her* house.

The door suddenly crashed open, and Tom fell into the room.

Courtney screamed, 'Get out, get out! It's too late. You were never a good enough brother to me, you let me down.'

Tom glanced at me and held his hands out in front of him. 'I tried, Annalise, I tried. But I was hurting too. And you have always been wild; it was not always easy to help you. I mean look at this, this isn't you.' Tom looked behind him; there were flames licking up the stairs; he had managed to get in just in time, but the only way out was down. Tom eyed the window and jabbed his finger at me and then the window. I knew this was my only option; going back down the stairs would be a death sentence. But jumping... how the hell was I supposed to do that?

I stood at the edge of the broken window as shards of glass crunched under my sandals. I felt a piece slice through my toe, a sharp pain, then the slow warm trickle of blood. I ignored it. I was acutely aware of my surroundings, from the wind whistling through the building to the sound of voices below the window. Were they chanting? Egging me on to do it? It was hard to tell, they were so far away, so very far below me. It was funny how my fear of heights had suddenly dissolved. Where I usually felt fear, I now only felt numb. I listened to Tom trying to coax Courtney, no, Annalise – was that what he had called her? She was his sister. They were brother and sister. I felt dizzy, the fire was burning up all oxygen, even with the broken window I was finding it difficult to breath.

I took a small step forward and I looked down. My thoughts turned to the line from *Peter Pan* – 'To die would be an awfully big adventure' – the one part of the film that had always struck a chord with me. For here I now was, ready to literally take the step into the unknown. What was waiting for me? What would it feel like? Whatever it – death – was, it had to be better than the alternative. Staying here amongst the madness and chaos.

I could hear the tiny voices of the crowd that was forming beneath me. I wondered what they were saying. It was all such a blur now. I didn't need to know. I edged further forward; both of my feet were now teetering over the edge. I surprised myself at how calm I felt; the beginning of the day now seemed so far away, and I could no longer recall the steps I had taken to get here. But it didn't matter any more. Too much had gone on recently. Was this finally the end? Surely I could not survive this next part. Because maybe I wasn't supposed to. Because maybe this was finally it.

For a brief amount of time, I had been the luckiest girl, now I was standing here, wishing I didn't exist.

I listened to the voices calling me, telling me to do it. Was that Blake? I had definitely heard Matt's voice. I took a deep breath – heard the crackle of cracked glass under my shoes as a thousand faces from my past and present shot in front of my eyes. I took one final step, so it was only air between me and the ground. I instantly felt my stomach being pushed into my chest, then I simply floated down.

Down.

Down.

49

NOW

I bounced. I didn't expect to bounce. Even though I had seen there was some sort of soft safety cushioning below me, I still expected to hit a hard surface. I thought it was the end. Then there were people around me, pulling me as I tried to make my way to solid ground.

A blanket was thrown around me and then Blake was there embracing me.

'Are you okay?' He had raw panic in his eyes. I began to laugh. This was a joke, right, all these people here for me? This didn't make sense.

'We need to treat her for shock and smoke inhalation,' a woman in a uniform said next to me and I was escorted to an ambulance and helped up inside. An oxygen mask was placed over my mouth whilst the lady asked me questions that only required me to nod or shake my head.

I noticed a figure lurking by the edge of the ambulance, and pulled the mask off my face.

'Can I?' I said to the paramedic.

'If you feel able. I'll just fetch you some water.'

Matt moved forward into the light so I could see him better.

'How are you feeling?'

'I don't really know. I feel weird.'

'It's the shock.' The paramedic handed me an open bottle of water.

'It must be a shock. A lot to take in,' Matt said.

'I don't know what the hell has just happened.'

Matt took a deep breath. 'Well, I only just found out, for the record. Annalise, or Courtney, whatever she wants to be called, I think Courtney is her middle name, I've always called her that, anyway, she came round after work a couple of nights ago and just blurted it all out to me. She set you up in this house for a game, and then the incident with Lucy happened. I was shocked at that. I had no idea. I thought you were the one who did it. Not on purpose.'

I looked down into my lap. 'But I still took that bar into work, without thinking it was full of nuts and seeds and all the other stuff Lulu was allergic to.'

'But it was stuffed right down in your bag apparently. Courtney made sure it was right where it would be seen. Lucy was a curious girl, by all accounts. The family want you to know they never blamed you. Grant said he saw you in Citrus. He tried to talk to you then, to ease your guilt. He told Denim when he passed him in the street. Anyway, I've passed on that bit of information, so you can do with it what you like. I'm glad you're okay.' He smiled.

'How come you're here, I mean, you and Tom?'

'Courtney told me everything and I spoke to Tom and then, when she stole his phone, he tracked it on his other phone. We had sort of figured that she was going to do something rash, I mean, she had already done something pretty out of the ordinary by setting you up in this place, pretending that you'd won it. I mean, it's mental!'

I sat upright as I suddenly thought about Tom.

'Tom, is he okay, did he get out?'

Matt looked behind him. 'Yep, he jumped out after he pushed Courtney out. I think she'll be doing a stretch in a psychiatric unit after this.'

I touched my chest in relief.

'In fact, here he is now, you can talk to him yourself.'

Tom appeared and he and Matt had a man-style half-hug and Tom patted Matt on the back before Matt walked away.

'Wotcha,' Tom said, and I felt all the emotions flood out of me. I climbed down from the ambulance, and we put our arms around one another. For a few seconds, as he held me, I imagined everything that had happened between us just melting away and that there was hope for us. But even as I felt the tension of the last few months slowly begin to ease, flashes of my life with Tom before the tragedy with Lulu came back to me. Whatever had happened to him growing up had clearly affected both him and his sister. Whilst Courtney had eventually lost the plot, I knew Tom had so much inside that he needed to expel.

'Thank you for coming.'

'Well, I wanted my phone back,' he said dryly. He looked pained, as though he had endured a lifetime of this.

He stepped back and we assessed one another.

'So, she's your sister?'

'Annalise Bethany Courtney Bridely. This has even surpassed my expectations. She was a handful when we were kids, but this. Faking an entire company to trick you into thinking you had won a house. One of many of her houses, in fact.'

I shook my head. 'Why didn't you tell me, Tom, that she was your sister? I worked with her every day, I told you how awful she was.'

'I tried to, but it became too complicated in my mind. I thought the best plan was to get you out of there. I could have offered any job to you, but you wanted to be a waitress. Just like my sister.'

'But she didn't need to work? Surely?'

'God, no. Neither of us do. I make safe and reliable investments. Annalise just plays games.'

'So, it was a game to her?'

'Yes, getting you into Willow Cottage, setting up the fake competition company, enlisting that guy, paying him a small fortune. Except the waitressing. She's like you. She does it because she loves it. I knew she was starting to tip over the edge. I kept trying to help her, but she kept pushing me away. But that was before the Lucy incident. I think she really began to lose it after that.'

I thought about the chocolate protein bars that had arrived. I had presumed they were from Tom, but it was the exact bar that Lulu had eaten, the one that had killed her. She had been trying to blame me then. And the bird nuts, just another dig to make me believe I was responsible for the death of a small child. But Lucy, my dear puppy Lucy.

'I had a dog, she died. I think it may have been your sister who poisoned her.'

Tom sucked in a breath and shook his head. 'That dog incident, I think I told you about it. That was a turning point in Annalise's behaviour, she was about eight or nine then. She became attached to the dog instantly. And then it was gone. She really started acting up then. I always wondered if she saw something, witnessed what my dad did with the dog when he took it off her.'

I let out a really long sigh and shuddered.

'Here, get back in the ambulance. We'll get you sorted with some warmer clothes or something,' Tom said.

'I packed my belongings in my car already. I was leaving tonight anyway, to go back to my flat. '

'You still have that tiny flat?' Tom almost laughed. I glared at him.

'Yes, Tom, I have my tiny flat and I was very happy there. I will still be happy there.'

'Okay. I'm sure you will be. Do I have permission to rummage in your luggage for a warm sweater or something?'

I smiled. 'Yes, please.'

Tom disappeared and I picked up the water bottle and had a few more sips.

Another head appeared tentatively around the edge of the ambulance.

'Is it safe to come and check on you or will I get my head bitten off by that paramedic again?'

I went to stand up again.

'Don't, I'll get in.' Blake hoofed himself up into the back of the van.

'I'm not sure you're allowed in here. It's for the sick and injured only,' I said with a slight playful tone, surprising myself after what I had just endured. But some of the pain had lifted, and I was beginning to feel lighter than I had done in months.

'Ah, sick and injured my arse. I saw that jump you did; it was practically Olympic level.'

I laughed loudly this time and, for the first time in a long time, it felt real.

'Ah, she laughs.'

I sighed. 'You were probably wondering when you were going to see a fun side to me.'

'I've seen plenty of sides to you, they are all intriguing. But yeah, I knew there was something pretty big going on that you weren't ready to tell me.'

Tom appeared again. 'One sweater... oh.' He clocked Blake, who had sidled up next to me on the bed.

Blake leant forward and took the jumper and handed it to me then shoved his hand back out to Tom.

'Blake, I'm Kit's neighbour. Well, I mean, I live up the road there.'

Tom shook his hand and nodded. Then looked at me and smiled. 'Right, okay. Probably quite a bit of paperwork to deal with here, so I had better get on.' He backed away, already reaching for his phone.

'All as mad as a box of frogs. The whole family,' Blake murmured. 'So I've heard,' he added. 'Listen, the police want to question you, so if you're up to it, I suggested to do it at mine. I have some of my brother's famous cider, it's just come in by the crate. I don't know what to do with it all.'

I smiled. 'Come on then, let's get this over with.'

Blake jumped down first and helped me step down, then I bundled myself up in the jumper. I looked up at Willow Cottage. The fire engine had extinguished the two small fires. One had been in the sunroom and the other in the master suite, where I had ended up with Annalise.

I shook my head as I thought about what I had been through these last few months and how none of it had to have happened.

Annalise was standing next to the police car. Her head was bent, she looked completely dishevelled. But as I looked at her, she must have felt the weight of my stare, and so she looked up at me one more time, her eyes locked on mine, and all I could think was that she seemed so very sad. I knew that no matter what I had been through, Annalise was the one who was suffering the most. I wasn't responsible for Lulu's death; I knew that now. It was just going to take some time to settle in, and eventually I would accept it and begin to like myself again. I thought about my little flat waiting for me, and I felt the grip of a hand on mine. I looked towards Blake, who was smiling at me. And through tears of shock and relief for a life that I was leaving behind, I smiled back.

ACKNOWLEDGMENTS

Thank you to the usual Boldwood crew, Amanda Ridout, Nia Beynon, and Claire Fenby, for the time spent thinking about *The Waitress*, all the great work you do, and our marketing meetings, which are always so exciting. I am so glad we all finally got to be together this year for the Boldwood summer party.

I managed to meet with my lovely editor, Emily Ruston, for the first time for this project. We spent a long lunch talking over the plot, characters, and twists and it made a real difference to how I felt and connected with the story. Thank you for pushing me to 'kill the dog.' I have sometimes struggled to take my novels where I know they need to go and so this is my new mantra for all future books.

I often advise those I meet who are still thinking about their career that they need to wait tables at least once in their life. Despite the dark theme in this book, waitressing was one of the best jobs I ever had, and I learnt a lot about people and myself. I also made a lot of good friends and the social life was just the best.

Thanks once again to my lovely readers who are growing in numbers. Thank you for your messages which mean the world to me. I have lots more books to come and I'm so glad you're all on this journey with me.

BOOK CLUB QUESTIONS

1. What were some of the main differences between Kit and Tom's upbringing and how did that impact their relationship?
2. Do you think Kit should have given it another shot with Tom or was Blake the one for her?
3. The saying goes, that money doesn't buy you happiness. Discuss.
4. Did you see the connection between Tom and Courtney and did you foresee how her character was going to impact Kit's life?
5. Have you ever worked as a waiter? Why do you think Kit loved her job so much?
6. Were there any moments when you thought the book would go one way and it went another?
7. What secret did you think Kit was hiding?
8. Which characters did you like the most and why?

MORE FROM NINA MANNING

We hope you enjoyed reading *The Waitress*. If you did, please leave a review.

If you'd like to gift a copy, this book is also available as an ebook, digital audio download and audiobook CD.

Sign up to Nina Manning's mailing list for news, competitions and updates on future books.

http://bit.ly/NinaManningNewsletter

Explore more gripping psychological thrillers from Nina Manning.

ABOUT THE AUTHOR

Nina Manning studied psychology and was a restaurant-owner and private chef (including to members of the royal family). She is the founder and co-host of Sniffing The Pages, a book review podcast.

Visit Nina's website:
https://www.ninamanningauthor.com/

Follow Nina on social media:

 twitter.com/ninamanning78

instagram.com/ninamanning_author

 facebook.com/ninamanningauthor1

bookbub.com/authors/nina-manning

Boldwood

Boldwood Books is an award-winning fiction publishing company seeking out the best stories from around the world.

Find out more at www.boldwoodbooks.com

Join our reader community for brilliant books, competitions and offers!

Follow us

@BoldwoodBooks

@BookandTonic

Sign up to our weekly deals newsletter

https://bit.ly/BoldwoodBNewsletter

Made in United States
North Haven, CT
29 July 2022

21984495R00154